MW01179059

Cheating FATE

Cheating FATE

AUDREY
PFITZENMAIER

thistledown press

Library and Archives Canada Cataloguing in Publication

Pfitzenmaier, Audrey, 1959–
Cheating fate / Audrey Pfitzenmaier.

ISBN 978-1-897235-41-6

I. Title.
PS8631.F48C44 2008 jC813'.6 C2008-900080-3

Cover photograph ©Hans Neleman/zefa/Corbis
Cover and book design by Jackie Forrie
Printed and bound in Canada

Thistledown Press Ltd.
633 Main Street
Saskatoon, Saskatchewan, S7H 0J8
www.thistledownpress.com

Saskatchewan Arts Board

Canada Council for the Arts Conseil des Arts du Canada

Canadian Heritage Patrimoine canadien

We acknowledge the support of the Canada Council for the Arts, the Saskatchewan Arts Board, and the Government of Canada through the Book Publishing Industry Development Program for our publishing program.

I would like to offer a special thanks to Alison Acheson and Michelle Superle for their comments and support through the writing process.

For Opa and Grandpa

Prologue

SUKH SLOWED THE SNOWMOBILE AT THE bend right where the shore neared the road and the forest no longer blocked the view of the lake. He stopped and idled the snowmobile, blowing warm breath onto his cold hands. While he waited for the others to catch up, he turned to his passenger. "What do you think, Jeremy? Should we cross the lake?"

Both boys turned as the second snowmobile came to a stop beside them. Cassidy, the passenger, covered her red ears with her hands to warm them up. She impatiently tapped her booted toes on the footrest. "What's wrong?" she asked.

The cold mountain air had brightened Jeremy's cheeks and made his nose run. He wiped his sleeve across his nose and called loudly enough for his voice to be heard over the sound of two machines idling. "I don't know, man. My dad said the ice isn't safe anymore." He looked to the driver of the second snowmobile. "Kyle, what should we do?"

Kyle looked across the white surface of the lake to the trees on the far shore — to Cassidy's house. It looked safe enough. "If we go the road way, it'll take forever to get there," he answered.

Sukh added, "The lake's way faster."

Cassidy nudged Kyle with her knees, "Go for it. I've got less than ten minutes to get home and get my room clean. If I don't, I'll be grounded for a week. I won't be able see anybody!"

Not see Cassidy for a week? Kyle gunned the accelerator. The snowmobile started over the snow bank and across the lake.

Sukh faced Jeremy, his eyebrows raised, silently seeking his permission to follow. Jeremy shrugged and nodded. Sukh squeezed the handle and rushed after the snowmobile carrying their best friends.

I
Fate

KEN LOCKETT RAISED THE HAMMER AND swung it down, burying the nail in the fence post. A warm gust of wind blew up from the lake and swayed the fir branches, the spruce and pine trees. The sound reminded him of a fast-running creek. He stopped working and turned his aged face into the mid-afternoon sun. He loved the feel of the wind on his skin, unusually warm so early in the season. It should be a decent summer this year, he thought.

In the mountains of BC's Cariboo, summer came late and winter came early. Daffodils and tulips, already in full bloom on the temperate southern coast, remained hidden beneath frozen ground. Ice as thick as timbers still stretched across the lake. Deciduous trees remained barren, with not a hint of a bud. Russet grass still lay flat, twisted and burnt by autumn frosts and snow sat in shaded patches across the ranches' many hay fields. Only the conifers, stretching up to the clear blue skies, stood as always, barely changed, dark and green. On a clear day the temperature often rose and fell more than twenty degrees from sunup to sundown. Hail and snow had been known to fall during any month of the year.

Ken had lived on this ranch for over forty years, so he knew the place as well as he knew the calluses that roughened his active hands. He knew that some years there'd been no autumn and no spring, just ten months of winter and two months of summer. This April, though, there was a spring. For the last few days, all day and most of the nights it had been above freezing. Unusual for this early in the year, but appreciated, especially by the ranchers.

In winter, the whine of snowmobiles racing across the lake was common. But today, while he repaired the barbed wire on his east fence, the sound niggled at Ken's subconscious. Because of the patchy snow, most snowmobiles had been stored away. Gravel roads and exposed logs were cruel to the snowmobiles' expensive tracks. Local riders would have more respect for their machines. Besides, the lake, though still covered with ice, would be a dangerous place to ride today. Who was riding on the lake?

Ken squinted into the glare of the sun bouncing off the ice desert. There, just passing the island, were two snowmobiles. They were racing across the lake toward the access road that bordered Ken's acreage. He recognized one of them as the Kendalls' old Arctic Cats, the one young Jeremy rode, and he was doubling someone on the back. The other snowmobile, also carrying two riders, was too far behind for Ken to tell who it was. Probably Sukh Sangera. Those two were inseparable. And odds were that Cassidy Sampson and Kyle Aspen were the other two riders. Ken shook his head, rolled his eyes and thought, "Kids! What are they thinking?"

He turned back to his work.

When the roar of the wind in the trees died down and the branches settled their swing, Ken noticed that the sound of the snowmobiles had changed. Instead of the high-pitched whine of the two-stroke engines, he heard a lower rumble, almost a gurgle: the sound of machines hitting pockets of slush on top of the ice.

Ken knew from experience the scary feeling a snowmobiler got when they suddenly found themselves riding through water in the middle of a frozen lake. The shifting and expanding of the ice caused harmless cracks, and water seeped up slowly from underneath. The snow that sat atop the water hid it from view and the snowmobiler wouldn't know it until they rode through. The ice below was still thick and safe, but the water from the seepage mixed with the snow to make slush, bogging down the machine. It happened to every snowmobiler at one point or another. Aside from getting wet feet and having to wait for help from fellow riders to lift the machine onto packed snow, it was not a big deal. Those kids had better find some packed snow, he thought, or they were going to have a tough time pulling those machines out of the slush.

The back door of the house opened and Ken's wife, Erika, walked out onto the porch. Ken glanced back and noticed she was carrying a dishtowel and a pot she'd been drying. He knew she too was concerned by the sound of a crippled snowmobile. She scrunched her eyes to look into the sun toward the lake, showing the many laugh lines etched deep into her face from years of living in this dry, cool climate.

"Is that one of the Sangera's?" she asked, recognizing the machine.

"Maybe the second one," Ken replied, "But the first one is Jeremy Kendall's."

"What first one?" she asked.

Ken looked back to see if the boy had stalled the machine, but the lead snowmobile was gone. He quickly scanned the lake, squinting and raising his hand to shield the sun from his eyes. Nowhere! The two riders on the second machine, now in closer view, seemed to be trying to change direction and sweep to the right of where Ken remembered seeing the first one. But it was slowing down, probably hitting slush and bogging in the water. He could hear the motor revving harder, but watched the machine move more and more slowly.

It was bogging down, all right, but instead of coming to a stop, it disappeared.

"Oh my God!" screamed Erika. "They've gone through the ice!"

Ken turned and ran toward the barn, hollering over his shoulder to his wife, "Phone 911! Call all the neighbours! Bring blankets! Ladders! Ropes! Get Jack over here with his diving gear. Tell 'em four kids are in the water!"

Inside the barn, Ken threw on a lifejacket and grabbed two coiled ropes. From a wooden storage box, he seized two ice picks. On his way out he grabbed two more lifejackets and unhooked the large extension ladder hanging under the eaves of the roof, carrying it under his arm.

Then he ran.

2
Cassidy

YEARS OF HARD WORK KEEPING HIS own ranch kept Ken in great shape, better than many men his age, but the weight of the ladder slowed him. His lungs burned. The muscles in his legs ached. His shoulders were numb from the awkward bulk of the ladder and gear. To make matters worse, he felt the apprehension of a soldier stepping through a minefield, not knowing which foot might go through thin ice to dark, cold water. Trained as a volunteer fireman, Ken knew he should never trust ice that someone had broken through, but he also knew that snowmobiles were heavier. *A five-inch thickness of ice is safe for snowmobiles and trucks; four inches for people.* He still felt solid ice beneath his steps, but his feet were starting to get cold as the slushy water seeped through the seams of his work boots. *Keep running! Every second counts! Keep running!*

Ken tried to look at his watch to determine how long the kids had been in the frigid water, but he couldn't get his sleeve up high enough to see without stopping. He was not going to stop running to see. He estimated they'd been in the water for close to five minutes. As he neared the area where he suspected the machines had gone through, he slowed down and held the ladder firmly with two hands. If he, too, broke through the ice, the ladder could act as a horizontal support, suspended across some solid ice over the water. If he let go, he could just as easily slip under the ice and become another victim.

Now he could see the water and the opening in the ice — about fifteen feet wide. But there was only one person floating in the exposed water. Sobbing and trying desperately yet unsuccessfully to scramble onto the ice was fourteen-year-old Cassidy Sampson. He did not want to think about where the other three were, but he knew that hypothermia would be setting into this one very soon. When it did, she would lose much of her muscle coordination and sink beneath the deep and murky depths. Dropping the ropes and ice picks, he threw one of the life jackets to her. Extending the ladder to its maximum length, twenty feet, he placed it directly across the ice hole as close as he could to Cassidy's head.

"Hold on Cassy," he soothed. "You just try to hold onto the ladder and the life jacket, honey, and I'll pull you up."

Cassidy tried to stop shivering and sobbing and do what she was told. In the process of letting go of the ice and reaching for the ladder, she sank momentarily, then came up gasping for breath, coughing, and resumed sobbing. She grabbed at the life jacket, but her arms, cold and numb, would barely move.

Her lips were already blue and the heavy snowmobile jacket was weighing her down. She was still shivering, but Ken knew that in a very short time her body would no longer be trying to generate heat with the muscular contractions of shivers. "Cassy, you are losing body heat. I want you to hug the lifejacket to your tummy. That's right," he continued to talk to her as he carefully climbed along the ladder. *Keep talking to her. Keep her conscious and focused.*

Cassidy sobbed. Her eyes were wide and fearful. Ken continued to reassure her, his thoughts conjuring up memories of his survival and rescue training. *H.E.L.P. — the Heat Escape Lessening Posture*. Calmly, he said to her, "Pull your knees up into a tuck position, cross your ankles." He tried to keep his voice light to prevent her from panicking. To keep himself from panicking. "Atta girl. Squeeze your elbows into your sides." Ken went down on his hands and knees, gripped the ladder and crawled the remaining distance.

"Here I am. Don't struggle, Cass. Just relax, or we'll both go in, and I just don't feel like swimming right now." He tried to laugh, but he knew it sounded false.

By the time Ken got to the middle of the ladder, Cassidy was neither talking nor crying. He suspected she was falling into another, more serious level of hypothermia. He reached behind her head and grabbed the collar of her jacket. On his knees, he shuffled along the ladder to the edge of the ice and pulled Cassy, still in the water, along with him. There, he stood up on the part of the ladder that was over the ice and pulled the inert girl out of the water.

Before Ken could decide whether to take Cassy to shore or to try to find the others, he heard shouts from behind. Looking back he saw some of his neighbours running out to help him. *Thank goodness Erika was able to reach someone at home!* Ken recognized the large man in the lead as Jack, another volunteer fireman and appropriately nicknamed "Bear" for being well over six feet tall with a huge chest and strong arms. His wife Donna was with him and they were pulling his scuba gear on a sled. *Great!* The sled would be a good way to take Cassy ashore so someone could warm her, and he could stay to help find the boys.

In seconds there were five more people beside Ken, laying down ladders for support and all wearing lifejackets. Ken rushed through his explanation: "Two snowmobiles went through, and there are three more kids in the water." Glancing at Cassidy, and at the same time taking a huge breath, he continued. "Cassy is the only one who found the hole; the rest of them must be somewhere under the ice. I'm pretty sure it's Jeremy Kendall and Sukh! I'm not sure, but odds are that the third is Kyle Aspen!"

"Probably," said one of the newly arrived. "I saw them all together a little while ago."

Jack, still breathless, started fumbling with his jacket zipper, which caught on the fabric and refused to budge. Exasperated, he stepped into his dry suit, thankful he'd invested the extra money in it, because it was roomy enough to go over all his clothes, including the jacket. Had he worn a wet suit he knew he would have chilled quickly in the freezing water. He'd need a lot of time if he had to find three kids under the ice.

Ken, catching a mouthful of air, watched two women start to take off Cassy's wet jacket. Between breaths he coached them through the important re-warming procedure. "Warm her torso first; leave her legs and arms for later or she could suffer from *afterdrop* and die."

Seeing the confused looks on the women's faces, Ken said "Afterdrop could give her a heart attack and lower her body core temperature even further. Her legs and arms have the coldest blood in them right now but the body is not letting that colder blood come near her organs. If you trick the body into thinking the cold has passed, it will allow that frigid blood to circulate and if it gets to her heart, it could give her a heart attack and kill her."

"So what should we do?" one of the women asked.

"Right now just warm her trunk," Ken continued. "Lie down beside her and use your own body heat under the sleeping bag."

Donna helped load the oxygen tank onto her husband's back. Frantically trying to zip the suit while slipping one arm at a time through the tank harness, Jack listened to Ken's advice to the women. Then Jack added, "Breathe into her face. She should try to inhale your warm breath. That helps to warm her faster, too."

More people arrived to help. Ken knelt down on the ice and, with wet fingers starting to go numb, began tying a rope to one of the ice picks. When it was knotted securely, he held the pick with two hands up over his head and with all his strength swung the pick down and stuck it into the ice.

"Do you know how long they've been in?" asked Jack, slipping his feet into his flippers.

Ken looked at his watch. "I'm guessing about ten, twelve minutes, now. This is getting real bad, Jack." Ken handed Jack the end of the rope. "Here's a guide rope for you to find your way back to the hole. Tie it to your belt. Some of us will sit on the ladder and kick our feet in the water. If any of those kids have found an air pocket under the ice, they might hear the splashing and swim over to it. But, it's been so long . . ."

His voice trailed off as he looked over at Cassy. She looked so blue. If she was already unconscious from the cold, the others would probably be, too.

Ken's morose thoughts were abruptly halted when one of the women let out a startled scream.

Cassidy stared at the crying child for a long time before she spoke. "Why are you crying?" she asked.

The boy did not stop. He did not look at her. It was as if he'd not even heard her.

"I'm too big to cry. Aren't you?" she asked.

She waited a moment. "Do you want your mommy?" She was torn between comforting the little boy and feeling ashamed for him.

The little boy, cheeks shining with shed tears, stopped sobbing momentarily as he turned to look at the blonde girl who had asked him the question. He resumed crying, louder now than before. He would not speak to the teacher, the little girl, or any of the other children around him. He just wanted to go home, away from these people, and this place!

Mrs. Cleveland crouched down at eye-level with the boy and continued to speak soothing words to him. Nothing she said calmed him. She stood. "Cassidy, it's circle time, now. We will leave Jeremy." She turned to face the small girl. "He's feeling a little sad this morning. Maybe he'll want to come and join us in the circle."

Cassidy took Jeremy's hand. "Come on, Jeremy. You can sit beside me."

Jeremy pulled his hand away and continued crying. Again, Cassidy took his hand to lead him to the other children but again he pulled away from her. He screamed, "No!" and ran to the farthest corner of the brightly decorated classroom, where he sat down on the floor, his back to the other children. There he sat crying, but silently, except for the odd hiccup.

Cassidy walked over to the other children and sat down cross-legged. She immediately reached for the hand of the boy beside her and he didn't pull away. Kyle liked holding the pretty little girl's hand. She leaned over and whispered into his ear: "He's a baby!"

Kyle giggled.

Mrs. Cleveland walked to the circle and sat down on a chair. With her hand in the air she waited for quiet. Then she said, "I'm going to read you a story. Who thinks they know what this story may be about?"

She held up the book. On the cover there was a picture of a bright yellow school bus.

A knock turned everyone's attention to a man standing in the doorway with two other people and a small child. Cassidy recognized the school principal. The others were not only strangers but also looked very strange.

Holding the small child's hand was an older woman dressed in what looked like pyjamas. If they were pyjamas, they were the most beautiful Cassidy had ever seen. The pants were a silky gold fabric with bright red trim, and the top, long enough to be a dress, was made of the same pretty fabric. On her feet she wore what looked like slippers. Over her head, covering most of her grey and black hair, was a veil of delicate white lace that crossed at her neck, one end draping over her shoulder, and hung down her back. Cassidy had never seen anyone with such dark skin, or eyes so dark they seemed black. Not here in town, on any of the ranches, or at neighbourhood barbecues. But the strangest thing about this woman was the shiny red jewel stuck to the side of her nose.

Standing on the other side of the principal was a very tall man with skin as dark as the woman's. He, too, wore brightly coloured clothing, with the same type of baggy pants and dress on top. He had a long grey beard and on his head was a strange-looking wrap of dark red cloth. Cassidy was certain nobody in class had ever seen anyone like these people before. They were certainly not from the Cariboo.

"Mrs. Cleveland, we have another student for you," said the principal. "This is Sukhwinder and he's with his grandparents."

Mrs. Cleveland rose from the chair. "Hello, Sukhwinder," she said. "I'm Mrs. Cleveland. Would you like to come in and meet the other children?"

All the children stared at this new boy. What an odd-looking kid, Cassidy thought.

He had large brown eyes fanned by the longest eyelashes she'd ever seen. His skin was dark brown and his hair, what she could see of it, was black. But the oddest thing was what the boy wore on top of his head. Cassidy thought he had an egg on his head at first, but then she realised it was a white cloth covering his bound hair. Wispy curls of black hair escaped the sides of the cloth and framed his very frightened little face.

Some of the students stood up to get a better view. He stared at them and they stared back. Mrs. Cleveland walked over to take his hand. She continued to talk to the man and the woman in the strange clothing.

The children continued to stare. Even Jeremy in the corner stopped crying to watch the little boy. Sukhwinder's eyes fixed on the boy sitting alone in the corner. He stared back at Jeremy. Then he pulled his hand out of Mrs. Cleveland's and walked toward Jeremy, stopping only when Jeremy was at his feet. Both boys stared, hypnotised. A long moment passed as the two faced each other, the entire class watching. Sukhwinder then looked up, beyond Jeremy, to the far wall. Following his gaze, Jeremy saw that the little boy had fixed his attention on a toy car garage and some plastic cars.

As Sukhwinder walked past him toward the cars, Jeremy rose and followed. Without a word, both stopped at the toys and began to play, oblivious to other children.

"Bye, Mr. and Mrs. Sangera," said Mrs. Cleveland as she turned back to the students, still sitting in the circle, but completely enraptured by the two boys making car noises across the room.

Before she left with the man, the older woman waved and called strange words as she looked over at Sukhwinder. The children were mesmerized as the little boy called back with equally odd words.

Kyle looked at the teacher. "What did he say, Mrs. Cleveland?" he asked. "What did he say and why does he wear that thing on his head?"

Mrs. Cleveland sat back down on her chair, relieved to see that Jeremy had stopped crying. She announced that the students could go to a play centre of their choice. All the children rose to find a place to play, but kept a wary eye and considerable distance from the two boys playing with cars in the corner.

All except Cassidy and Kyle, who raced over to the toy cars to play with Jeremy and the little boy with brown skin.

3
Jeremy

ALL EYES TURNED TO DONNA, WHO stood with a stricken look on her face. She was pointing toward the ice hole, her other hand over her mouth. There, floating in the middle of the water, was one of the boys, face down, only the back of his head above the surface. Somehow he was floating. Maybe there was a large enough air pocket, trapped under his heavy jacket, acting as a buoy. Maybe he'd been treading water under the ice and only recently lost consciousness. But before he could slip beneath the surface again, two men ran to the ladder and began crawling across to reach him. Ken threw the other life jacket into the water in case they needed one.

As they pulled him up and out of the water, Ken saw that it was Jeremy Kendall. Brown hair, usually curly but now straight and wet, framed an ash-grey face. His eyes were open, staring vacantly into a sky as blue as his lips. To Ken he looked dead, or as close to dead as he could be. Some of the women started crying. Ken went down on his knees and reached for the boy's wrist to check for a pulse. Either Ken's fingers were too cold, or the pulse was too weak, but he felt nothing. He knew that almost all the near-drowning victims revived with CPR, Cardiopulmonary Resuscitation, rarely recovered completely. If Jeremy survived but hadn't been breathing for more than a few minutes, he would probably have permanent brain damage.

He was just about to begin chest compressions when he heard Jack yell, "Wait, Ken! Give him a minute!"

Ken's first thought was that Jack was hypothermic and too cold to make any sense.

But Bear continued, his voice excited. "The mammalian diving reflex! Somebody — who has a watch? Time a minute! Check, then wait another one."

He picked up his powerful waterproof flashlight and waddled toward the hole in his cumbersome fins. He pulled at the collar of the neoprene hood to make sure it fit snugly around his neck and forehead and lowered the dive mask over his eyes and nose. He checked that the pressure regulator was working properly. Then he slipped the mouthpiece between his lips and, making sure the rope was secured at his waist, stepped off the edge of the ice into the lake. Instantly the dark waters swallowed him as he and the soft glow of the dive light disappeared from view.

The two men nearest the hole sat on the ladder and began kicking and splashing water.

Ken thought about what Bear had said. *Two minutes?* He looked down at the boy he knew so well. He felt helpless — and useless — sitting for two minutes and doing nothing to save him.

He forced himself to bide his time by explaining to the others: "The mammalian diving reflex is something that Bear, er, Jack and I have talked about before, when Jack was taking diving lessons and both of us were training for the fire department." He placed his hand on Jeremy's forehead and lovingly wiped the hair back. He took a slow, long breath, fighting the tears and the cracking of his voice. "Diving mammals . . . like seals and whales, have a natural reflex when they descend in cold waters to . . . to deny oxygen to their extremities, by slowing down their heart and blood flow and applying most of the oxygen to their heart and brain." Ken ached to pick up the still boy in his arms, tears threatening to blur his eyes and run down his cheek. With broken voice, again he went on, stuttering, "The . . . the theory . . . is . . . is that humans have the reflex, too, but . . . but it is very weak."

He paused, then shouted, "My God! How long has it been?" He turned to Donna, whose arm was up, her eyes glued to her watch.

"Only forty-five seconds," she announced, forcing herself to remain emotionless.

Ken started to rock forward and back, still on his knees. His body held pent up energy that he wanted to use to resuscitate the boy — now! He forced himself to wait, taking another deep breath and slowly releasing it. He continued, a slightly brighter thought racing through his head as he spoke, "When people, usually children, fall into icy waters, their lungs and heart sometimes will trap the air inside and . . . and shut off the oxygen travelling to their legs and arms . . . sending it to their vital organs only. It's a, I guess, a survival reflex and it doesn't happen very often."

"One minute, Ken!" Donna almost screamed it.

The men kicking the cold water ceased. Ken reached again for Jeremy's wrist. Everyone was silent, holding their breaths as Ken looked skyward willing his fingers to feel the slightest tremor beneath Jeremy's skin. A few moments went by and the rescuers needed only to see the sag of Ken's shoulders to know that he felt nothing.

Donna thought aloud. "I'm starting another minute."

Ken looked over to see if Cassidy looked any healthier. What he could see of her between the two women was not encouraging.

He turned back to Jeremy and continued to bide his time, forcing himself to continue talking in a textbook voice: "It, the reflex, can't happen if the victim gradually gets cold in less than icy water. It's only been known to happen when the water's very cold and chills the body instantly."

He looked up at his neighbours and forced a smile. "Some children have been known to be underwater, not breathing for more than an hour and have a full recovery. With no permanent brain or tissue damage!"

He watched a flicker of hope in some of the women's eyes as one of them voiced the thoughts of all of them. "You mean there could be hope for Jeremy and the other two boys yet?"

Ken said, "Jeremy's heart may actually be beating, but instead of the normal sixty beats per minute, his metabolism may have slowed down . . . to two or three beats a minute. And I don't want to interfere with Jeremy's metabolism by giving CPR if his heart and lungs are working, even that slowly. Interfering could cause them more damage and a heart attack."

Ken's voice trailed as he looked down at Jeremy again. Did he look greyer? He'd waited as long as he could physically bear but Jeremy was still not breathing on his own. To hell with it!

The energy burst from Ken's body in a flurry of determined activity. For the third time that day, he tried to find Jeremy's pulse. When he still detected none, he began CPR, pressing his joined hands into the young boy's chest. "One, two, three, four, FIVE! One, two three, four, TEN! One, two, three, four, FIFTEEN!" He stopped pressing his palms into Jeremy's chest and slowly breathed two breaths into his mouth and nose. Then he resumed counting compressions as the people around him, the energy contagious, began to move in an effort to feel useful.

Donna, realizing the watch was no longer needed, looked past her wrist at a movement up on the shore. She called, "There's the ambulance and fire department. They're at Ken's place!"

Two of the men stood up to wave their arms, whistling and calling to attract the attention of the ambulance attendants and firemen. "We're here! Here!"

Their calls could not possibly be heard from so far away, but Ken's wife, Erika, guided the emergency crew to the shore. A fireman acknowledged the crowd on the lake with a wave and began to run out to them, leading the others carrying stretchers. By this time Cassidy, barely conscious, lay on the sled, her torso wrapped in sleeping bags and her legs and arms still chilled beneath her wet clothes. Jack's closest neighbour and his wife, pulling the sled, broke into a run toward the attendants and their stretcher. Another ambulance and the RCMP had just pulled into Ken's driveway so Erika waved them, too, down to the edge of the lake.

Ken, his arms aching from performing chest compressions, asked Donna to help him. He suspected she had CPR training, just as his own wife did, being married to a fireman. She knelt beside Jeremy's cold frame and confirmed his suspicion when she began to count with him, "One, two, three, four, FIFTEEN and SWITCH!"

At the last word, Ken lifted his arms and pulled away only to have his hands expertly replaced by Donna's smaller ones. He leaned over and applied two breaths to Jeremy's mouth. Donna was now in charge of Jeremy's fate, and Ken could rest his aching shoulders.

His rest was short-lived. The two men who waited at the edge of the ice for Jack's return noticed the bubbles rising from Jack's underwater breathing apparatus were growing larger.

One of them pointed and hollered, "Here comes Jack. And . . . he's got someone!"

~ ~ ~

The day his mother left him — him and his dad — Jeremy felt that his heart had busted and could never be fixed again.

He knew his mother was not happy about living at the lake, isolated from town. She was from Vancouver, the Coast, as everyone here called it, where the winters were warm and wet and the grass was always green. She would tell him stories about the neighbourhood where she grew up and the things she'd done there. She described her apartment above her parents' small store and how she and her friends would spend hours going from shop to shop in the small strip. She talked of taking the bus from one end of the city to the other, just for something to do, and about fast food restaurants on every street and giant chain stores where you could buy anything you wanted. She always complained that so many people from across the country wanted to move to the Coast, so why had she moved away? Jeremy's grandparents still lived there and every few months he and his mom would go down to visit them.

But never his Dad. Jeremy figured his Dad didn't like the long drive from the Cariboo-Chilcotin to Vancouver. Even Jeremy didn't like it. It took almost all day and was very boring.

Jeremy would never forget the day he and his dad went into town to buy some things from the hardware store. It was a Sunday, and he had no school and his dad had no work. They had left first thing in the morning and his dad bought him breakfast — pancakes — at the truck stop along the highway in the middle of town. By the time they finished their errands in town and got back home, it was already time for lunch. There would be a few chores to do and then he could still meet up with Cass, Sukh, and Kyle, to play Manhunt in the woods for a little while before it got too dark and cold.

"Oh, your mother let the fire go out," his dad commented as they drove down the long, forest-lined driveway toward the small, two-storey log house that sat beside the lake shore. Jeremy looked up and sure enough, there was no smoke coming from the chimney.

"Before you go in, Jeremy, get some kindling and a couple of logs."

His dad stopped the old pickup, pulled on the emergency brake and turned the key to withdraw it from the ignition. Then he gathered up his bags of purchases and headed toward the work shed while Jeremy headed to the side of the log house to the woodshed.

When Jeremy got into the house, he noticed right away how cold and empty it seemed. "Mom!" he called.

He walked through the kitchen. "Mom!" he called again.

Jeremy stopped when he got to the wood stove and dropped the logs and kindling to the floor. He knew he should try to make the fire before he continued, but he had a strange feeling about the silence. He walked through the main living area and up the stairs.

"Mom?" he called again.

When he got to the top of the stairs he listened at his parents' closed bedroom door. Could she be sleeping? He gripped the doorknob and slowly opened the door while he called, in a loud whisper, "Mommy?"

All her dresser drawers were open. And empty. The closet, usually full with almost no room for Dad's stuff, was bare. Only some of Dad's pants, a suit, and a few hangers were left. There were no women's shoes on the closet floor. Her nightgown was not on her bed; her bedroom slippers were not on the floor. He looked past the bedroom to the ensuite, usually cluttered with hairbrushes, makeup and perfumes. The counters were clear. The only things Jeremy could see that belonged to his mother were a pair of snowmobile boots and her snowmobile suit, hanging on a hook beside the window. And that was when he knew.

Jeremy stood there with his hand on the doorknob for a long time, staring at the unmade bed. Even when we go to visit Grandpa and Grandma, she never takes all her clothes, he thought.

She was definitely gone.

Jeremy heard the screen door slam shut downstairs and his father call, "Honey?"

Silently he stepped back out of the room and shut the door, turning the knob so as not to make the slightest click. He tiptoed down the hall to his own bedroom and, as quietly as possible, lay down on his bed. He crossed his ankles and folded his hands together on his stomach. He looked up at the ceiling, at the little dark spot he stared at every night before he fell asleep.

Then he waited for his dad to come looking for his mother.

4
Kyle

JACK BROKE THROUGH THE SURFACE OF the lake, cradling the lifeless form of Kyle Aspen in his huge arms. The two men waiting at the hole reached down to pull the boy onto the ice. Ken rose from his knees and ran over to where poor Kyle lay, just as ashen as Jeremy had looked. Finding a pulse proved to be just as unsuccessful, so Ken checked his watch and began the wait to see if Kyle would breathe on his own, all the while praying that the firemen and ambulance attendants would make it out to them soon.

Jack, still partly submerged in the water, called, "I found him at the bottom of the lake." He struggled to catch his breath from the exertion. "It's not too deep here . . . maybe, I don't know, thirty feet." He panted. "I saw Sukh, too, but he's under the snowmobile. Gotta go back down . . . to get him!"

And with that, he replaced the mouthpiece and sank below the surface.

Kyle followed the shortcut through the woods to Cassidy's house. Since he had discovered this path he no longer had to take the road all the way around the point to go and play with her. Now if he turned off the road past the big rock, he could travel along the game trail that followed the barbed wire fence beside the Lockett Ranch. And because the trip there and back was so much shorter, he was allowed to go by himself, even though he was only eight years old. As long as he remembered to phone home when he got there.

He just had to remember to leave her house well before dark, because it was always much darker in the forest. One time he waited too long and Cassidy's mother made Cassidy's older brother walk him home. Kyle wouldn't have been scared if he'd gone alone. As it was, Jeff had terrified him. During the entire walk home Jeff told him story after story about savage bear maulings and cougar attacks, and one story about a rabid chipmunk. He even tried to tell Kyle there were sharks in the lake. Kyle's mother was very concerned when her son arrived home as white as a sheet. For a long time after that Kyle wouldn't use the shortcut, not even in daylight. And he never let the darkness trap him at Cassidy's again.

"We're going to the Sampson's house today," his mother told him one summer Sunday morning. She was gathering up towels, a beach blanket, sunscreen and some country music CDs.

"We're all going? Cool. What are we gonna do there?" Kyle asked.

"There's going to be a neighbourhood barbecue. I'm baking some buns right now and we're bringing hamburgers. You can go and help Daddy get the lawn chairs. Mrs. Sampson says you can try waterskiing, so bring your lifejacket."

The Sampsons had the coolest ski boat. It was a Moomba with a tricked out tower, fat sacks for weight and giant speakers for the stereo system. And Cassidy's brothers were the best skiers and wakeboarders on the lake. Cassidy was pretty good, too, but she was too young to be impressive. She could *go all the way around the bay without falling, and maybe she could cross the churning waters of the boat wake. But big deal. Her brothers could do three hundred and sixty degree turns and tantrum flips. Kyle had tried to ski a few times, but he couldn't get up and out of the water. They'd kept telling him that wakeboarding was easier, but his pride was too wounded to try; he might bomb at that, too.*

"How are we going to get there? Boat? Car? Or walking?" asked Kyle.

"Daddy says he wants to drive, to carry everything, so I guess we'll take the truck."

"Can we go now?"

"Not for a while yet. I have to let the buns rise before I can bake them. They'll take about a half an hour to bake." His mother was calculating in her head. "I figure maybe not for another hour or so."

"I'm walking, then," Kyle decided. "I want to go now."

"Fine," she answered, then called out after him, "Call us when you get there!"

Kyle followed the dirt road until he got to the trail. As soon as he turned off the road he saw Mr. Lockett on the other side of the fence.

"Hey, Kyle. How are you?"

"Fine. We're going to a barbecue and water-skiing at Cassidy's house."

"Well, doesn't that sound like fun? As a matter of fact, we're going to a barbecue at the Sampson's today, too," he answered with a wink and a smile. "I wonder if it's the same one." He walked closer to the fence. "And Mrs. Lockett is going to bring some apple strudel."

"Wow, I love her apple strudel. So do Jeremy and Sukh."

Mr. Lockett replied, laughing, "I think everyone loves Mrs. Lockett's strudel. That's what made me fall in love with her when I met her in Germany thirty years ago. She made the best apple strudel then and I have never tasted a better one."

Ken and Kyle heard voices coming from along the dirt road. "Well, look who's here. If it isn't Sukh and Jeremy."

"Where are you guys going?" asked Kyle.

"To Cassidy's for a barbecue. Our whole, entire families will be there," said Sukh.

"Your whole, entire families?" Mr. Lockett teased. "Even Naniji and Grampaji?"

"Even them. Naniji is bringing samosas and pakora," answered Sukh.

"And my dad is bringing some fresh trout we caught yesterday," added Jeremy.

Mr. Lockett smiled and said, "Well, it sounds like we're going to have an absolute feast. Just remember, if you get there first, save some for me. I'd like to have a little bit of everything. You do that for me and I'll be sure and save you guys some strudel."

The boys nodded and giggled. Mr. Lockett looked serious for a moment. "Listen, boys. I heard something snooping around my garbage cans last night. I didn't see anything, but the lids were all flipped off this morning. There could be a bear around, so be careful, okay?" He looked up the trail and added, "I'll see you at the Sampsons'." He winked again, turned and headed back toward his house.

"Bye," they answered as they continued down the path, deeper into the forest.

A few moments later Jeremy reached into his pocket and pulled out some brightly coloured little balls. "Look at this," he said to the others.

"Wow, where'd ya get those from?" asked Kyle.

"My uncle brought them from the Coast. I have a whole jar full of them at home."

Sukh looked at the balls and finally asked, "What are they?"

Kyle answered, "They're paint balls, dummy. People at the Coast get all dressed up in army clothes and run around a forest trying to shoot each other with these special guns and these balls. If it hits you, they splatter coloured dye all over your clothes. And you're dead, or at least you're out of the game!"

"Do they hurt?" asked Sukh.

"Nahh. They're not supposed to." Jeremy reached back and pulled a slingshot out of the back pocket of his jeans. "Watch that tree."

Jeremy stretched the rubber of the slingshot back as far as he could, took aim and released. Instantly, a bright orange splat appeared on the trunk of a large pine tree.

"Cool," commented Kyle.

"Sweet," said Sukh.

"Here, you guys run ahead and I'll see if I can hit you."

Kyle and Sukh ran up the trail a little ways. Jeremy took aim with another paint ball and fired.

Sukh stuck his thumbs in his ears and wiggled his hips, saying "Nahh, Nahh! You missed me! You missed me! Now you have to kiss me!" Just like Cassidy always said. Then he pursed his lips dramatically and made kissing sounds.

"I'll kiss you . . . right on your butt with this!" Jeremy let another paint ball fly.

Sukh quickly turned and dodged so as not to get hit in the face. The orange paint ball slapped him on his backside, staining his blue jeans with a bright orange circle. "Ow!" he cried. "That smarts!"

He rubbed his backside. The initial pain was just a little jolt, but now it spread out in a burning circle. He wanted to cry, but started laughing instead. Then he began jumping up and down, continuing to rub his injury. "That really hurt."

Jeremy and Kyle laughed as their friend's pain gradually diminished. "You think it's funny. Here, let me try to hit you," Sukh demanded.

As Jeremy handed over the slingshot and some paintballs, a cracking sound made them turn and look sideways. Something big and black was moving through the forest. They could only get glimpses of it through the trees. It was not coming toward them, but was moving parallel to them. Almost circling them. All three boys froze. Another crack *behind them made them step closer together and swing their heads around again. They were surrounded by something.*

Jeremy whispered, "A bear?"

"It would have to be two of 'em," answered Kyle, his voice quiet and frightened.

"Aw, no," Sukh moaned, then whispered, "If there's more than one, it must be a mother and a cub. We're dead!"

Another noise in front, followed by bleating. The boys let out a collective sigh of relief.

"Cows," Sukh said, as he watched one step through the trees into a clearing nearby.

"Whew," replied Jeremy. "Must be the Lockett's." Then he looked at the boys with a big grin on his face. All the boys got the same idea together.

"No dumb cow is going to scare us. Take that," said Kyle. He drew back the band of the slingshot and let the paint ball fly. The shot hit the target. The black cow, now with a bright yellow bull's-eye on its side, began to run away from the boys. It didn't take much to spook the other cows, still invisible to the boys because of the trees. Within seconds, at least twenty cows, some brown and some black, stampeded past them, heading in the direction of the black one. When the dust settled, the three boys doubled over laughing.

Then they continued down the path toward the Sampsons' house, eager to tell Cassidy about their adventure.

5
Sukhwinder

WHILE THE REST OF THE RESCUE group waited for the minute to be up, the firemen and ambulance attendants finally reached them, bringing stretcher baskets. Ken recognized all of them from working and training together; they'd all been locals for years. He informed Johnny Schwartz, a fellow rancher and volunteer fireman, of Jeremy and Kyle's conditions.

Johnny said, "Two of the guys have taken the girl back to the ambulance. They've got some humidified oxygen in there. It's heated — helps hypothermia victims. We're here to transport the boys. Is there anyone still in the water?"

At Ken's nod, he raised a hand-held radio that crackled with static before he spoke into it. Ken didn't hear what Johnny said, or what the gravelly voice blared back in reply. But Johnny turned to him and continued, "One of the ambulance attendants has already radioed into dispatch and asked for a medi-vac helicopter to come out here to transport the fourth child. These kids are too ill to wait in an ambulance. We're transporting!"

Ken was torn between going with Jeremy and staying with the rescue. He figured Jeremy's dad would probably meet the boy at the hospital. Better for Ken to stay, even though he wasn't on duty. He felt a responsibility to the other kids, who were also his friends and neighbours.

"Johnny, I'm staying here," said Ken. He lowered his voice so the others wouldn't hear him. "I'm worried Jack might suffer from hypothermia, with the water being so cold and all."

Johnny nodded and said, "I'll leave Steven here, too. Steve! You stay until everyone's out of the water. I'll help get these two kids to the ambulance. The RCMP will be out here any second." Ken watched him leave with Jeremy and Kyle cradled in the stretchers, while Donna ran along beside them supporting an attendant giving CPR. Ken turned back to face the quiet hole in the ice. He thought of Sukhwinder trapped for so long in the frigid waters and whispered, "Hail Mary, full of grace, the Lord is with thee . . ."

Sukhwinder was the first person in his family to learn how to swim. Neither his mother, father, his grandparents — Grampaji and Naniji — Uncle Raman and Auntie Manisha, nor his three older cousins (whom he called his sisters), had ever learned how to swim. There was no concern about them learning. Their large home had a lake view but was actually up a huge cliff, far from the water's edge. But since Sukh spent so much time with his three best friends who did *live on the lakeshore, he simply felt compelled to learn how.*

Near Kyle's home was an old tree that had fallen over one day in a violent wind storm, but had wedged itself in between two trees that crossed each other. This 'X' provided a great support for the fallen tree to lean far over the water of the lake. Kyle's dad had tied a long rope to the tip of the tree, knotted the end with a series of handles and attached a platform with a makeshift ladder to the tree's base. On hot summer days Jeremy, Kyle and Cassidy spent hours at the rope swing, swinging out as far as they could, then letting go and landing with giant splashes in the cool water. But when the others called to invite him over, Sukh's parents wouldn't let him go to the new hangout.

One day the children were going to play at Kyle's house after school. It was one of those rare hot days in June when the school bus was sweltering hot because all the windows were kept closed to prevent the children from gagging on the dust swirling up from the dirt road. When they passed the part of the road where the rope swing hung Kyle said, "Hey, let's go for a swim. Last one to the rope is a loser!"

As soon as the bus stopped, the children raced out and ran back to the swimming hole. When they neared the water's edge, backpacks fell and clothes flew in every direction. The children had no towels, no swimsuits and no permission, but they didn't care. The last one to the rope swing was a loser.

Everyone was giggling when Cassidy made it to the top of the old tree first. She wore only a pair of panties. The boys had on boxer shorts. Only Sukh had something else on, a patka, the modified version of the turban his father and Grampaji wore to cover their hair.

"Three, two, one, go!" Jeremy and Kyle chanted to Cassidy. She lifted her feet, swung out to the farthest reach of the rope and let go.

"Yahoo!" she yelled before the cold waters of the lake consumed her. The rope swung back to Jeremy and he caught it. When Cassidy emerged from the water, she let out a loud gasp and a yell. "It's freezing!" she called.

"Whee, look at me!" called Jeremy as he released his grip on the rope and landed in the water in a cannonball splash.

Kyle always did the most impressive swings. When he released his grip on the rope, he lifted his knees over his head, did a full turn and landed feet first in the water.

Everyone clapped and cheered, except Sukh. He was standing as far out on the platform as he dared. The rope swung back to him a second time and still he didn't catch it. He looked down at the dark green water. From where he stood, the rocks far below the surface looked to Sukh dangerous enough. But the water between him and the rocks seemed an even bigger threat.

"Come on, Sukh," called Cassidy. "Catch the rope."

Sukh didn't move. By now the rope had stopped swinging and hung straight down to the water. Kyle waded into the lake to retrieve the swing and throw it up to Sukh.

"Here, Sukh, catch it," he called. Sukh still didn't move. He would not talk, not move, not swing.

The children waited, confused. Then it dawned on Jeremy: he'd never seen Sukh in the water without a lifejacket. He gave Kyle a little shove with one hand. When Kyle looked at him to see what he wanted, Jeremy opened his eyes wide and nodded toward Sukh above them. Then he shook his head.

Kyle didn't understand Jeremy's body language. "What?" he asked.

Again Jeremy shook his head to indicate "No."

Cassidy noticed the silent communication between Kyle and Jeremy. "Sukh, you can't swim, can you?"

Sukh stepped down off the platform. He climbed down the old ladder to the children on the ground. He walked over and began to pick up his clothes.

"It's okay, Sukh," began Kyle. "We'll teach you."

"Yeah, we can teach you," said Jeremy. Cassidy nodded.

Sukh stopped. "Really?"

The children showed Sukh how to blow bubbles with his face in the water, how to hold his breath and float. They taught him to tread water and to flip over on his back. They made him reach down in the deep water for coloured rocks and challenged him to float on his torso, face down and feet kicking, from one of them to the other. He wasn't stroking yet, but he was floating. Gradually, the cold water got the best of them and they climbed out onto a large, warm rock to dry off in the sunshine.

Sukh was ecstatic. "Wow, I can swim now." He looked up to the rope swing. "Next time, I will be ready for that!" He added, "Well, maybe . . . with a lifejacket."

Then he started to unwind his patka. All the children watched. They'd never seen Sukh without the traditional headdress, not since he had graduated from the little white cloth on his hair to this larger, more ornately wound one. When he finished, Sukh laid the cloth down on the rock beside him to dry in the sun. Then he shook out his hair to let it fall down his back.

Cassidy gasped. Jeremy and Kyle sat with their eyes and mouths wide open. Sukh's hair was longer than Cassidy's. It hung in black waves all the way down to his boxers.

Wow!" Cassidy said.

Sukh looked at his best friends' faces and laughed. "I have never cut my hair in my life. If God meant for our hair to grow, why would we cut it? Yours would be this long, too, if you never cut it."

Cassidy reached out to gather the long strands. "Can I braid it?"

All the boys laughed at her request.

Cassidy's face fell. "Oh, come on, you guys. I don't have a sister and I never get to play with any girls. There're no girls living around here. Just you guys and my stupid brothers."

Sukh considered that Cassidy had just taught him how to swim, something he'd wanted to do for a long time.

He looked at the other boys and sighed. Then he said, "Promise not to tell anyone about this?"

"What are ya gonna do if we tell?" asked Kyle.

"I'll tell everyone you guys were swimming naked," answered Sukh. "Then, I'll tell everyone you are a couple of girlie-girls."

"Girlie-girls? Spoken by a guy about to get his hair braided?" asked Jeremy.

"Promise . . . or not?"

"Fine," answered Jeremy.

"Yeah," replied Kyle.

"Pact," said Sukh. All four children reached out, forming a circle of fists touching knuckles to knuckles.

Cassidy's face lit up. "Goody," she said, as she positioned herself behind Sukh.

They knew they'd all catch heck when they got home that day, but they continued to sit on the rock, laughing and joking and allowing the afternoon sun to warm their bodies, while Cassidy made dozens of thin braids out of Sukh's long, dark tresses.

6
Out of the Water

THERE WERE ONLY FIVE PEOPLE LEFT waiting at the silent hole. The now familiar feeling of uselessness and the agony of waiting engulfed Ken again. He felt oddly alone. Was it the silence? Was it fear for the childrens' lives? He looked up to his house, wondering what his wife was doing. He wanted her reassurance that everything would be all right, but the 911 operator would have asked her to wait there for the police, ambulance and firemen.

In his driveway he saw the Kendall's and Sangera's cars parked, their drivers' doors open. He couldn't see the parents in the yard, but he knew they had to be nearby. Ken wouldn't even try to imagine their fear and grief. The afternoon's stress sparked an odd thought: funny that both boys' frantic parents had burst out of their cars and left the doors open. He wondered if the keys were still in the ignition and if the *ding, ding, ding* of the "key left in the ignition" alarm was driving anyone crazy. Would the interior car lights left on drain the batteries dead? Dead. How long would it take? He felt like running across the lake and up the driveway to shut the doors. Instead, he made a mental note to find his jumper cables when he got home so he could jump start their cars later.

He glanced at his watch. Since Jack's last appearance, six or seven more minutes had gone by.

"I wonder if he's having trouble getting the machine off of Sukh," one of the men commented, not expecting an answer.

Another minute ticked by.

"Come on, Bear," Ken muttered.

From the distance a new sound began, small but very clear. It grew louder until the men could hear and feel the *thump, thump, thump* of a helicopter, flying low enough to sway the tops of the tallest trees lining the lakeshore.

"Search and Resc," the man closest to Ken said. And he began to wave his arms and call to the giant bird.

The helicopter flew overhead, creating tiny tornadoes of snow that danced around them, dusting their faces with icy crystals. It landed in the closest snow-patched pasture, about a hundred metres away. Two rescue workers, fully outfitted in bright orange jumpsuits and white helmets, leapt out of the side of the helicopter. They leaned back into the opening and brought out a stretcher. Then they raced out to the men on the ice.

"And here's Jack!" yelled the other man, detecting the glow of the dive light. The small group of men cheered as Jack again split the surface of the water. He was pulling Sukh by the collar of his jacket. Eight hands stretched forward to pull the boy to safety. Ken, exhausted, stepped back to let the search and rescue workers, fresh from the helicopter, take control of Sukh's life-saving procedure. He was too drained to face another lifeless teen.

Jack tried to pull himself out of the water, slipping on the ice just as Cassidy had. Two of the men struggled to assist by pulling on the rope still tied to Jack's waist. Ken suspected that Jack would be feeling considerable muscle weakness from the cold, cold water and from rescuing Sukh from under the machine. He couldn't help but think of his nickname; he reminded Ken of a bear, splashing around in a deep pool, fishing for salmon.

"Bear!" he called so he had the big man's attention. "Here, use this."

Ken slid Jack an ice pick. He watched the giant man hammer it into the slippery surface and use it to hoist himself out of the water.

When he was safely out, Jack sat down on the ice and took off his mouthpiece, mask and hood. For a few moments he just sat there, catching his breath and staring down onto the ice. Drops ran down his cheeks. Ken wondered if they could have been tears and the thought caused Ken's own vision to blur. He took a deep breath and looked up into the sky to stop the tears from brimming over his eyelids. He was unsuccessful.

Within minutes, Sukh was expertly loaded onto the helicopter. The helicopter's motor revved higher as the rotor blade's speed increased. They all watched the copter rise slowly straight up, do a one hundred and eighty degree pivot, then charge through the air toward the local hospital.

Jack, still sitting on the ice, watched the helicopter disappear over the tops of the trees. "Did we resuscitate any of them?" he asked with dread, already knowing what the answer would be.

Ken put his hand on Jack's broad shoulder. No one said anything. Silently, they all began to gather the ropes, equipment and ladders. An RCMP constable joined them but, sensing their mood, held off asking questions for his report. He quietly helped to gather Jack's scuba gear, then walked to Ken to help carry the other end of his ladder. Without a word, all six neighbours departed in the directions of their homes, leaving the gaping wound in the icy lake.

A short while later, bone-weary, Ken entered his house. An orangey glow from the waning sun bathed his home in gold.

The only sounds were the whispers of his wife praying with the shiny black beads of her rosary. He wanted her to hold him, but he felt those kids needed her prayers more than he needed a hug. He walked over to the chesterfield and sat down. Dazed and adrenaline-charged, he tried to will his heart to stop pounding. He stared at the floor. His gaze fixed on a tiny piece of candy wrapper balled up under the coffee table. He tried to convince himself that this day did not happen.

7
Opa and Oma

JEREMY WAS COLD. COLD AND NUMB. His eyes were open. A bright light was blinding him. He tried closing his eyes but the light stayed just as bright. What was going on? Voices. Whose voices were those? They sounded frantic. He looked around, but all he could see was the light. A bright, fiery light. Was something on fire? Would somebody please stop shining that thing in his eyes? The voices started to fade. Everyone seemed to be moving farther away. Even the light was dimming . . .

When Jeremy was ten he decided he didn't need a babysitter anymore. It wasn't that he didn't like going to the Locketts'. He did. He just felt that after school care wasn't necessary anymore. And he didn't want to hurt his dad.

When his mom left, Jeremy's dad asked Mr. and Mrs. Lockett to baby-sit him after school. Because they worked the ranch from their own home, the Locketts were always there to meet the school bus, which went past their house everyday anyway. Mrs. Lockett was a great cook and always had homemade German food waiting for him, like the breaded meat called schnitzel, and bratwurst and even sauerkraut. Sometimes there was apfel *strudel and German chocolate cake and his favourite cake,* sachertorte. *And after closing up the business every evening in town, his dad usually was invited to stay for dinner when he picked up Jeremy to take him home. His dad greatly appreciated the hot meals, eating as he wearily talked about the business he was forced to run alone. Sometimes Bear and Donna came for dinner, too, and Jeremy would fall asleep in the spare bedroom as he listened to laughter from the dining room.*

After a while Mr. and Mrs. Lockett asked Jeremy to call them "Oma" and "Opa." He liked the names; they sounded funny. It was a long time later that Jeremy found out that the words were German for "Grandma" and "Grandpa," but he didn't care. They acted like what real grandparents should be, and he hadn't seen his own since his mom left.

Some days after school, Jeremy had Sukh, Cass and Kyle over to the Lockett's place, just as he would sometimes go to their houses. The bus would stop and four kids — always four, never two or three — would run down the slope to the ranch house, eager to eat some warm apfel *strudel dusted with icing sugar before they ran out to the lake, the pasture or the barns. As each of their parents came home from work they would swing by the Lockett's ranch and pick up their child, often staying for a short visit or one that would stretch into the evening.*

One cold, snowy day, just after a cold snap in the Cariboo, the kids were coming over to the ranch. Opa had a surprise for them. The kids ran from the school bus to the mudroom off the kitchen and dropped mittens, toques, and snow boots before Jeremy noticed a pile of ice skates in a box on the floor. Cassidy recognised hers right away. They were a well-worn hand-me-down pair from her brothers.

"What the . . . " Cassidy began, stupefied. "What are my skates doing here?"

Kyle, Sukh and Jeremy had never really done much skating, even though they lived on the lake and could skate every winter day if they chose. In the box were three other pairs of skates, not new, but barely worn.

Mrs. Lockett came into the room saying, in her thick German accent, "Don't take off your snow pants yet! Go out and see what Opa has done for you."

Curious, the children all said "What?"

Jeremy tried to look out the window, but could see nothing through the frosty pane. "Where is he?"

They put their boots back on and ran down to the lake.

Before they got near the shore they slowed down, overwhelmed with what they saw. A rectangle half the size of a full hockey rink was cleared of snow. Its edges were smooth and straight with walls of packed snow. Opa was at one end, pushing a snow blower. Snow sprayed out from a spout metres beyond where he was walking. His eyebrows, moustache and toque were covered with snow crystals, making him look like the abominable snow monster. As he slowly pushed the machine, his feet slipped slightly on the smooth surface of ice on the lake.

And standing straight up on the edge of the ice, stuck into the snow, were five brand new hockey sticks.

"Hockey!" yelled Sukh.

"Let's go back and get on the skates!" cried Cassidy.

"I'm goalie!" shouted Kyle. The three of them turned to run back to the mudroom.

Jeremy stood watching Opa. For some strange reason he felt like crying, but he was really happy. He put his hand to his mouth and began to call out, but the cracking of his near-tears-voice embarrassed him. Besides, the noise of the machine would hamper a call, so he put his fingers in his mouth to whistle for Opa's attention. Opa stopped and looked up. He waved to Jeremy. Jeremy stood still, not knowing how to respond. Finally, he raised both hands and gave the two thumbs up signal. Then he turned and ran back to the mudroom to put on a pair of skates.

By the time Jeremy's dad came to pick him up that evening, Sukhwinder's Grampaji stood in one goal, his turban glistening with frost crystals. He wore snow boots and held a corn broom for a goalie stick. Naniji stood behind him with the hood of her parka covering her hair, her baggy pants tucked into her snow boots. She was ready to rescue any wayward pucks before they got lost in the deep snow behind the net. Cassidy's older brothers skated circles around the younger children, occasionally passing them the puck to make them feel important.

It was adults against kids, so Ken Lockett, his friend everyone called "Bear" and Kyle's dad were on the opposite team. Cassidy's dad had hooked up some trouble lights, strategically placed on trees lining the shore. Erika served hot chocolate from a thermos to anyone who was forced to the bench because of penalties, cold feet or just plain fatigue.

Mr. Kendall stood on the edge of the ice rink, no expression on his face. He listened to the laughter and watched everyone having fun. He watched Bear skate too close and too fast near Jeremy, then lift the child around the waist to put him down behind him, avoiding a collision. He listened to Jeremy giggle and call after him, "No fair, that's cheating!" He watched Ken skate fast to Jeremy, still sitting on the ice where Bear had dropped him, and stop suddenly to spray the child's face with shaved ice. He listened to Bear and Ken roar with laughter as Jeremy sputtered snow from his mouth and laughed along with everyone else. He knew Jeremy loved this. But he was too tired to join them. And he was jealous.

"Jeremy!" he called.

Jeremy looked up, blinking snow from his eyelashes.

"Hey, Dad, watch this!" He got up and skated as fast as he could to the other end of the rink and back. Kyle passed him the puck and he dribbled it back and forth from one side of his stick to the other. He passed the puck to Cassidy's oldest brother, then skated back to his dad to wait for his praise.

"Come on, Jeremy. We're going," said his dad.

Jeremy's face fell. That was not what he was expecting. "No, Dad," he whined. "Not yet, this is too much fun."

"Now! Right now, Jeremy!" his dad replied sternly.

Erika Lockett walked over to them and said, "I have some dumplings with gravy for dinner. Please stay."

"Yeah, Dad. I haven't eaten yet. I've been playing hockey since I got home."

Jeremy's dad did not smile. Slowly and deliberately, he replied, "This isn't home, Jeremy." Then he pointed to their pick-up. "Now, get your things and let's get going."

Jeremy didn't know why his dad wouldn't stay. For a long moment he looked at his dad. Then he skated to the middle of the rink and yelled back, "I'm not going!"

By then every skater had noticed the tense moment happening between father and son. The laughter ceased, the game paused and everyone skated to the far end of the rink to make small talk. Everyone except Kyle, Sukh and Cassidy. They stood together on the ice and faced Jeremy's dad. Opa skated back to where Jeremy had stopped on the ice. He whispered something to Jeremy, who replied, "No!" without taking his eyes off of his dad. Jeremy crossed his arms in front of his chest and took a deep breath.

Erika called to Jeremy to come, but Jeremy turned away from her and skated over to stand beside his best friends.

When Jeremy looked back, he saw his father get into the pick-up and slam the door. He heard the engine start, watched his father back up the driveway, spin on some ice and take off down the road.

That night, when Jeremy bedded down in the Lockett's spare bedroom, he listened to the whispers of Opa and Oma. He couldn't hear what they were saying, but he knew they were talking about him. He lay there for the longest time, on his back, his ankles crossed and his hands folded on his stomach. He wondered what his dad was doing. He wondered if his dad was still angry.

He decided he was too old to have a babysitter. And too old to still call the Locketts Opa and Oma.

8
So Long, Childhood

CASSIDY COULD HEAR HER MOTHER'S VOICE calling her over and over. And her mother was crying. What's happened? Why is Mom crying? Cassidy felt cold. Very, very cold. Her hair was wet. And something very heavy was on top of her. She tried to kick it off with her arms and her legs, but it wouldn't move. What was on top of her? Burying her. Cassidy panicked. Burying her! She felt as if she couldn't breathe very well. Her legs and arms wouldn't move. Was it because of the heaviness she was buried under? Please, stop crying Mom! Get this thing off of me! She thought she could hear some people coming closer. Were they coming to help her? She tried to scream for help, but no words came out . . .

She was eleven but almost twelve. It was exactly six weeks before her twelfth birthday. It was the day she became a woman. At least that's what her stupid brother told her. Her mother told her it was just part of growing up. And she hated it.

Her mother surprised her by driving her into town to go shopping. Shopping was one of those chores her mother did, but always alone. She said she liked to get to the crowded stores for some peace and quiet, away from the rat race of raising three boys and a girl who acted like a boy. Cassidy was curious as to why she would be so privileged. Or punished. She didn't know which because she hadn't ever shopped with her mother.

When they got to the only department store in town, her mother took her straight to the hair notions aisle. "Here, Cass, look at these. Aren't they cute?"

"What are they?" Cassidy asked.

"They're for your hair. See, you clip it on and it hangs down the back."

Cassidy looked at the beaded pink clip. Her only thoughts were how to keep it from getting tangled in a tree branch, or how her head would hurt with a snowmobile helmet pressing it against her scalp. "Why would anybody want one of those?" she asked.

Her mother turned to look at her. "Because it's pretty. And wearing pretty things makes a girl feel pretty. I'm sure you've seen some of the kids wearing them at school."

"Yeah — girls," Cassidy answered. "But none of my friends do. Not even Sukh." She giggled.

Her mother sighed. "I can't believe how much I wanted a daughter to dress in pink frills and put bows in her hair. And I thought my prayers were finally answered when you were born." She rolled her eyes. "Just tell me, when do I get to dress you in pink and curl your hair?"

Now it was Cassidy's turn to roll her eyes. "Oh, Mom. Oh, please."

"Come on, you. Let's head over to the women's wear." Her mother hooked her arm through Cassidy's. "You need some clothes."

"Nothing pink, lacy or with bows, Mom. 'Cuz I won't wear it."

Her mother looked straight ahead, unable to look into Cassidy's eyes as she continued. "No, I was thinking more along the lines of white and lacy with a little tiny bow in the middle."

Without releasing her mother's arm Cassidy stopped walking, jerking her mother back to a full stop. "What are you thinking?"

Her mother would not make eye contact with her. "Honey, it's time for you to get some support."

Cassidy did not want to hear anymore. "No, it's not. I know what you're talking about. I think."

"Cassidy, you need a bra."

Cassidy raised her hands and covered her ears. "No, No. I can't hear you."

Her mother faced her, pulled her daughter's hands away from her ears. "Yes, honey, you need a bra. A bra! It's not a big deal. Every woman wears one."

"But . . . but. The guys. They're going to laugh at me. They're going to tease me. I'll never hear the end of it, Mother."

Her mother laughed. "Yes, you will. They won't even notice. And if they do, so what? You're growing up. I'm sure they're going to notice that."

Cassidy's face was getting hot. She could feel her skin turning red. Oh, why does this have to happen? Why do I have to have . . . stupid breasts? But she allowed her mother to lead her to the lingerie section.

When it was all over, her mother took her for lunch to the little truck stop on the edge of the highway in the middle of town, where she talked to Cass about her changing body, her menstrual cycle, and sex. Puke!

A few days later, during another hot drive in the school bus coming home, Kyle called, "Last one to the rope swing is a loser." Kyle, Sukh and Jeremy ran to the swimming hole, while Cassidy walked. The boys stripped down to their boxers. Cassidy did not even take off her backpack. Jeremy was the first one to the end of the tree, followed by Sukh, then Kyle. Cassidy leaned against a tree near the edge of the water. She held a long blade of wild wheat, picking off one green seed at a time, while the boys swung, one by one, landing in the cool water.

"Coming, Cass?" Jeremy finally asked.

"Nah," she answered. "I just don't feel like it today." She really didn't.

"Cassy is a loser. Cassy is a loser," chanted Kyle.

Sukh looked at Cassidy, then asked. "Come on, Cass. It's not that cold. I know you can swim." He winked and smiled at her.

Jeremy held onto the rope for a few seconds, looking out to the shimmering water. A thought struck him. He raised his eyebrows and glanced down at Cassidy, who looked up to meet his gaze. She watched his eyes look not at hers, but at her chest. He knew and Cassidy knew he knew. She folded her arms to protect her chest from his penetrating look. Her face turned red. He smiled at her, let out a quiet chuckle, then lifted his legs to swing out to the welcoming lake.

But thankfully no words were spoken about her uncomfortable, constricting, pinching, strangling, annoying, unpleasant, white lacy garment with the little white bow that she wore under her baggy sweatshirt.

9
So Long, India

THUMP, THUMP, THUMP. *SUKH FELT A pounding in his chest. He heard nothing, but with each thump he felt his heart grumble. It was like . . . the heavy bass from a stereo system . . . or thunder when the lightning struck very close by, or . . . an explosion. People. Strangers. Oh, that feels so nice and warm . . .* thump, thump, thump . . . .

When Sukhwinder was twelve he cut off his hair.

His parents were livid. They were traditional Sikhs and their hair should not be shorn. But Sukh was tired of being one of the only Sikhs in town, the only one in school wearing a turban and the only student to need assistance (to help him with his reading vocabulary, they said) in class. He was tired of translating Punjabi into English for Naniji and Grampaji everywhere they went. And he was tired of driving to the Coast to visit the Temple. He wanted to be just like everyone else.

The day he did it was the day his older cousin told him she was getting married. Raveena had spent the last three months in India with Naniji and Uncle Ramen. When she came back to Canada, she brought the news that she was getting married. It had all been arranged on her visit to the Punjab, a province in Northern India, where Grampaji, Naniji and Sukh's parents were originally from.

"You're marrying a guy you barely know," he said to Raveena as she unpacked her suitcase. "I can't believe it."

"Well, believe it."

"But you don't even know this Rajwinder guy. You're crazy."

"I'm not crazy. I'm respectful," she said, hanging a sari in her closet.

"Respectful? To who?" he asked.

"To my family. To my culture. To his family."

"To your family? Your family won't care if you don't marry him." He thought about his older cousins and Raveena's older brother, Jaskirat, all living on the Coast. "Jaspal and Jaswinder won't do it. They have tons of girls to choose from right here in Canada. There's no way they're going to go to India to get a wife they barely know. And they wouldn't care if you didn't either."

Raveena looked at Sukh. She sighed, thinking about her wild cousins and her own brother, Jaskirat, living in Surrey. "Jaspal and Jaswinder don't seem to care about a lot of things this family believes in," she said quietly.

Sukh turned to face her. "What's that supposed to mean?"

She turned away from his question. After a long moment she finally said, "They just seem to have given up on a lot of . . . well, a lot of what we believe in."

Sukh lay on the bed, tossing a football in the air and catching it. He considered her comment. He knew that they'd cut their hair a long time ago, but other than that, he couldn't think of any other things he believed in that they'd given up on. Sure, they didn't dress like Grampaji, but then neither did his dad or his uncles. "Well, I think they're cool. I want to be just like them."

Raveena turned back to face Sukh. She quickly walked to the edge of the bed and caught the football in the air. Snatching it to her side she looked into his eyes. Sternly she told him, "Don't you ever talk like that. I mean it Sukhy. Those boys are up to no good. I don't want you to think that they're cool, because they're not. Do you understand?"

His hands were still reaching up in the air to catch the football but his eyes were wide as he looked at her. The tone of her voice scared him a little. He swallowed and nodded, but his curiosity took over. "What do you mean?" he finally asked. "What'd they do?"

Raveena realized she'd said too much. She tried to smile, but it was forced. "Never mind," she began, but decided to put his mind at ease. "Nothing, Sukh. Nothing." She smiled again, more genuinely this time, and tossed the football back to him. She held her hands out to accept a toss back from him. "Just remember," she added, "neither of those boys are married yet. They still might agree to an arranged marriage."

Sukh considered this for a moment and tossed her the ball. "Well, I'm never gonna let Naniji and Dad pick me a wife. I'm picking my own."

Tossing the ball back to him, she said, "You'll change your mind. I felt the same way when I was your age. But things change when you get older. I mean, with the divorce rate in this country being almost fifty percent, how much worse can an arranged marriage be?"

"Way worse. For all you know, this Rajwinder could be an axe murderer."

Raveena laughed, "No, I know he's not an axe murderer. Naniji has known the family forever. If there were any axe murderers in the family, she would have heard." She turned to continue emptying her suitcase.

"Still, he could be nuts, or a child molester, or a wife beater. You don't know." Sukh pressed the ends of the football between his open palms. "Where are you going to live? Here or in India?"

"Oh, here, of course. It's considered a great opportunity to marry a woman with Canadian citizenship. I think that was part of the arrangement. Kind of like a dowry." Raveena was putting the last of her clothing away.

"Raveena, any man should be paying you for the chance to marry you. Doesn't he know how lucky he is to get you?"

Raveena stopped to look at her cousin. Even though they weren't siblings, she always treated Sukhwinder as a brother. "You are so sweet, brother."

Sukh blushed. "Tell me you aren't going to do this."

"Look, Sukhy. I've made my decision. I've given my word. I will marry Rajwinder. You have to accept it."

Sukh knew he was dismissed so he got up from the bed and left the room. Then he left the house to start up the road to Jeremy's place, which was becoming the hangout for the four friends. Jeremy's dad was rarely home because he worked so late at the store and that meant there was no one to nag them about doing chores, or homework, or to eat fruit and vegetables for a snack. They could listen to their own music as loudly as they liked. They could use four-letter words. And they could play stupid games without someone making them grow up.

When he got to the house Jeremy, Cass and Kyle were watching TV in the family room. They were all on the couch. Jeremy's feet were up on the coffee table and Kyle was eating potato chips from a bag resting on his belly. Cassidy was sitting beside Kyle, her feet curled up under her as she ate chips.

She was the only one who looked up when Sukh entered the house, "Hi, Sukh. What up?"

"Hey, I need a favour," Sukh answered. He walked over to a drawer in the kitchen and rummaged through until he found a pair of scissors.

Jeremy looked back. "What are ya doin'?"

Sukh walked back into the family room with the scissors in his hand. "Who's going to cut my hair?"

Cassidy screeched and jumped up from the couch. Kyle stopped chewing, with a large potato chip still in his mouth. Jeremy continued facing the television and said, "It's about time!"

"What are you talking about?" Cassidy asked, first glaring at Jeremy, then turning to Sukh. "You can't!"

Sukh walked toward the couch. "The hell I can't. Who'll do it? Kyle? Jeremy?"

Kyle stood up, spit the chip out of his mouth and said, "Hell, no. Not me. Your parents will kill you first and then me."

Cassidy, her eyes wide, just shook her head.

Sukh walked over to Jeremy. "Will you, Jeremy? I'll tell my folks I did it myself."

Jeremy stared at the TV. He reached out his hand. Sukh gave him the scissors and went to sit on a chair in the kitchen. He unravelled his patka.

Jeremy got up from the couch with a sigh. He walked over to Sukh, held up a large lock of hair and, before he cut, asked, "Just tell me why."

Sukh looked straight ahead. "Because I want to pick my own wife. Cut!"

10

The Great Tree

KYLE TRIED TO SCREAM — TO CALL FOR help, but when he opened his mouth to scream, it filled with water. Cold, icy water. Cold enough to make his teeth hurt. To make his throat freeze. To chill his lungs. He could hear voices. People were coming. Will you help me and my friends? Is that why you're here? To help my friends? But I can't find them. I don't know where they've gone . . .

Kyle was in love with his best friend, but she didn't know it.

At school, Mikey Mike came up to him in gym class and asked, "What's up with you and Cassidy Sampson?"

"What do you mean?"

"You know. What's up? Are you going out with her?"

Kyle was shocked. "Going out, like dating? No. Eeewwww. That sucks."

Now Mikey was shocked. "What do you mean, 'that sucks'?"

Kyle still did not comprehend what Mikey was talking about. "I mean, that sucks. It's Cassidy. She's like a good friend. Like a sister. Dating? No way!"

Mike leaned close to Kyle and continued, "In case you haven't noticed, Cassidy Sampson is hot. She's one of the hottest girls in grade nine. Have you looked at her lately?"

Kyle thought about her. He tried to picture her face in his mind. Yeah, she had long blonde hair, big blue eyes, a nice body, but . . . she was Cassidy. It just didn't seem right. He walked away, shaking his head.

Mikey watched him walk away then called after him, "What are you, a fag?"

Kyle continued to ignore him and walked to the changing room. Mikey likes Cassidy. I wonder if Cassidy likes him. Should I tell her?

During the next class change Kyle caught up with Jeremy as he walked down the hall. He tried to make his voice sound light-hearted and teasing. "Guess who likes Cassidy?" he asked.

Jeremy looked at Kyle's face. "You mean 'Guess who doesn't *like Cassidy'. That list is shorter."*

"What?" Kyle asked, dumbfounded. "Who?" He suddenly felt left out of the loop.

"Here's Sukh. Hey, Sukh," he called. "Tell Kyle who likes Cassidy."

Sukh laughed. "Well, there's Kevin and Mikey and Spencer." He was counting off his fingers. "And Mike J. and Reese and . . . do you want me to go on?"

Kyle was very quiet for the rest of the school day. On the bus ride home he sat alone in a double seat watching Cassidy sit with Sukh. Jeremy sat in front of them, but faced behind to talk with them the entire drive home. Kyle tried not to think about his conversation earlier with Mikey, but he couldn't get the words out of his mind. His hands curled into fists each time he remembered Mikey saying, "Cassidy Sampson is hot." He didn't know what he was feeling, but he knew he didn't like to hear it. He thought about all the other boys, his friends, who liked her, too.

Cassidy laughed at something Jeremy had said. Kyle's thoughts swung back to the present. To Cassidy. Now he couldn't stop watching her. She was pretty. He could see it. Actually, she was quite beautiful. How could he have been so blind? She was hot, just like Mikey said.

Just before the bus stopped at Sukh's house, Jeremy asked if the gang wanted to come over to his place. It was a beautiful sunny day in April. They could get a snack and then go for one last boot on the snowmobiles.

Cassidy said, "My folks said it's too late for the snowmobiles. Ours are already put away."

Kyle got up from his seat and walked over to them. "Ours are put away, too."

"Mine is still out. I'll bring it over to your place. Be there in a bit," said Sukh. The next stop was his, so he stood and walked to the driver. When the bus stopped, he got off, waving to his friends.

Kyle looked outside at the patchy snow. "Are you sure you wanna go for a ride? It looks pretty bare."

Jeremy laughed. "My old machine is a piece of crap. I don't care if it gets a few more scratches."

Cassidy suddenly remembered. "I can't be late today. I promised my mom I'd have my bedroom cleaned up before she gets home from work at 5:30. If I don't, I'm grounded for the rest of the week."

Kyle wanted Cassidy to come. "We'll get you back before then, I promise."

When the bus stopped in front of Jeremy's house the three got off. Soon they could hear the whine of Sukh's machine, then the rumble of it stopping right outside the house. He came without a helmet, and since Cassidy and Kyle didn't have theirs either, Jeremy decided not to wear his.

Kyle had an idea. "I know a great place to go. I found this tree out in the woods just off the forestry road. It must have been struck by lightning last summer, because it was all blown up in pieces. I swear you can find chunks of the tree a hundred metres away. It's the coolest thing." He looked at Cassidy. "Here, I'll drive Jeremy's machine and show you where. Jeremy, you can double with Sukh."

Jeremy walked over to Sukh's machine. Kyle sat on Jeremy's old Arctic Cat. He patted the seat behind him and said, "Here, Cass. You can ride with me."

Cassidy sat down behind Kyle. She was just reaching for a place to hold on to when Kyle gunned the machine. The jerk forward caused her to lurch and lose her balance. Leaning backward, almost falling, she reached her arms forward around Kyle's waist, then pulled herself forward to regain her balance . . . Then she held her arms tight around Kyle's waist and rested her chin on his back. She muttered something in Kyle's ear about being a lousy driver. Kyle smiled and revelled in the feel of her body pressing up against his. Then he took off down the road, zigzagging to find large patches of snow to protect Jeremy's machine as much as he could and to force Cassidy to hold onto him more tightly.

The tree was off the forestry road, down a tiny path dotted with patchy snow. It stood, cold and angry, beside a clearing. It looked just as Kyle had said: orange, dead needles decorated the ends of charred branches near the top; blackened bark, huge chunks missing, trimmed the inside; a split twisted its way down the trunk.

"It looks like a two-by-four's been stripped right out of it. Look at that," said Sukh, pointing to the middle of the tree.

"It's true," said Kyle. "I found this place because I saw what I thought was a two-by-four lying in the middle of the forest and I wondered, 'What the hell? What's this doing here? Is somebody building something?' Then I saw the tree."

He walked to the clearing. He suspected it wasn't a field at all but a pond under the frozen crust. He kicked his heel against the snow and saw the smooth, frozen surface of ice.

"Hey, you guys! Look at this. It's a pond. This is a really cool place."

"We should come here in the summer. I'll bet it's beautiful then, too," said Cassidy.

Sukh nodded, but Jeremy was silent. He continued to look up at the tree.

"What do you think, Jer?" Cassidy asked.

It took a moment or two for Jeremy to respond. Without taking his eyes off the altered tree, he spoke as if to himself. "It's like it just exploded." He then added, very quietly, "The power of God."

Cassidy nodded and looked at her watch. "Oh, my God! My mother is going to be home soon. I'm dead! I am so dead!"

All four jolted into action and ran back to the machines. One pull from Kyle started Jeremy's snowmobile; Sukh's needed a few more pulls. And they were off!

11
The Funeral

THEY CHOSE CREMATION. IT WAS PERFORMED in a western crematorium, but it was reminiscent of the traditional pyre familiar to the mourning Sikh family.

They filled up the local motels: men in turbans, women in saris and dark-eyed children in western-style clothing. Cassidy saw them in restaurants, at gas stations, at the grocery store. She watched these people — Sukh's people — come into town to pay their respects. They'd been here for only a few days to help with the preparation for the funeral, but they already appeared to feel quite at home.

Cassidy sat with her family. Tears streamed down her cheeks as she thought of Naniji. She couldn't see anything but the backs of the people in front of her. She found the room too hot, too stuffy, too smelly, too loud. She couldn't hear the speaker because Sukhwinder's family, taking up the entire front half of the building, wailed in their grief, deep, grating, unnerving cries that echoed off the walls of the small room. She thought back to her grandfather's funeral, when everyone cried discreetly with silent tears and the occasional sniffle. *Why can't they cry quietly, like we do?*

She hated the smell of too many spices lingering on their too-bright-coloured-for-a-funeral clothing. *And why is it so hot in here?*

She looked around the room. It was crowded. There were people standing in the aisles, along the back wall, through the doorway, and she knew there must be others still outside hoping to get in. Glancing behind her, toward the wall, she was able to see Jeremy and his dad. And directly behind them was Kyle sitting between his parents. Kyle was looking at her. He winked. She smiled, turned her face down and again faced the front of the room. She felt a little better.

Something different was starting to happen. The people at the front were standing and turning toward the aisle. Gradually they stood and left their pews, filling the aisles, inching closer to the front of the room. The wails were getting louder. Some of the crying women had to be supported by others. Everyone in Cassidy's pew stood, faced the aisle and slowly inched down the aisle to the front of the room. Cassidy, still unable to see anything but the backs of the people closest to her, allowed herself to be led to the front, following her oldest brother. She felt her father behind her, his hands rest on her shoulders, steering her forward.

Forward, forward. Her brother stepped to the left, following the person who walked ahead of him. As he stepped away from in front of Cassidy, Naniji came into her view.

Cassidy gasped. She'd never seen a dead body before. *Oh, Naniji!* She lay on the table, her face a mottled grey. Her long grey hair, usually hanging in a heavy braid under her veil, lay freely at her sides. Bright coloured fabrics, red, gold and purple, covered her and the table. Cassidy knew it was Naniji, but that body lying in front of her just didn't quite look like the Naniji she remembered. Or maybe she just didn't want her to be Naniji.

No more Naniji. Never again would Sukh's grandmother be around to join the Sunday afternoon parties with her delicious samosas and pakora or for an after school snack with Sukh and his friends. Or to teach Cassidy some words in Punjabi. Or braid

Cassidy's hair in the traditional way most of the Punjabi women wore it. Naniji always enjoyed touching Cassidy's hair. Sukh said she touched it because in India, few people had hair the colour of gold and the colour always reminded Naniji of the Golden Temple in Amritsar, the favourite place of Sikhs in India.

Naniji would never again be waiting at the bus stop for Sukh or the gang when they visited the house after school. Not that Naniji had done that in years, but she'd always been waiting there in the rain or snow or searing hot sun in her veil and baggy, bright clothing on that dusty dirt road when Sukh, Jeremy, Kyle and Cassidy were little. Naniji's English was not very good, but between her beautiful dark, twinkling eyes and perpetual smile, everyone understood her. And when they couldn't, Sukhwinder always translated. And she used to say the nicest things to everybody.

A sob escaped Cassidy's throat. She couldn't look at the body lying on the table a moment longer. The heat of the room and the stuffiness and the smells were overwhelming. She felt light-headed. The room was spinning. She pulled at her collar. *Why can't I breathe and why is it so hot in here?*

She felt an urge to get out of this room, this building. Outside. *I have to get outside. What's the matter with me?*

Cassidy looked for a door. There was the one in the front that the people were walking through, but it was far too crowded to get through quickly. She looked behind her, past her father and saw only masses and masses of people behind him. The walls seemed to be moving. Closer and closer to her. The ceiling, too. She was suffocating. She felt the blood drain from her face. She felt nauseous. Her eyes were wide and she was panicking. She felt dizzy. So dizzy.

And then, nothing.

12
The Cousins

"Hey, Kyle!"

Kyle looked outside the sliding doors of the Sangeras' house and saw Jeremy and Sukh waving to him as they stood with some older boys. He walked outside and through the yard, crowded with the people from the funeral. Tables and tables of food were set up. Sukh's mother had greeted his family at the door and had led them to the patio. Kyle could see Grampaji, looking suddenly very old and hurting, sitting on the couch in the living room while women in colourful gowns fussed over him. Kyle saw Opa Lockett and Bear speaking in hushed voices in the dining room, while Oma Lockett walked from person to person carrying a platter of samosas.

A sense of mourning and depression permeated the house. People looked at each other with sombre faces. But outside, with the beautiful sunshine and gorgeous view of the lake, the atmosphere was more cheerful. People here were holding drinks, chattering, smiling. It was a celebration. A celebration of life: Naniji's new life.

"Hey, guys," Kyle answered when he joined the boys, all dressed in black. Black jeans, black shirts, black shoes, black belts.

Sukh, his eyes slightly puffy and red from recently-shed tears, introduced Kyle to the group. "Kyle, these are my cousins from the Coast, Gurinderpal, Jaspal, Jaswinder and Jaskirat," said Sukh. "Their friends call them Paul or Jas." He continued in a happier voice. "They all tend to answer at the same time. It's funny when someone calls their house because whoever answers the phone always goes and gets the wrong person."

Everyone laughed. Kyle nodded to each of the teens. They looked much older than Sukh's fifteen years. Their eyes and skin were as dark as Sukh's. Their hair was cut short in the western style and each had facial hair shaved into some kind of thin beard framing his chin. They appeared menacing to Kyle, even when they smiled at him. Each of them held a beer.

Kyle watched Sukh peer through the crowd, then, completely unexpectedly, grab Jaspal's beer. Then Sukh ducked behind his cousin and took a long drink from the bottle while his other cousins laughed and looked around to see if an` adult had seen. The only person who looked at them, though too late to see the transgression, was an older woman wearing a sari. She had a frown on her face that suggested to Kyle she was displeased with laughter at a funeral reception.

Jeremy turned to Kyle. "How's Cassidy?"

"Oh, she's fine physically, but emotionally she's a mess. She just fainted. The room was too stuffy and standing for so long got the best of her. Then she either was too embarrassed or too emotional to do much but cry, so her parents took her home," he answered. He stepped behind Jaspal to talk directly to Sukh and continued, "Her family sends their condolences."

Sukh stepped back into the circle of boys to say, "Man, I thought she hurt herself or something. The way she kept crying. What happened, anyway? I was in the next room already, so I didn't see anything. All I saw was her dad carrying her to the car."

Jeremy spoke first. "She seemed to be okay. She was walking forward, then boom! She fell over."

"I saw her walking because I was still in my pew," Kyle added. "Her face went white as a sheet. She started to, I don't know, freak out like she was terrified of something. Then, just like Jeremy says — boom! She collapsed. Lucky her dad caught her before she was flat out."

Jeremy cut in. "Then her mom started shrieking and people started to crowd around her. When she came to, all these people were staring at her and that must have freaked her out even more because she started to cry really loud like all those women were. Her dad picked her up and got her outside fast."

Jaspal listened intently, then asked, "Was that the blonde hottie you guys were in the snowmobile accident with last year?"

The group grew uncomfortably quiet. Sukh turned away to look out at the lake. Jeremy looked at the ground. Kyle looked straight at Jaspal, an unreadable look on his face. He balled his hands into fists.

More silence.

Oblivious to the change in mood, Jaspal looked at each of the boys. "Well, was it?" he asked. He felt a nudge against his ribs, then looked at Gurinderpal. He finally seemed to sense he'd done something wrong. "What?" he asked. "What'd I do?"

Jaskirat had heard from Raveena that Sukh never talked about the accident last spring. Ever. Nobody knew why he wouldn't talk about it. The counsellor had asked the family to try to get him to discuss the events, even with his friends, but it was apparent to Jaskirat now that they were all still silent on the topic. Recognizing the change in mood, he said "Jeremy, Kyle, you want some beer? Here, take a pull."

Everyone except Kyle looked around to see who was looking. Reaching quickly for the beer, Jeremy turned his back to the crowd and took a long swig. Then he stepped in front of Kyle, hiding the beer between their two bodies. He tapped the bottle on Kyle's arm. Kyle didn't respond. His gaze still bore into Jaspal; his hands were still balled into fists.

Again Jeremy tapped the bottle on his arm. Kyle turned his head, adjusted his eyes to Jeremy's face, then looked down at the bottle of beer, still being offered. He accepted the bottle, took a swig and offered it back to Jaskirat. But, just as Jaskirat reached to take it from him, Kyle drew back his hand, faced the lake and downed the entire contents of the bottle. With a determined look on his face, he drew back his arm and with all of his might, threw the bottle off the cliff, the small group watching as it sailed down to the lake.

Jaskirat looked at the others, about to say something, but only shrugged. He walked over to a cooler, opened the lid and lifted out four more beers.

13
The Campfire

"Beer tastes crappy," slurred Kyle, lying on the bench and staring up into the stars.

"So does coffee," added Jeremy.

"And cigarettes," continued Kyle. "Why does anybody like this stuff?" He sat up and flicked the barely smoked cigarette into the campfire.

Jeremy sat up and took a drag from his own cigarette. "They like it because of the alcohol buzz."

"And the caffeine buzz," suggested Kyle.

"And the nicotine buzz," added Jeremy.

"That's a lot of buzzes," Kyle replied.

Jeremy snorted out a laugh. Kyle began to giggle. He looked at Jeremy, the firelight revealing a wide smile, and continued to laugh. Both boys began to laugh harder and louder, Kyle holding his belly and falling back onto the bench.

They were alone at Kyle's place. Jeremy's dad and Kyle's parents were still helping out at the Sangeras', serving food and tending to guests. When it began to get dark Kyle and Jeremy left Sukh with his cousins and went to Kyle's to make a small campfire. Out here they could hear a car coming from a long way off and had plenty of time to hide the beer and cigarettes, both gifts from Sukh's older cousins, before any parents caught them.

"That's a lot of buzzes!" repeated Jeremy. "That's a good one . . . a lot of buzzes!" Still laughing, he stood and raised the last beer above his shoulders. "A toast to Naniji. An incredible grandmother and someone who knows what it's like to die!" Then he took the last sip and threw the bottle into the darkness. It fell into the lake with a slight splash.

Both boys became quiet, the sputtering and cracking of the campfire the only sound. The comment about Naniji knowing what it's like to die got Kyle thinking. The beer loosened his thoughts and they began to spill over each other in his head, never quite coming clear. He felt the bench spin a little, distracting him, but always coming back to the words "knows what it's like to die".

"Jeremy," Kyle began. "Do you ever think about that day . . . the day we went through the ice?"

For a long time Jeremy said nothing. He sat back down on the bench. He flicked an imaginary ash from his thigh. He ducked his head and squinted, protecting his eyes from the campfire smoke. Then he reluctantly spoke, "Think about it how?"

Kyle rose to a sitting position, facing Jeremy across the fire. "Just think about it. I don't know 'how.' Do you ever think about it?"

Jeremy feigned shock. "Well, all four of us almost died," he answered. "We were in the news all across the country because of that mammalian diving reflex thing. Hell, we were news all over the world! Of course I think about it."

Kyle was silent for a moment, collecting his thoughts. "Not the *news* part of it," he answered quietly. Then he spoke louder. "The rest of it. The 'happening' part of it."

Jeremy pondered the question. "I don't know what you mean by the *happening* part of it," he answered, too quickly. He continued to stare into the fire, refusing to meet his friend's eyes.

Kyle leaned forward, his eyes looking intently at Jeremy, willing him silently to look up face to face. The sound of a small animal scampering up a tree in the darkness distracted him for a moment, but just a moment.

"You know," Kyle continued, "while we were in the water. Do you remember anything that happened while we were in the water . . . or while we were, like . . . dead?"

Jeremy refused to look at Kyle. He took another drag from his cigarette. "What do you mean, dead? We weren't dead. Our body systems just shut down; we just looked dead. I don't think we were actually dead."

Jeremy's answer was nothing new to Kyle. He'd heard it from everybody: doctors, ambulance attendants, neighbours. They were the Miracle Teens. All four of them had survived with complete recoveries. The doctors could find nothing physically wrong with any of them. Not even frostbite! Their faculties had remained intact — no brain damage. Some people called it the power of prayer; others found the scientific explanation more acceptable, which suggested that they were all very much alive through the entire experience. Still, they remained in the news for weeks after the accident.

Kyle continued hesitantly. "Were we having . . . a Near Death Experience?" he asked.

Jeremy released his breath, not realizing that he'd been holding it. He rolled his eyes. "Now, what the hell is that?"

At first Kyle was surprised by Jeremy's ignorance. "You've never heard of a Near Death Experience?" he asked. Then he remembered how he himself had learned about it, researching it. "I looked it up on the Internet. It's something that happens when people nearly die. It's really kind of freaky." He tried to focus on his thoughts, to express them clearly. "All these people who actually seemed to be dead, like in the hospital after a heart attack or in an accident when they have to be resuscitated. They all remember stuff that happened when they were dead."

"Stuff like what?" Jeremy's voice was clear and sober.

"Well, stuff like what people were doing in the next room and things people were saying. Some people remember the doctors working on them . . . They say their body felt kind of, like, detached from themselves. They didn't feel any pain and they felt like they were floating."

Jeremy did not look interested, but asked, "What else?"

Before Kyle continued, he looked toward his house, completely enveloped in darkness. He thought he should go in and turn on a light for his parents, but decided not to interrupt the conversation. "They also said they remember their whole lives passing before their eyes. Things that happened to them over their lifetimes, like flashbacks. And they remember a bright, warm light."

"Anything else?" asked Jeremy.

Kyle shook his head. After a moment, he asked again, "Were we having a Near Death Experience?"

"How the hell should I know?" Jeremy answered. He leaned away from the tower of campfire smoke, a moment ago so straight but now bending toward his face. He held his breath and counted quietly to himself, mentally willing the smoke to change direction so he could breathe again. "We were nearly dead, I know that. But actually dead?" He shook his head, stifling a cough as he awkwardly inhaled the last drag of the cigarette and flicked it into the fire.

Kyle watched the curl of smoke from Jeremy's mouth mix with the smoke of the campfire. "Dead, nearly dead. Who cares which? Do you remember anything from that time?" he asked again.

Jeremy took a deep breath and released it slowly, in part to relieve some of the pressure he began to feel in his chest and in part to think about what to say. "Yeah," he answered, then said "No." He didn't know what he remembered. Was he too tired? Or too drunk? Or too scared to talk about it? But he was curious. Finally he said, "I don't know." He looked out into the darkness, toward the lake. "What do *you* remember?"

"I asked you first," said Kyle.

"Well, I asked you second. Big deal. What do you remember, Kyle?" Jeremy asked, beginning to feel a little impatient.

"Me? I don't know. Not a lot, I guess." Now Kyle looked back to the fire. He sat up straight. "Well, yeah. Actually, I do remember something. The flashbacks. I remember having flashbacks. There were two of them." He looked across the fire to Jeremy, hoping to meet eye to eye. Jeremy was still facing the lake. He continued, "I remembered when we paintballed those cows one time a few years ago . . . and the other time was at school, one time in gym class." He wouldn't continue. He didn't want to talk about Mikey's comments about Cassidy, or about visiting the big tree, or about why they'd been on the ice in the first place.

Jeremy waited a long moment before he spoke. "Actually, I remember flashbacks, too."

Kyle waited patiently for Jeremy to continue, then finally said. "Of what?"

Jeremy took a deep breath before he answered without looking at his friend. "The time when Opa made the hockey rink and we all played hockey, and . . . " The memory brought fresh pain to his chest; it radiated to a lump in his throat.

"And?" Kyle helped.

"And . . . the day my mom left," Jeremy answered, almost in a whisper.

"I'm sorry, man." Kyle paused a moment, He looked away, then turned back. "Anything else?"

Jeremy sighed. "Nah. No other flashbacks, anyway."

"Anyway?" Kyle was optimistic. "Anything *other* than flashbacks?"

Jeremy lay down on his own bench, folded his arms behind his head and looked up at the stars.

Kyle waited. "Jeremy? Anything else?"

Jeremy said nothing.

"Because I remember something else," said Kyle. "Something really weird."

Jeremy was torn. He wanted to know what was really weird. But he couldn't bring himself to talk about the painful times of his life that he usually refused to even think about. In the end, curiosity about Kyle's statement won out. He turned his head and made eye contact with him. "Weird, like how, Kyle?" he asked.

In the firelight Jeremy watched Kyle's lips move to form a word, then stop. Kyle took a deep breath and again appeared as if he would speak, but said nothing. Jeremy was astounded. Kyle, at a loss for words? Did hell freeze over?

"Hello? Kyle, what was weird?" Jeremy asked. "I remember something weird, too. But you say first."

Kyle finally looked toward Jeremy. "Okay, okay. I remember . . . " he took a deep breath and released the breath as he uttered, "a . . . sort of . . . book."

Jeremy gasped. His eyes grew wide. He muttered, so quietly that Kyle almost didn't hear him, "Oh, my God!"

14
The Book

KYLE FELT A TIGHTNESS BEGIN TO form in his chest. The adrenaline in his body was spreading to all of his muscles. The hair on the back of his neck stood on end and he could feel goosebumps growing on his arms. He returned Jeremy's stare. He suddenly felt very sober. "You saw it, too. Didn't you?"

"Uh, nah, uh, a book?" Jeremy wanted to deny it, but he knew he'd already given too much away. Curiosity had turned to fear. He could feel his face drain of colour, the blood racing to his heart as though he'd just run a wind sprint. *Deny! Deny!* The thought pounded inside his brain. *Deny just as you have all year long,* he told himself.

But before he could stop himself, Jeremy said, "I don't know if it was a book. I didn't see any book, really."

He knew Kyle wouldn't accept that. Before he could stop himself Jeremy continued, his words unchecked. He felt as if he were at confession at church: you couldn't lie to God, so what was the use even trying? "It was more like, I don't know, like a page. But I wouldn't say that it was a page of paper. At least not what I think of paper to be like."

Kyle looked at him with knowing eyes. It felt like those eyes were boring into Jeremy's brain, reading all his thoughts. He was suddenly afraid of Kyle.

"And it had names on it, didn't it?" asked Kyle.

Jeremy was stunned. He couldn't speak.

"Didn't it, Jeremy?" Kyle almost yelled. Kyle wanted answers. He'd waited an entire year, thinking about this. An entire year just wondering what it all meant. "It had people's names on it; strangers' names. Didn't it?"

Jeremy cringed. He wanted to escape from his friend, or at least from his friend's persistence. But Kyle would never let him alone until he'd extracted from Jeremy's head all his memories of that fateful day in April. "Names?" said Jeremy.

"Yeah. Names of people we don't know. Didn't it?"

"I, I guess."

"Come on, Jeremy. So far, you've remembered everything the same way I do. It had names of people." Then he shouted: "Didn't it?"

Jeremy jumped. "Okay, okay. It did," he answered obediently.

Excitement radiated from Kyle's face, his body language, his voice. "But not our names, right? It had other names."

Jeremy looked away. He moved to the far end of the bench, as far from Kyle as he could. He prayed his dad would come to get him, or that Kyle's parents would drive up right then. He strained his ears for the sound of a car on the gravel road. He looked across the lake for the twinkling signs of headlights through the trees. Anything to change the subject.

But Kyle got up from the bench and moved across to the other side of the campfire. To Jeremy's side. "It had a date," Kyle said, "in weird writing and names in weird writing, but I know that it said April third, the day we went through the ice. I don't even know what kind of writing was on it, but I could sense what it said, kind of."

Kyle was right. He was speaking Jeremy's own memories. Could it be true? Did it really happen? Did Kyle remember the same things from that day? Jeremy turned back to Kyle. He was starting to feel less scared and more angry. His memories from that day were so confusing. He was feeling persecuted by one of his best friends. Kyle knew what he knew. He could no longer cower on the bench, exposing his mind and heartache to this onslaught. He stood.

"I know!" he yelled, his face inches away from Kyle's. His voice softened. "I could never identify the writing if I saw it again, but for some reason, I think I know what names were on it."

Kyle moved closer to Jeremy. "I'd never heard those names before. Now I'll never forget them as long as I live. Adam Eaton Schuler," he breathed, pointing at Jeremy's face.

"Oh, God!" moaned Jeremy. His legs felt weak; he had to sit down. Anger turned to fear again. Backing away from Kyle's finger, he sat down on the bench and looked at the fire.

Despite Jeremy's discomfort, Kyle sat down on the bench beside him and continued: "Ann Elizabeth Johnson . . . "

Jeremy knew what Kyle was going to say next, so he added, each boy speaking at the same time, "Joseph Anthony Smith."

The boys turned to stare at each other, silently trying to make sense of their revelations. Kyle whispered slowly, "Holy shit!"

15
The Names

THE SORROWFUL CALL OF A LOON pierced the night. Both boys jumped, startled, and looked into the blackness that was the lake. The large bird had to be right off shore, but the darkness protected its image from the audience just a short distance away.

Kyle wasn't going to let a loon change the topic, so he continued before Jeremy could digress. "But our names weren't on that list."

Jeremy sighed, in exasperation that the topic wasn't closed and because he knew that what Kyle said was correct. "No, I know."

"They were on another list. In another part. Much farther into the book, right? Did you see it?"

Jeremy lashed out, "It wasn't a book, okay? It was . . ." he rested his elbows on his knees and rubbed his hands through his curly dark hair. "Aaaurgh, I don't know."

"Who cares what it was? It had our names. Yours, mine, Sukh's and Cassidy's. And other people, too. Their names in between our names." Kyle was oblivious to Jeremy's discomfort. "What names did you see, Jeremy?"

Again Jeremy sighed. "Do I have to say? This is so creepy." His voice was going to break. "I thought it was a dream. I've never talked about that day. Not to my dad or the counsellor or any of those doctors. Not even to any of you guys. I just don't want to talk about it."

"I haven't told anyone either. But you were there with me. You know what I know. It couldn't have been a dream, not if we both saw it. What names did you see with ours, Jeremy?"

Jeremy walked to the edge of the lake. He had to take some slow, deep breaths instead of the rapid, shallow ones he suddenly realized he'd been taking. *Relax. Settle down.* He picked up a rock and skimmed it out into the darkness. He could hear the skips: five. He could do better. Bending over, he tried to find a flatter stone in the darkness.

"Jeremy!" Kyle yelled. "Tell me!"

Without thinking, Jeremy blurted out, "Jamieson Frank Otters! Catrina . . . "

" . . . Elsa Birgman. You saw them, too." Kyle walked to the edge of the lake to join Jeremy. "What does it mean?"

Jeremy faced Kyle. He whispered, "I don't know." Then he repeated it mournfully, almost yelled it to whoever could hear across the still water of the lake. "I don't know!"

Kyle felt Jeremy's anguish. But he couldn't end the conversation, not yet. "I've been wracking my brain for a whole year trying to figure out what it means." He paused a moment. "Do you think we're going to die?"

Jeremy looked back at Kyle, his arm stopping in mid throw. "Of course, you dope. Everyone dies. That's what you came up with in a year of wracking your brain? 'We're going to die'? Oh, brother!"

Kyle was too keyed up to be embarrassed. "I mean together. I think we're all going to die together." He watched Jeremy roll his eyes. "I think that first page, with all those names on it, was people who were supposed to die on April third, and we weren't on that list. That's why we didn't die then."

Jeremy looked at Kyle, unblinking. He'd had the same thought, that they'd all die together one day. A wave of fear squeezed the air from his lungs. He took another long breath and reminded himself that this was speculation. Only speculation. He asked, "Did you ever think the whole thing was just a dream? One big, bad dream?"

Kyle bit the inside of his mouth and shrugged, "Yeah, I did."

Jeremy was beginning to sense that Kyle may have doubts, just as he had. "For a year," Jeremy continued, "I kept telling myself it was a dream. Yeah, we went through the ice. Yeah, we almost died. But all those pages were just one big bad dream. I didn't want it to make sense. You don't have to make sense out of a dream. You have them and you forget about them." He grabbed Kyle's shoulder so they were face to face. "Why do you think you have to make sense out of it?"

It was Kyle's turn to look away. He pulled out of Jeremy's grip, bent down and picked up a rock, but didn't throw it. "I guess," he answered, twirling the rock in between his fingers, "I guess because I can't forget about it. It isn't like other dreams. It's more real, but at the same time, so . . . surreal. Is that the word?"

Jeremy lifted his hands, helpless. He knew what Kyle meant. He'd felt the same way. "Now," said Jeremy hopefully, "I accept that if you saw those pages too, they must be real. But that's not what it means . . . necessarily."

"Okay, Smarty, what else could it mean?" Kyle scoffed.

"Well," Jeremy began, "have you ever talked about this to Sukh or Cass?"

Kyle's response was to turn away and finally throw the rock in his hand. He tried to listen for the landing, but Jeremy disrupted the sound.

"Why haven't you? Why did you wait until you had a few beers to even bring it up? Maybe they never saw anything like what we saw. Sukh never said a thing to me. Has Cass said anything to you?"

Jeremy could tell by Kyle's lack of response that this was the first time either one of them had ever talked about that day and he was pretty sure that Cass and Sukh had probably never mentioned it to each other either. This was too big a secret to keep.

"It wasn't the beer," said Kyle.

"Maybe it was just a coincidence that we saw those names. Did you ever think that maybe they were just a flashback, something we don't remember? Yeah, that's why we both saw the same names. It's a flashback of a part of our lives that we shared. Maybe they were the names of teachers in our school or, . . . or nurses and doctors from the hospital that we were born in. Huh? Did you ever think of that?"

Kyle recognized desperation in Jeremy's voice. "Oh, yeah, sure. You were born on the Coast and I was born up here. Same doctors, my ass. And there was never a teacher in our school with any of those last names," Kyle reasoned. "Besides, I just sensed all of this. It's not that I was told anything, or read it, I just sensed it. Didn't you get that sense, too?"

Another loon called in the darkness, quickly answered by its mate. The campfire was no longer burning, but glowing an eerie red in the fire pit. The boys looked again out toward the lake, trying unsuccessfully to make out the shape of the large birds, when the moisture inside a charred log exploded in the fire, spitting a large spark onto the grass at their feet. Both boys jumped and then stared at each other.

Jeremy spoke first. "Look, Kyle, this is too creepy for me. And it's creepy out here tonight. I don't want to talk about this now." Then, as if in answer to his prayers, the sound of car wheels spinning out rocks on the gravel road echoed through the trees. Jeremy looked up toward the road where the glow of headlights made a halo around the conifers. The sound of one car slowing to take the turn in the driveway was joined by another car farther up the road. His dad and Kyle's parents were here. Jeremy looked to Kyle as if waiting for an answer to an unasked question.

Kyle sighed. His chance to fully understand would have to wait.

"And if you mention this to anybody," said Jeremy, "I'll just deny it. Then you'll look like a whacko. A nut. A schizophrenic."

Kyle was scared to push Jeremy too far. "But can we talk about it again?" he pleaded. "Tomorrow?"

Jeremy sighed. "I don't know. I'm going home." He turned and walked toward his father's waiting car. He didn't look back.

16
The Note

SUKH AND JEREMY SAT ON THE couch in Jeremy's family room. As usual, his father was at work and the boys had the house to themselves. Without a knock, the side door opened and in walked Cassidy and Kyle.

"Hey, guys," said Cassidy.

"Hey," answered Sukh. Jeremy, an X-box controller in his hand, wouldn't tear his gaze away from the television screen.

"Notice anything different about Cass?" Kyle asked, his voice rising at the end of the question.

Cassidy walked in front of the TV screen to capture their attention. Sukh put down his controller, but Jeremy moved to try to look around her at the screen. "Move, Cass," he begged. "I'm finally winning this stupid game against this so-called friend and you're spoiling it!"

Cassidy folded her arms across her chest. Jeremy tried once more to look around her, even getting up from his seat. But finally he dropped the controller on the coffee table and threw his hands in the air. He sat, leaned back on the couch and said, "She's finally big enough to wear a bra!"

"Hmphh?" chuckled Sukh. "What, Cass? Is it true? Are you finally big enough to wear a bra? And you're only fifteen years old?" He winked at her. "Wow. I'm impressed."

"Ha! Ha! Not funny! I've been wearing a bra for years. Look again," answered Cassidy.

"Look higher, you perverts," Kyle responded.

Sukh pretended to concentrate. "Higher, you say. Hmmm, she coloured her hair?" suggested Sukh. "Wow, it looks great. I hated the other colour."

"Seriously," suggested Jeremy. "She should be a blonde. Blondes have more fun. That other colour was just nasty."

"I didn't colour my hair! I have never coloured my hair!" Cassidy shrieked.

"Oh, for crying out loud. Look at her face, you idiots." Kyle stood behind Cassidy, grabbed her shoulders and gently pushed her forward so the boys would be distracted by nothing but her face.

"Wow! She pierced her nose!" Jeremy was astonished. "Oh man, did it hurt? What did you do that for?"

Cassidy touched the amethyst stud twinkling in the light on the side of her nose. Then she looked at Sukh, who was silent. "I did it for Naniji, Sukh. I feel so bad that I fainted at her funeral and didn't get to your house to give my condolences." Kyle gently pulled Cass's hand away from her nose. "I, I wanted to do something to make up for it," she said, stammering slightly. "And, I don't know . . . I kind of thought that this would help me remember her. Every time I touch it, I think of her. I really miss her." She absentmindedly touched the stud again.

Sukh was silent. He opened his mouth to say something, but instead closed it, got up and walked over to Cassidy. He held onto her shoulders so he could get a good look at her nose. Tears welled up in his eyes, then he smiled, sighed and hugged Cassidy, who also fought back tears.

Jeremy and Kyle looked at each other, a lopsided grin on each of their faces. Jeremy flicked at an imaginary tear on his cheek and said, "Aaaaaaah. I feel a group hug coming on." He jumped up from the couch, stepped on top of the coffee table and threw himself, arms spread, at the two who were hugging. As he fell into the couple, he reached out to pull Kyle into the hug with him.

Everyone laughed as they fell off balance and tumbled to the floor in a heap. Kyle yelled, "Dog pile on Cassidy!"

"Guys, no!" Cassidy struggled out from under the boys, cursing them. "You guys, I can't bump my nose! It's still too tender! And if this stud falls out it'll be a total waste of money!" She jumped up onto the couch to safety. She touched her nose stud to make sure it was still where it belonged.

The boys began a struggle to the top of the pile using some wrestling moves, getting more intense all the time, and with no intention of ending the match too soon. Absently fingering the stud on her nose, Cassidy watched them for a few minutes, then began to play X-box to the sound of their grunts, groans and giggles. It still hurt a little, but she felt it was well worth the pain.

After a short while, Kyle called out, "Cassidy, she said no touching it. You'll get an infection!" He climbed out of the wrestling match and on to the couch to play X-box with Cass. Sukh and Jeremy, exhausted and out of breath, lay on the floor, still laughing.

As Sukh sat up, he found a piece of folded paper on the floor beside him that must have fallen out of someone's pocket. "What's this?" he asked quietly and opened the paper to read it. His eyes moved from side to side as he read. He gasped.

They all looked to see what had startled their friend. Sukh's eyes were wide, his mouth open and his brown face pale.

"What's the matter, Sukh?" asked Cassidy. "What's that?"

Kyle jumped up, ran to Sukh and snatched the paper from his hands. He refolded it and stuffed it into a front pocket of his jeans. "It's nothing," was all he would offer.

"Kyle, what is that?" Cassidy begged. She turned to Sukh. "Sukh, what's wrong with you? You look like you've seen a ghost!"

Sukh's eyes were still wide, staring blankly at Kyle's knees in front of his face. He looked as if he'd stopped blinking, breathing, living.

Cassidy turned to Jeremy, a questioning look on her face. Jeremy looked from Cassidy's face to Kyle's and finally to Sukh's. He shook his head and shrugged. He got up and walked over to Kyle. He reached into Kyle's pocket and pulled out the paper so quickly that he had it before Kyle had a chance to react.

"Hey," responded Kyle, trying to grab the paper back. "Give me that!"

Jeremy walked away, putting the couch between himself and Kyle. Cassidy held onto Kyle's arm so he couldn't retrieve the note. Reluctantly, Kyle didn't try to pull himself from Cassidy's grasp, so Jeremy opened the folded paper. He knew almost immediately what it said. Then he looked at Kyle and shook his head. "You just couldn't leave it alone, could you?"

"Look at him," Kyle motioned toward Sukh. "He knows. He knows the names."

"What names? What's going on?" Cassidy stomped over to Jeremy and snatched the paper from his hand.

"Gimme that," she snapped, walking away from any threat of the boys taking it away from her before she read it. Kyle and Jeremy watched her back stiffen and her body freeze, the paper slipping between her fingers and floating, feather-like, to the floor. She turned back to face the boys, her brow furrowed. "I've heard these names. Where'd you get these from?"

Jeremy folded his arms across his chest. He looked at Kyle menacingly. "Yes, Kyle," he said, sneering. "Tell us where you got those names from."

17
Sukh's Secret

Kyle walked over and picked up the piece of paper from the floor. "Why, Cass? What do *you* know about those names?"

Cass looked at Sukh, who still sat on the floor, stunned. She turned to look at Kyle. His eyes were riveted on her. She looked at Jeremy, who for a long moment stared at her, but broke eye contact before she could speak. "I don't know," she began. "I don't know those people."

Kyle walked over to her. "Maybe not, but you know those names. Don't you?"

"I don't know," was all she would say.

"Come on, Cass," he continued, then turned to Sukh, "You both recognize those names. You've seen them before. During the accident. I know you've seen them or heard them or sensed them, or whatever the hell happened. Jeremy and I have, too."

Jeremy interrupted. "Says you, nutbar."

Kyle looked at Jeremy and rolled his eyes. "Cut it out, Jeremy. You already admitted it. What is with you guys? This is so important and it's as if you want to pretend it didn't happen."

Cassidy finally spoke. "Okay, I know those names, or I remember them, I think. When I was in the accident. I don't remember anything about them, but apparently, when I was starting to wake up, in the hospital, I was repeating those names over and over again. I thought it was a dream, but one of those dreams that seems so real you just never forget. My mom asked me about them later. I didn't know why I repeated them, but I still remembered them. Why? Did she tell you about them, Kyle?"

"Well, now we're getting somewhere," Kyle responded, ignoring her question. "Did you have any flashbacks, Cass?"

"Flashbacks — what do you mean?" asked Cassidy.

While Kyle explained their conversation of the night before, Jeremy walked to the window and stared out into the forest surrounding his house. His head hurt and his stomach felt queasy, probably from the beer. A hangover, like his dad had occasionally complained about. *Why do people drink that stuff?* Trying to ignore what Kyle was saying, he watched a squirrel run along a branch, then jump to another tree, barely able to hold on. When it had regained its balance, it continued along the next branch without fear. Jeremy wondered how the squirrel could so easily dismiss the possibility of falling. How could it just continue along its precarious path?

Cassidy sat down on the couch, grabbing her ankle and sitting on it. "Yeah, now that you mention it, I had two flashbacks. One was of the first day of Kindergarten, when I met you guys. It's weird, though. If you'd asked me the day before the accident what I remembered about Kindergarten, I wouldn't have remembered that day. But it all came back, so vividly. Jeremy was crying." She looked at Sukh, who was still sitting on the floor, not focused on any of them. "And Sukh, you came in with Naniji and Grampaji and the principal. And you couldn't speak any English, barely. And Kyle, you were my only friend."

Kyle looked at her. "I don't remember that."

"Neither did I. It's not like it was an important event or anything," said Cassidy.

Jeremy still looked out the window as he asked, "What was your other flashback, Cass?"

"Well, it seems so stupid. Actually embarrassing. You mean these flashbacks are supposed to be major events in our lives?" She scrunched up her face as though she smelled something foul. She looked to Kyle and Jeremy for an answer. Both boys just shrugged.

"I remembered," Cassidy said, "the day I got my first bra, with my mom."

Jeremy chortled. "You mean you had a flashback about today?" he asked.

"I didn't get my first bra today, you dope." She laughed as she reached down and picked up an empty CD case from the coffee table. She hurled it toward the window at Jeremy. They all laughed.

Then in a more serious tone, Cassidy said, "But I remembered going back to the rope swing with you guys, too."

The clattering CD case shook Sukh out of his trance. He was finally able to focus his eyes on the others.

Sukh spoke slowly, as if he were choosing his words very carefully. "The rope swing." He turned to look at his friends. "That was what my flashback was about. When you guys taught me how to swim. And when Jeremy cut my hair. Those were my two. But the names. What about the names, and those people and the heat? What about that?"

Jeremy and Kyle spoke together. "Heat?" Kyle continued, "What do you mean, 'heat'?"

Sukh finally stood up, looking at each and every one of their faces. "When the people got there. The people with the names on that list. And the heat or flames or whatever."

Jeremy spoke first. "You saw the people with those names? Really?"

Cassidy had tried to follow the conversation, but was falling behind. "Wait a minute, guys. Where did you see the names?"

Kyle said, "I didn't see any people. And neither did Jeremy. Just names. These names on this paper-like thing." He continued, explaining about the strange book with their own names written in it.

"Well, I didn't see any of that," said Cassidy. "*Our* names, too? Ooooh, this is too weird. What does it mean?"

"I don't know," said Kyle, "and Jeremy doesn't want to know. But it makes sense that you don't know much about it, Cass, because you were dead the shortest amount of time."

"We weren't dead, Kyle!" Jeremy yelled. He softened his voice. "We were suffering from a natural phenomena. Uncommon, but possible. Mammalian Diver's Reflex. It was all over the news."

"Whatever! It was also all over the news that it almost never happens to kids our age. Usually it happens to babies. We weren't babies. And it was so incredible that it happened to all four of us at the same time. Hell, we are written about in an international science journal." Kyle paused a moment, then continued, "Sukh, what about those people and the heat?"

All eyes turned to Sukh, who looked paler than before, if it were possible. His gaze was riveted, trance-like, to a spot in the middle of the room.

Cassidy walked over to where Sukh was sitting on an ottoman. She touched his shoulder and said gently, "Sukh? Where are you, bud?"

Cassidy expected Sukh to snap out of his trance at her touch, but he didn't. She shook his shoulder gently, "Sukhy," she called, then laughed gently. "Earth to Sukhy!"

Still no response.

"Guys, what's wrong with him?. He doesn't look very well," Cassidy's voice expressed concern. "Sukh!"

Kyle and Jeremy walked to where Sukh sat. "Yo! Sukh!" hollered Jeremy. Kyle shook his friend harder than Cassidy had. Finally Jeremy reached down to Sukh's arm and pinched it.

Sukh said nothing, but stood up, rubbing his arm where he'd just been pinched. He looked at everyone, wondering why they were staring at him. "You guys just don't get it," he said finally, shaking his head. "You just don't get it."

He walked to the window and for a long moment just stared out. He turned back to them. The attention the three gave him made him uncomfortable. He turned and looked out the window again.

He finally spoke: "We're all going to die!"

18
Revelations

All were silent except for Cassidy, who let out a tiny gasp. The only other noise was the territorial chattering from a squirrel outside.

Moments went by before Jeremy released his breath in an uncomfortable laugh and responded exactly how he had when Kyle said the same thing the night before, "Of course, you dork. Everyone dies!"

"Yeah," Sukh responded. "Everyone dies. But us, we're going at the same time. Together." He paused a moment to let it sink in, then repeated it to make sure they understood. "We're all going to die together."

Kyle looked at Jeremy with an I-told-you-so glance, then asked, "How do you know that, Sukh?"

Sukh shrugged. "It's like you thought, Kyle. Cassidy knows the least because she was dead the shortest. I was dead the longest, sooooo . . ."

This time Cassidy said it: "We weren't dead!"

Sukh looked at her and smiled. "Well, is there a word for being right between dead and alive? Gone and still here?" He shrugged. "I don't know. Not from what I've learned from being Sikh, there isn't. Reincarnation? Yes, I've heard of that. But, nobody ever told me that there's a stage between death and life."

Jeremy answered, "I've heard of Purgatory, but what I thought about Purgatory from going to church with Oma and Opa, is that it's a place between Heaven and Hell. A place where you have to pay for your sins here on Earth before you can get to Heaven. I've heard of the pearly gates and St. Peter guarding them so no evil can pass to heaven, but I didn't see anything like that." He looked to Kyle for support.

"Search me," said Kyle, shrugging. "I never went to church."

"Do you think that means we're too evil to get to heaven?" asked Cassidy. She waited for an answer, first from Jeremy, then to Kyle, then to Sukh. Each of the boys turned away from her questioning eyes.

Kyle looked back to Sukh. "Look, man, you gotta tell us what happened. What you remember."

Sukh sighed. "I've never talked about this to anyone and I vowed to myself that I never would, but I guess you guys experienced parts of the same thing. I think the names of the people on that list are the people who died that day. I never tried to prove it because I didn't want it to be true. Our names were on another list, and the way I figure it, we are all going to die together in the future sometime. Don't ask me when, because I have no idea. And there are some other names of people who will probably die with us . . . "

"Catrina Elsa Birgman and Jamieson Frank Otters," replied Kyle.

Sukh shook his head. He had difficulty believing that Kyle knew those names. "Now, I have no idea how I know this is true. It's just something I . . . absorbed? Is that the right word for it? Then these people suddenly appeared with this incredible blast of heat. And I just knew they were the people with the names on that first page thing."

Jeremy closed his eyes and shook his head. Kyle turned to Sukh. "I remember the names on the first page," said Kyle, "and the page with our names on it. Jeremy doesn't remember much, but then I was dead longer than him."

Jeremy's eyes flew open as he and Cassidy spoke in unison and exasperation: "We weren't *dead*!"

"I have an idea . . . how we can see if this whole story is true," said Kyle.

Sukh asked, "How? Are you going to jump off a bridge and see if you die?"

Kyle looked at Sukh, contemplating the idea and said, "Hey, that might work, but I have another idea. We just find out if those people did die, and on what day."

"And how do we do that?" asked Jeremy, his voice almost a sneer.

"We can look up old obituaries," said Cassidy.

Kyle shook his head. "You know, if all of those people died together, it would be news wouldn't it? Think, guys, how could three people die at the same time?"

"I'm sure thousands of people die every second in this world. What makes you think only three people died at that time? Or even together?" asked Jeremy. "Why would there only be *three* names on that list? This is stupid."

"Well, maybe they were related to us and that's why those names were exposed to us," suggested Cassidy. "Maybe we know them, but we just don't know how we know them. You know, that theory that everyone in the world is six degrees apart."

Sukh raised one eyebrow in confusion. "What are you talking about?"

Cassidy sighed. "You know that theory that says you know everyone in the world within six relationships? I know you and that makes everyone you know one degree from me, and you know your cousin's husband and everyone he knows in India is two degrees from you and all the people they know, well that's three degrees and they know someone in, let's say, Tibet, who knows someone in Taiwan, who knows someone in France, and so we all know everyone within six degrees. You haven't heard that?"

Sukh rolled his eyes and shook his head. "That's insane. So why would we have some special relationship with the people who died if the whole friggin' world is related to us? We'd have a relationship with *everyone* who dies."

"I don't know. I haven't thought this through yet. I just found out about those names today."

Kyle walked past the other boys to the far end of the room, turned on the computer and logged on to the Internet. He began plugging words into a search engine. Cassidy and Jeremy walked over to watch.

They heard car wheels on the gravel driveway. Sukh walked over to the front window, saw Jeremy's dad open the pick-up's door and step out. "Your dad's home, Jeremy," he called. "Look guys, should we still talk about this stuff in front of him?"

"Hell, no," answered Jeremy. Without waiting for consensus, he closed the web browser. Before anyone could argue with him, he turned off the computer.

Sukh looked at Kyle. "I'm with Jeremy on this. I don't think we should tell anybody, at least not until we have some proof it's true."

Everyone looked at Cassidy. "What am I gonna tell?" she said. "I don't even know anything."

Jeremy's eyes grew wide with fear. "I don't think we should ever tell anyone. Ever. Never!"

Kyle nodded his head. Shrugging, he added, "Who would believe us, anyway?"

All four came together, held their fists to touch each other's and said, "Pact!"

19
The Proof

JEREMY LEANED FORWARD ON HIS MOTORCYCLE; the engine still idled but the wheels no longer turned. He pressed the kill button as his foot searched for the kickstand. He swung his right leg over the back of the bike, unstrapped and removed his helmet, then hung the helmet on the right handle. He rubbed his sleeve over his face to remove the inevitable dirt kicked up from riding on the trail to their meeting spot in the forest. Sukh's dirt bike, already cold, leaned against its own kickstand. Off to the other side of the trail stood Cassidy's horse, Paintbrush, on a long tether; it was named after the pretty red flowers that coloured the forest floor.

The horse quietly munched wild roses and grass, unimpressed by the horsepower of Jeremy's motorbike. He walked over to gently pat her back. Scratching between her ears, he whispered, "Hey, beautiful." Then he looked around: no sign of Kyle yet.

Even though he was close enough to hear Sukh and Cassidy talking quietly and occasionally giggling, this part of the forest was so dense he still couldn't see them. He followed the game trail, created many years ago by deer, bear and other wild animals, to the treasure that lay beyond the trees. He stepped over the old tree that had fallen across the trail last winter, passed the large rock and reached the meeting place they'd established in the year since the accident. A pond lay twinkling in the sunlight, butterflies flitting from plant to plant by the water. And there, to the right, was the giant tree, or what was left of it after lightning had twisted it into a charred and tattered obelisk, standing forever as a warning to everyone of God's wrath.

Cassidy and Sukh sat on an old log, facing the pond. As Jeremy walked behind them, he overheard the names from the list again and knew that the conversation begun at the house was continuing even without him and Kyle. He stepped on a small stick, snapping it in two. The small sound was enough to alert the two, who looked back to see him.

"Hi, Jeremy," Cassidy spoke first. "Did you see Paintbrush back there? Is she still tethered?"

"Paintbrush? No, I didn't see her," Jeremy teased, "I figured you doubled on the back of Sukh's motorbike."

Cassidy looked stricken. "What?" She jumped up and was ready to bolt down the trail when Jeremy laughed.

"No, just kidding. She's back there and she's fine."

Cassidy put her hand to her chest in a mock heart attack, breathing a sigh of relief. "You jerk," she said, a slight smile beginning on her face.

Sukh asked, "Do you know where Kyle is?"

As if on cue, the whining of a two-stroke motocross bike screamed through the forest. Jeremy cocked his head and looked toward the sky. "Judging by the sound of a Yamaha TTR125, and knowing that you can hear them from miles away, and that Kyle only goes that fast when he thinks he's far enough away from home so his parents can't hear . . . " He took a deep breath and continued, "But they can because two strokes are so friggin' loud. I'd say that he just hit the forestry road and his estimated time of arrival is in," he considered for a moment, "four and a half minutes."

Sukh stood up. "I say his ETA will be less than four. Two bucks." He dug into his jeans' pocket and pulled out two loonies. He placed them on the log beside Cassidy.

"You're on," answered Jeremy.

Cassidy wanted a piece of this action. "Are we talking about here at the tree or at the start of the path?"

"Here," said Jeremy.

"I say five minutes," said Cassidy. "Closest one without going over wins. Here's my two bucks." She dug into her jeans' pocket, pulled out a toonie and placed it on the log beside Sukh's and Jeremy's money. Then she raised her left arm to pull her sleeve off her watch and began timing. Jeremy started skipping rocks into the pond, counting the spreading rings of water, while Sukh found a horizontal tree branch and began doing chin-ups, silently pulling his taut body up to chin-level with the branch. He could do only five before his form seriously suffered. When his arms started to tremble, Cassidy laughed. Sukh let go and jumped to the ground.

"I'd like to see how many *you* can do," he said, panting.

"Okay," she replied, getting up off the log and ignoring her watch. "But you have to lift me up to the branch. I'm not as tall as you."

"Nobody is," interjected Jeremy, still skipping rocks. "How tall are you now, Sukh?"

"This tall," answered Sukh with a growl. He swooped down, grabbed a shrieking Cassidy around her waist and pulled her into a sitting position on his left shoulder. Then he stood up, wobbling slightly, Cassidy now towering over Jeremy, the branch at her chin level. She was afraid, then excited as she felt the power of being up so high.

"Wow, I'm the queen of the castle," she sang as she gripped the branch with two hands. Sukh stepped back.

As she struggled to pull her body up so her eyes were level with the branch, Sukh smirked, then began counting, "One," he said, laughing.

Again Cassidy tried to pull her body up, trying to make her straight arms bend at the elbow and raise her body. Her arms were already shaking and she still hadn't done one correctly.

"One," Sukh repeated, stifling a fake yawn.

The sound of the motorcycle faded to a low rattle then stopped. Kyle was walking down the path by now.

Cassidy's arms trembled. Her face turned red. She was holding her breath and still she wasn't close to doing even one chin-up.

Sukh began to laugh. "Minus one," he finally said, just as Kyle stepped out of the forest to the edge of the pond. Without a pause, he walked straight over to an exhausted and dangling Cassidy, grabbed hold of her legs and hips, and lowered her carefully to the ground. Without any thanks to Kyle, she looked at her watch and called, "Four minutes and twenty-two seconds! Damn!" Then she took three enormous breaths.

With a chuckle, Jeremy threw his last rock into the pond, walked over to the log and picked up the coins. "Yes!" he called, pumping his fist.

Because they were offering no explanation about the money, Kyle simply shrugged, slid a small backpack off his shoulders and unfastened the top. He reached inside, pulled out some folded and crumpled pieces of paper and said, "Look at this, you guys."

Cassidy, still breathless from her attempted chin-up, reached for one of the papers and began to read aloud: "Three Die in . . . Fiery Crash on Highway 24 . . . Late Wednesday afternoon, three people died when the pick-up . . . they were driving in the Interlakes area when the vehicle veered off Highway 24 and struck a tree. Police Constable Rod Jackman — hey, Kyle, that's your cousin!"

Kyle nudged her arm. "Just keep reading," he said.

Cassidy tried to find her spot, her breathing gradually slowing to normal, then repeated,

" . . . Constable Rod Jackman said the accident seemed unusual in that there were no signs of any attempt by the driver to brake before the vehicle left the highway, indicating the driver may have fallen asleep at the wheel: 'There were no witnesses, but the people first on the scene said the truck was completely engulfed in flames when they arrived. The victims had no chance of survival.' Police are withholding the names of the victims until family members can be notified."

Cassidy finished reading and looked up. "I don't get it. Why is this important?"

"Look at the date of the article."

Cassidy looked for a date, turning the paper over to check the back. Nothing. "I don't see any date, Kyle," she said.

Kyle looked at the other papers in his hands. "Oh, sorry. Read this one."

As Cassidy reached for the paper, Jeremy stepped forward and took it before she could. "Accident Victims Identified," he read. "The victims of the fiery crash that took the lives of three people on April third have been identified as . . . " Jeremy stopped reading aloud. His eyes darted left to right, following the words on the paper. His lips continued to move, his voice trapped in his throat. He finally stopped reading and looked up at Kyle. He closed his eyes and released his breath. He handed the paper to Cassidy and walked away.

Cassidy quickly tried to find the spot where Jeremy had ended. " . . . have been identified as — oh my God!" Cassidy's voice was shrill. "It's them!"

Sukh was sure he knew what the article said. He felt his heart pounding in his chest. His pulse seemed to grow louder and move into his ears. He didn't want to move. He didn't want to breathe. His stomach suddenly felt queasy. If he stood very still, maybe he would feel better. He didn't have to see for himself, but . . . "Is it . . . ?"

Cassidy looked to Sukh. "Yup," she nodded, "It's them." Her eyes were wide, long eyelashes fanning her brow. She blinked hard. "They're the names that I was saying," she continued, "when I was semi-conscious, and the ones you guys saw first."

Sukh ran his hand through his hair. This was the proof that he'd wanted but was too scared to seek. This was the information that would have to be analyzed. He walked to the edge of the pond beside Jeremy. Each was oblivious to the presence of the other. Sukh quietly whispered, "Then it's all true. We're going to die together."

Cassidy continued reading the articles quietly to herself. She had to squeeze her eyes shut twice to refocus on the writing. The writing on the paper kept blurring. "Kyle, where exactly did you get this?"

"I went to Ourbc.com. It has news stories that date back a couple of years. I typed in the names of those people, and guess what? This second article came up. I went back a bit and found the first article." He looked past Cassidy to Jeremy and Sukh. Were they mad at him? He hated to be the bearer of bad news, but this was too important to ignore.

Cassidy considered his answer, then asked, "Well, how come we never heard about it before? Interlakes is so close to here. Why didn't we hear about a bad accident there?"

Kyle looked back at her. "Well, for one thing, we were in no shape to hear about it. We were probably in the water just as these guys were dying. It says it happened in the afternoon."

"Yeah, but somebody would have mentioned something later, don't you think?" asked Cassidy.

"Maybe, but then those guys aren't from around here. Where does it say they're from? Kamloops?"

"It says just outside of Kamloops," she offered.

"Yeah, could be Barriere. McLure. Any of those small towns. They were just passing through on their way to Prince George. Nobody from around here would know them." Kyle looked back to the other two. He wanted to draw them into the conversation, but they were still looking out over the pond. "And all the folks around here were too involved in the news about us to be talking much about strangers. They died at the scene." He shrugged. "So they probably never even made it to the hospital."

Cassidy shuddered. "That feels so weird, knowing that while we were in the water, freezing, somebody just over that ridge was dying in a fire," she said.

"That's why I felt that freaky, hot wind. When I saw them."

Cassidy and Kyle turned to look at Sukh. He had turned toward them, but still would not make eye contact. He was looking past them toward the disfigured tree. "It's because they burned in a fire."

"I guess you're right, Sukh," Kyle responded. "Did they look . . . burned?"

Still without looking at him, Sukh shook his head. "Nah, they looked like normal people."

Kyle rifled through some of the other papers in his hand. "Did any of them look like . . . this?" He held out a piece of paper that had writing and a small picture. The picture was a formal photographer's portrait of a young woman. She had curly dark hair that framed the sides of her face. She was wearing a graduation cap and a graduation gown over a lacy white blouse.

Sukh had been shocked too many times in the past two days to respond with more than mild surprise. He took the paper from Kyle and nodded. "That looks like her. One of them." He tried, but he just couldn't say her name anymore. He handed Kyle back the papers.

"She was a nurse in Kamloops. That picture was taken when she graduated from nursing school," said Kyle. "There were no pictures of the men who died with her." He looked at Cassidy and Sukh. Their attention was riveted on the picture.

Kyle looked at Jeremy, who continued to stand with his back to them at the edge of the pond. It annoyed Kyle that Jeremy would not look at the picture. He wouldn't look at any of them. For no reason he could understand, Jeremy's lack of interest frustrated Kyle. *Say something, Jeremy! Do something, Jeremy! Didn't he care about this? They might all die! Together! Maybe very soon.* Why was he ignoring this evidence? At least he wasn't throwing any damned rocks.

"Well, Jeremy?" Kyle asked, in a voice edged with irritation. "Is that the proof you need? Now do you believe we're all going to die together?"

Jeremy ignored Kyle. His silence was more maddening than an answer.

"Come on, Jeremy! Get with the program, man," Kyle hollered. "You wanted proof? Here's proof. Those people died," he yelled, "on the day we almost did! What does that tell you?"

Jeremy wouldn't turn; he wouldn't say anything.

Kyle was infuriated now by Jeremy's silence. "Now do you believe me?"

Sukh and Cassidy looked at Kyle and then at Jeremy. Why was Kyle getting so angry? Why was Jeremy so quiet? Did something happen between these two that they didn't know about?

Kyle walked toward Jeremy. He pushed the papers in Jeremy's face. "Look at them!" he yelled.

Jeremy swatted Kyle's hand away from his face, causing the papers to slip from his hand and fall into the water. Enraged, Kyle grabbed Jeremy by the arm, forcing him to face him. In an instant, Jeremy lifted his fist, ready to punch Kyle. He'd never punched anyone before, but he'd had never been pressed like this.

Cassidy screamed: "No!" She ran over to the two boys and stood between them, her hand on Jeremy's chest. "Stop it, you two! What the hell is the matter?"

Jeremy took a step back. He didn't want to hit Kyle, but he wanted to hit something. His arm shook with the tension of his tight fist. His lips were pressed together. He held his breath, but refused to take his eyes off Kyle. Neither spoke. Neither moved. Gradually Jeremy released his breath and relaxed his arm. After a long moment, Kyle turned and stepped away.

Jeremy ignored Cassidy's question and continued to look out to the pond. Cassidy asked again, "What's going on here?"

An uncomfortable silence ensued. Sukh walked to the far end of the small pond. He knew something was coming and he didn't want to be in the middle of it. The three boys stood in a big triangle with Cassidy in the middle. Silence.

Just as Cassidy was going to ask a third time, Jeremy looked at her. "Cassidy," he called, louder than he had to. "What do you think will happen now that we have proof?"

What did this have to do with Kyle and Jeremy's anger? "I don't know. I just want to know why you two are so angry."

"Never mind that," Jeremy said. "What do you think will happen now?"

She shrugged. "Nothing, I guess."

"What do you mean, nothing?" Kyle asked. He looked at her, astonished.

"I don't know. You tell me what'll happen, then." She waited a moment. "I just want to know why you guys want to fight."

"Just answer me, Cassy. What will happen now? Think about it."

Cassidy turned a wary eye to Kyle, making sure he kept his distance from Jeremy. She didn't know if the threat of a fight had passed. As if he sensed her eye on him, Kyle turned to face her. Folding his arms across his chest, he waited for her answer, but didn't move closer to Jeremy. Cassidy considered Jeremy's question.

"Well," she began. "I guess . . . if we're all going to die together, then . . . " She stopped. She bit her lip. She reached to pick a small pinecone from the bough of a tree and absently pulled pieces of it apart. She looked back to Sukh. Jeremy's point suddenly dawned on her. If they were all going to be together when they died, how would it happen? How could it happen? A car accident? Or maybe a boat accident? At school? Here? Would it be tomorrow, or when they were old and gray?

She suddenly realized: they shouldn't be together. Until just now she hadn't thought about the consequences of them staying together. They could all die. Anytime. Even right here at their meeting spot. It was too dangerous. Desperate, she asked, "Are you sure you don't know *when* we're going to die, Sukh?"

Sukh couldn't look at her. He lowered his eyes and slowly shook his head. He too had figured out what Jeremy and Kyle must have already thought of: the consequences of them staying together.

Cassidy was frantically sorting thoughts in her head. *How can we not stay best friends? But, how can we stay together if it means we can die at any time?*

She looked back to Kyle with pleading eyes. He was always the one with the answers. Why did she have to answer *this,* of all questions? *Help me, Kyle,* she screamed inside her head.

As if Jeremy knew her thoughts, he interrupted her. "No!" he yelled. "Cassidy, *you* answer the question. What are we going to do now?"

Tears of frustration started to form in her eyes. She blinked rapidly to quell them before they could spill over her lids. Stay together or stay apart? "Well," she began again, "it means that . . . that . . . I don't want to die!" She let out one heart-wrenching sob before she was able to collect her wits.

Watching her anguish was breaking Kyle's heart. He wanted to run over to Cassidy and hold her in his arms. He wanted to wipe her fears away and tell her everything would be all right. Things would never change. Everything was as it would always be. But he couldn't move. The question had to be answered. As much as he didn't want to answer it, he knew Jeremy would never let it go.

Jeremy's quiet voice brought Kyle some relief. "None of us want to die, Cass. But what should we do?"

Cassidy looked back at Jeremy. "Why me?" she implored. "Why are you asking *me*? Why can't we vote on it?"

Jeremy looked at her with eyes full of tenderness. He hated hurting her and she knew it. "A vote wouldn't change anything," he said. "If we voted on this, Cass, what do you think would change? Kyle would vote to stay apart." Jeremy turned to Kyle, who didn't deny it and simply stared at Cassidy.

"And I would vote to stay together," Jeremy continued. "And Sukhy . . . " All three looked to Sukh. "Well, knowing Sukh, I'm sure he would say he didn't care, whatever we decide."

Sukh smiled at Cassidy and shrugged.

"I know all this because you guys are my very best friends. But you, my pretty lady, are my wild card — and the tie-breaker. You're the girl, and — "

"I'm the girl?" Cassidy lashed out, "What difference does that make? You need an answer full of sugar and spice and everything nice?" She threw what was left of the pinecone at him. It fell to the ground at his feet. "Why should I be put on the spot? How the hell should *I* know what we should do? And why do I need the pressure of making this huge life or death decision?"

She folded her arms in front of her and turned away from Jeremy only to find herself facing Kyle. She turned away again but found herself facing Sukh. In frustration she unfolded her arms and swung back to face Jeremy. She tried to speak, but could only open her mouth. No words came to her lips, just an exasperated "Oh!"

She knew he was only the messenger, the one who dared to speak what they all were thinking. When she'd finished venting he looked at her and continued. "You are *the girl* and we all care so much about you. I think we'll all abide by your decision. What you *want* us to do."

Cassidy was instantly contrite. She knew they all cared about her and she cared so much for each of them. She needed these guys, her best friends. But she was so scared. And she suddenly felt all alone. She knew that deep down, whether she decided they should stay together or apart, they wanted the decision made because of her sugar and spice. She could make the decision to stay together, admitting that she needed them so they could continue to look like men, their masculinity intact.

And if she chose to stay apart, they would respect that because if she could live without her best friends, then so could they. *She* had to answer the question and for some reason, whatever her decision would be, she knew they would accept it.

What should she say? She raised her chin, looked directly into Jeremy's eyes and finally said, "I believe in leaving it up to fate."

Jeremy smiled slightly, not so much with his mouth but with his eyes. Kyle closed his eyes. His face was unreadable.

Their relief was short-lived when Sukh asked quietly, "Cheating it . . . or tempting it?"

Both Jeremy and Kyle looked to Sukh with raised eyebrows. What does that mean? They then looked back to Cassidy, as if she should know.

Cassidy was just as confused as they were. "Wh . . . what do you mean, Sukh?" she asked, nervously.

Sukh shifted his weight from one foot to the other. "I believe in fate, too," he began. "But to cheat fate would mean . . ." he paused, trying to find words. "It would mean we can never be all together again. Fate would never be able to catch us together . . . to kill us together. Therefore, we cheat it, and . . . death." Sukh looked up to the tree that had been struck by lightning. The top branches, now bare of anything green, pointed to the sky, like the fingers of a giant hand, directing the way to heaven.

Cassidy asked, "How do we tempt fate, then, Sukh?"

Still looking at the tree, Sukh said, "To tempt fate means we stay together." He looked away from the tree back to Cassidy's face. "And fate will be tempted to kill us . . . whenever it wants."

A sudden light wind began to rattle the poplars, pines and firs. It grew to a dull roar, not so much from intensity as from the movement of the many trees that were so easily disturbed by its presence. The tops of the giant pines rocked back and forth, sending pine needles, dried poplar leaves and old twigs falling. One small pinecone that had been trapped on a bough for months fell into the pond, sending growing circles of water to dissipate to the shore. Everyone looked up and around, suddenly uneasy about the dangerously twisting treetops that could snap in a moment and fall, crushing them. Killing them. The only object unresponsive to the spinning air was the old tree, too stiff and dead. It remained impassive to the pelting debris falling from the skies. Although the air was still warm and most of the gusts were high over their heads, Cassidy wrapped her arms around herself. She rubbed her hands up and down her arms to warm them. "I'm getting chills."

All three boys stared at Cassidy. They absorbed her words, and then rubbed their own arms. This wasn't fair. It was huge. This decision would affect the rest of their lives. Why should Cassidy have to decide? Nobody wanted to deal with Sukh's question and it wasn't fair to force it on her.

Kyle walked toward her. He reached one hand out and pushed back a few strands of long blond hair that had stuck to her glossy lips. He hugged her to him, wrapping his arms around her small frame. Pulling her body to his, he silently offered his own body heat. "I think we all are," he half whispered to her and half spoke to all of them.

Nobody said another word until the wind swept passed them to announce its presence to the trees far beyond the pond. Without looking up, her head still pressed against Kyle's chest, Cassidy asked, "What are we going to do?" She was near tears.

Kyle pulled his arms tighter around Cassidy's shoulders. Sukh and Jeremy could no longer stand back. They both envied Cassidy's security nestled in Kyle's arms. They all wanted to be wrapped in someone's strong arms and told that the problem would go away. Jeremy walked toward them. Sukh took Jeremy's cue and joined them at the centre of the invisible triangle. Everyone wanted a hug at that moment, but Sukh and Jeremy were both content to put a hand on Cassidy's shoulder and accept her touch as their own sanctuary. A decision would have to be made . . . but not just now.

20

The Decision-Maker

THE SCHOOL BUS CAME TO A full stop in front of the buffalo ranch beside the highway. A sixth-grader stepped off it. As the doors squeaked closed, the driver adjusted the gears and the vehicle lurched forward to continue along the daily route.

Cassidy rested her feet against the back of the seat in front of her. Jeremy sat low beside her, his head resting on the back of his seat with his pro-fit baseball cap tilted down over his closed eyes. Sukh and Kyle sat in the seat behind them, talking quietly about the latest NHL scores.

"I know you guys are coming to my place now, but what time are all your parents coming tonight for the barbecue?" Cassidy asked.

"Don't know," Sukh muttered quickly, almost ignoring the interruption.

"Yeah," answered Kyle, just as quickly, then continued to talk to Sukh.

Jeremy sat up straight, pushed the cap back above his eyes and said, without looking at anyone, "My old man is bringing someone."

Kyle and Sukh stopped talking in mid-sentence and turned away from each other to look at Jeremy, their eyes wide open.

Cassidy, equally surprised, turned to Jeremy. "What? Who?"

Jeremy cleared his throat, still looking straight at the road ahead, and said, "Some lady-friend." He indicated a quotation with his fingers around the words "lady-friend" signifying to his friends that they were his father's words, not his.

"Well, do you know her?" asked Cassidy.

"Nah," answered Jeremy. He feigned interest in one of the many trees the bus was passing, turning his head back to watch before it disappeared from his line of vision. His gaze returned to look up the road, ahead of the school bus. "She lives in town, and so far my old man has only dated her in town." Then he added, "I hope she stays there."

At first Cassidy was excited for Jeremy's dad, but she could tell it upset Jeremy, and her excitement turned to unease.

Jeremy sank lower into his seat. "She's supposed to be Mme. Lafleur's sister."

"The French teacher?" asked Cassidy.

Jeremy refused to look at her. "Yeah . . . the French teacher."

Kyle let out a low whistle. "Wow, then she must be hot!"

Sukh chuckled.

Cassidy rolled her eyes. "Well, then she must be very nice. Mme. Lafleur's cool. I think she's the nicest teacher in the whole school."

"Yeah right. The nicest *looking* teacher. I could sit in her class all day long," said Kyle, and sighed.

"Yeah, but it's not French you're thinking of." Sukh elbowed Kyle in the ribs.

"I hate French," said Jeremy.

The bus took the next bend in the winding, narrow highway.

As everyone continued to stare at Jeremy, thinking about this new turn of events, they watched his eyes suddenly open wide with horror. His hands darted forward and gripped the bar on the back of the seat in front of him. He forced his feet ahead, pressing an invisible footbrake. Cassidy, Sukh and Kyle looked forward, too, and froze.

There, taking up the entire highway, was a jack-knifed semi-trailer. Logs had spilled from the trailer and lay strewn across the road, some still rolling. The bus driver tried desperately to brake and turn away, but the sudden change in direction forced the school bus into a sideways spin. The wheels no longer rolled but slid sideways across the pavement toward the shoulder on the opposite side of the highway. Children began to scream. The bus driver moaned as he tried frantically to get control of the spinning vehicle, now facing toward the direction from which it had come. The bus lurched when the wheels left the smooth pavement and hit the gravel shoulder. The vehicle turned over on its side and slid down the embankment, coming to rest against some trees.

For a moment everything was quiet. The children, all in shock, said nothing. Slowly they began moving. Because the bus now lay on its side, everyone had been thrown onto the children who'd begun the journey on the left side of the vehicle. The windows that were now on the ground had all smashed. Broken pieces of glass lay everywhere. Some of the children were bleeding; some were moaning; some were crying.

The bus driver tried to get up, but his position made it awkward. His breathing was rapid and shallow. He looked up at the door that was now the roof of the bus. With his right hand he pulled on the steering wheel to lift himself, but his left side and shoulder were trembling with pain. There was banging. Someone was at the emergency exit windows on the outside.

He tried to call to the children to be calm and everything would be okay, but he could manage only a whisper. He again tried to move but the pain must have been excruciating; he passed out.

When the driver awoke, someone was walking on top of the bus. Fingers reached in between the two doors, prying them open. With a loud squeak, the doors separated and Jeremy's bloodied but smiling face looked down into the bus driver's. "We're all okay, Mr. Sanders, but how are you?" Then Jeremy had a good look and continued. "OOOh, not too good."

Mr. Sanders tried to smile back. He closed his eyes for a moment and rested his head against the broken glass that used to be his side window. There were more footsteps on the roof. Sukh and Kyle both jumped off the front of the bus and looked through the cracked windshield to smile at him. With their heads up, they raised their arms and walked around and out of sight to help the younger children down to safety. On the roof, Cassidy, was soothing some of those still crying. There were sirens. One by one the children came to the front of the bus to look at Mr. Sanders, to stare through the jagged, silvery lines of the shattered windshield. It was like a silent roll call. Some of them had small cuts, ripped clothes, oozing scrapes. Some were still crying. He tried to smile at them, to comfort them. There was shouting. Men shouting. At last . . . the fire department. Ken Lockett, his brow creased with worry, peered into the bus through the starburst of broken glass.

21
The Decision

"MOM, I'M FINE," CASSIDY WHINED. HER mother pushed Cassidy's hair away from her face and gently touched the bruise on her left temple.

"Are you sure, honey? A blow to your temple can be serious."

Cassidy rolled her eyes and looked over at Kyle and Jeremy, who smiled and looked away, grinning at each other. "Why don't you look at Jeremy's stitches? After all, it was my hard head that cracked his forehead open." Mrs. Sampson began walking in his direction.

Sukh's mother and father spoke in Punjabi to Sukh, and from their tone Cassidy could tell they were just as concerned about the bruises on his arm and shoulder. Cassidy's and Kyle's dads were at the barbecue, discussing the accident while they turned chicken pieces. Jeremy's dad and his dad's girlfriend stood nearby, occasionally adding to the conversation, but mostly whispering and giggling together.

And Jeremy didn't like her one bit. Her name was Bernadette and she was from Quebec. She'd moved out west a couple of years before and moved to the Cariboo only a few months ago. She was younger than Jeremy's mother, blond and attractive in a flashy sort of way, and she spoke with a French accent. At first that was okay, but the more he heard it, the more it began to grate on him. Today was not the day he wanted to meet someone new or share his father's attention. His head still hurt and the sympathy he was expecting — wanted, needed — to get from his dad was too brief. To his relief, she didn't look too interested in Jeremy or his injuries, so after his father inspected his stitches for a few moments, Jeremy took a seat well away from them and avoided looking in their direction, even when Kyle whispered to him about how nice she was.

The accident had caused quite a stir in town, and they almost considered cancelling the barbecue. But, all the children were released from Emergency with nothing more than a few stitches, and most with considerably less, and after all, everyone still had to eat and there was plenty of food at the house.

Everyone looked up at the sound of a car coming down the driveway. Ken and Erika Lockett were finally here. They would bring news of Mr. Sanders.

Mrs. Sampson met them as the car door opened. "How is he?" she asked.

Ken stepped out and walked back to the trunk to get their share of the potluck dinner. He lifted a platter covered in plastic wrap and draped with a clean dish towel. "Well," he began, "he's pretty serious, but it looks like he'll pull through. To quote the media: 'he has no life-threatening injuries'. A punctured lung, dislocated shoulder and two broken ribs." He looked at all of the adults walking closer to hear everything he had to say. "It was a miracle no one was killed. And all the kids are home safe."

"And the truck driver, how is he?" asked Kyle's dad.

"Broken leg," answered Ken.

Erika walked directly over to Jeremy. She tilted his chin up and stared at his face intently. "Ah mein schatzi," she said. "Are you okay, my treasure?"

Jeremy, who had felt so brave through the entire ordeal, felt tears well in his eyes. His Oma was here. He reached his arms around her waist and lowered his face to rest his cheek on her shoulder. Then he hugged her, tight. She squeezed his shoulders gently so as not to hurt any bruises she was not sure about.

Pulling away from him, she looked again at his face, especially at the stitches on his forehead. "Ah, *yow*," she said in her German accent, fighting tears herself. Her beautiful Jeremy was hurting and had a cut that would surely scar. Jeremy's dad came up behind Erika and touched her shoulder. She turned towards him and he hugged her, too. Jeremy wondered if Bernadette felt left out, that she didn't belong here today, but a glance in her direction showed her talking to the other men and laughing at a joke.

Kyle waited for Jeremy's attention, and when he had it, nodded toward the lake. Sukh and Cassidy were already walking toward the gazebo where the children's table had always been set up for them. Cassidy's older brothers had graduated from the gazebo to the patio to sit with the adults, but the four friends hoped they would never have to do that. They loved their privacy by the water. Kyle and Jeremy hurried to join the other two.

"Wow. All I remember was Jeremy's face. You should have seen yourself, Jer. Your eyes popped out of your head like you'd seen a ghost. The next thing I knew, I was falling all over the place." Cassidy poked Jeremy's shoulder.

"Yeah, more like you were falling all over *me*. First thing I felt was your boob, the next thing I knew I was seeing stars when your head smacked mine."

"Ha! That's what you get for touching my boob, even if it was an accident!" Cassidy said and laughed.

"Oh-ho!" said Kyle. "I wish I had a boob fall on me. Instead I got this huge kid — " He playfully shoved Sukh, " — and all the rest of the freakin' bus load of kids fall on me."

Sukh turned and faced Kyle, a big grin on his face. "I remember thinking how soft you felt when I landed on you."

"Soft? Ha! Ha!" Jeremy poked Kyle's belly.

Kyle feigned offence, but smiled when he said, "I'll have you know that I am not soft. Look at this six-pack. All muscle." He lifted his shirt to show a lean and well-defined abdomen. "Go ahead. Hit me."

Without a pause, Jeremy and Sukh pulled back their fists and stumbled over each other to get to Kyle first. Kyle, recognizing the gleam in their eyes, pulled down his shirt and ducked behind Cassidy, laughing. "Hey, one at a time, you guys."

Cassidy squealed and pulled her arms up to protect her stomach from Jeremy's and Sukh's fists, but both boys faked a punch to her belly and, leaning past her, punched Kyle in his ribs.

"Ow," he muttered, and everyone else giggled.

It was then that the women brought dinner out to them, telling them that because of their ordeal they wouldn't have to help clean up. Cassidy's brothers on the patio let out a collective moan.

As darkness began to surround them, Cassidy realized that they'd all only picked at their meals; even Sukh, who lately was always hungry. For the last little while they'd been silent, deep in their own thoughts. The earlier jovial mood had been replaced by a more pensive one. For the first time since they'd retreated to the gazebo, Cassidy was aware of the sounds of the adults eating dinner up on the patio. She knew that the subject of the accident had to be dealt with, but she didn't want to be the one to broach it. Adding another log to the fireplace in the middle of the gazebo, she took a deep breath.

"Guys," she began, "that was too, too scary. I thought we were going to die today. I'm still shaking."

A long moment passed. Cassidy wondered if they'd heard her. Finally, Kyle shrugged and said, "I'm sure everyone in that bus thought they were gonna die, Cassy. It was scary."

"It's over, Cass, and we're fine. You don't have to be scared anymore," added Jeremy.

Sukh looked at all of them, then made eye contact with Cassidy. "I think Cassidy means that, because of our destiny, she thought today was the day in the notorious 'book'." He continued to look into Cassidy's eyes. "Today we tempted fate." He leaned back in his chair, into the shadows beyond the campfire light.

Silence. Everyone had the same fear. Fate would not have had to work very hard to kill them today. It would have been so easy — so tempting — for them to have been killed in the bus.

Jeremy had a creepy feeling that fate was some kind of an invisible beast lurking around them, teasing them. *I could have killed you today if I wanted to,* it was thinking. *Or maybe tomorrow. Hee, hee. You'll never know. Just don't tempt me.* Jeremy shuddered and looked behind him into the dark forest. The hairs on his arms stood up. He leaned closer to the fire.

"I must admit, guys, when I first saw that truck across the road and no way around it, I thought then and there that, if I get through this alive, I'm finding new friends." Sukh's voice was serious and even in the darkness they knew he was not smiling. "I love you all, but when death looks you in the eye like that, well hell, I was wishing we'd decided to separate the other day." He looked out to the lake.

"Me, too," said Cassidy quietly.

Kyle looked to Sukh. "Yeah," he began, "I thought the same thing. But then I thought about those other two names: Catrina Bergman and Jamieson Otters. Those two are supposed to die with us, right? And they weren't on the bus, whoever they are."

"Yeah, but how did you know they weren't in the jack-knifed semi? They could have died in the truck," said Sukh.

"Yeah, or they could have hit the truck from the other side. Who knows? But they could have just as easily died with us today," added Cassidy.

Kyle shrugged. "I guess."

"The 'Miracle Teens', my ass," said Jeremy sullenly. "We're just accident prone." He was resigning himself to the idea that their future together would not be without risks, but he couldn't accept entirely the theory of them dying together. Today he was scared. Scared of what could have happened . . . and what he knew was about to happen.

The four friends sat quietly for a long time. The fire cracked and snapped. Laughter penetrated the darkness that separated them from the deck, where their parents had finished their dinner and were having coffee and dessert.

"Well, I think we all agree that we can't stay together," Cassidy said, looking at Jeremy. When she made eye contact with him he closed his eyes, sighed and turned to look into the fire. She knew this would be hardest on him, but she forced herself to continue. "I'm telling you right now. I can't give up all of you." She took a deep breath. "What do you think about us breaking up into two. That would be cheating fate, right Sukh?"

Sukh shrugged and answered, very quietly, "I don't know. I don't even know if we *can* cheat fate."

"Is it fate we're cheating?" asked Kyle. He paused. "Or is it God we're cheating?"

Jeremy looked at Kyle. "Do you even believe in God, Kyle?"

More laughter drifted over from the deck. Looking toward the colourful patio lights and tiki torches, the kids could see that Bear and his wife, Donna, had arrived.

Kyle looked bemused. He ran his fingers through his hair. "I don't know," he answered. "A year ago, I never gave it any thought. Now, with all these accidents . . . ."

Cassidy interrupted, "I know what you mean. I never went to church. We never talked about God, but man, I sure have been thinking about weird stuff lately."

Jeremy turned back to Kyle. "But, Kyle, if you don't believe in God, what *do* you believe in?"

"Aliens."

Jeremy, Sukh and Cassidy exploded with laughter. The pensive mood had lifted. It felt good to laugh. Kyle smiled. "It's true."

"What?" Cassidy asked, smiling. "You can't be serious."

Kyle leaned closer to the fire. "Now, hear me out before you tell me I'm crazy. I think that, just maybe, with all these supposed visits from aliens you hear about on TV and in those stupid magazines and tabloids, maybe it's true. Maybe there are aliens. And since they don't seem to be in a big hurry to blow up the earth because they've been coming for centuries supposedly and haven't blown it up yet . . . who knows? Maybe they haven't blown us up yet because they're helping us. It could be that they planted us here on earth, from another galaxy or planet or whatever. And they keep coming here to check up on us. You know, so *we* don't blow it up or something."

He looked quickly around to see his friends' expressions. "And I think every so often they send us somebody from outer space like a prophet, or Jesus or somebody, to tell us how not to be stupid. You know, that love thy neighbour stuff, don't sleep around because you'll die of some disease, rest one day a week. All that stuff that's supposed to be in the Bible or the Ten Commandments or something. Maybe *they* wrote the Bible. Or maybe they're quoted in it. 'Cause let's face it, the Bible is the owner's manual for how to keep humanity going, isn't it?"

"So, you think these aliens brought a shipload of people here?" said Jeremy. "When?""

Kyle smiled. "No, but maybe they had to bring a man and a woman and a little seed of everything to start it here."

"Adam and Eve and The Garden of Eden," mumbled Jeremy.

"I guess," answered Kyle, shrugging.

"So where did all the animals come from?" asked Cassidy.

Kyle pondered this for a moment. "I haven't figured the whole thing out yet, Cass."

Smiling, Jeremy said, "Maybe the Bible is a little wrong and the animals came over on Noah's spaceship, not on an Ark."

"That's stupid," responded Cassidy.

Sukh looked at her. "Why is it stupid, Cass? What do you believe in?"

"Me?" she asked. She leaned back in her chair and lifted her feet up onto the edge of the fireplace. She raised her left eyebrow and tried to look up into the creative side of her brain. "Well, I keep thinking about something that Mr. Lightman said."

"The science teacher?" All the boys asked the question at the same time.

Cassidy laughed. "Yeah, the science teacher. He said something once about atomic structure and how the atom works, and I haven't forgotten it." She stopped talking and waited. Hearing no scoffing, she carried on. "He said the atom has one nucleus and that there are other particles, electrons — there are a number of those, not just one — that spin around the nucleus inside the atom. Then he said something that still gives me chills."

"Well, what was it?" asked Sukh.

Cassidy enjoyed their suspense. "He said it was almost the same way as the planets rotate around the sun. Like the Earth is an electron and the sun is the nucleus."

Kyle asked, "Why would that give you chills?"

Cassidy looked into the fire. "Well, if you think about it, that would mean that our universe, our huge and vast universe of all the planets and the sun, is just an atom. So, what if our universe is an atom in the make up of another . . . Being? Can you imagine how great that Being must be?"

Jeremy whistled. "Well, I know that God is supposed to be bigger than anything we know. But can you imagine how huge that would be?"

Sukh shuddered. "Man, that gives me shivers, too."

Cassidy said, "I also think that there might be a tie somehow between astrology and the atomic structure thing. The sun and planets make up the zodiac, you know, so I've found myself looking up stuff on astrology and our signs. For instance, Sukhy, you're a Pisces. Born in February, right?"

Sukh nodded.

"So you tend to be a rule-breaker, lucky, deceptive and a have a tendency toward addictions."

Kyle asked, "What am I supposed to be like? I'm an Aries."

Cassidy smiled. "You fit your sign to the bill. Aries are bold, self-confident, impulsive and they want to conquer the world."

Jeremy chuckled. "What are you, Cass?"

"Me? I'm a Scorpio. I like to inspire others, be loyal to my friends, and I'm supposed to be jealous and emotional. I'm not sure exactly how they tie together, but I think that astrology has some connection to God — if God is that huge and powerful Being that our universe is only a tiny particle of."

"You know, it's really weird how we all believe in different things, yet our beliefs are so similar," Jeremy said. "I went to church with Oma and Opa and took Catechism classes for them. My dad says he's Catholic, but he only goes to church on Christmas and Easter. Oma and Opa go every Sunday. I didn't like going, but I guess a lot of it sunk in, because I do believe in the Father, the Son and the Holy Spirit." At this, he did the sign of the cross, touching his right fingertips to his forehead, his chest, his left shoulder and then his right shoulder. Then he said, "Especially we believe in Jesus, the Son of God. But even as a Catholic I know there's still a God who's bigger than Jesus."

"I thought Jesus *was* God," said Cassidy.

"He is."

"But you just said He's the Son of God."

"Jesus is the human form of God. Maybe God is Kyle's alien or your atomic structure. But somehow he had to come here in a human form to teach us forgiveness so we'd listen to Him."

Sukh kicked at a log that had fallen away from the fire and was only smoking. "I believe in God, too," he said.

Jeremy looked surprised. "I thought you believed in, like, nine gods."

Sukh smiled. "Ten, but they're not really gods. They're more like prophets, I guess. Kind of like Jesus. And they even taught us the same stuff as Jesus: forgive your enemies; all people are equal; share the wealth. Stuff like that. Only one God, though." He shook his arm to raise his long sleeve. A silver bracelet gleamed in the firelight. "This is my Kara. It's supposed to remind me not to sin. Our future fate depends on how well we behave in this life. Our belief is that most sins are done by the hands, so a bracelet is to remind us to think about what we're doing . . . before we do it."

"Well, I've seen your hands sin tons of times, so when are you going to start thinking about it?" Jeremy chuckled and ducked away when Sukh jokingly raised his fist to punch him in the shoulder. Cassidy and Kyle laughed.

"See, he just sinned again!" yelped Jeremy, rubbing the spot on his arm his friend had just abused.

The log that Sukh had kicked burst into flame. Four pairs of eyes watched the orange and red gases lick at the poplar branch, each of the four lost in thought again. Their irises flashed gold, reflecting the flames.

Jeremy finally spoke: "So it's like I said. We all believe in God, except maybe for Kyle, who believes in aliens."

"Wait a minute!" Kyle jumped to his own defence. "I didn't say I don't believe there's a God. People all around the world — people who haven't gotten along for thousands of years, different languages, different cultures, people who live in lands completely isolated from the rest of the world, almost all of them believe in some kind of God. And they have for thousands of years. Who am I, a stupid teenager in this century, to say that there's no God? I just think, well, maybe He's an alien."

A splash near the shoreline, followed by a quack, brought their attention to the dark water. A duck must be nearby, and was probably in danger of being attacked by a much larger loon. The silence that followed alerted Cassidy to the fact that the adults were no longer out on the deck. The warm spring days always ended in cold evenings, especially so near the water, where a cool breeze escaped from around the point. Since the adults didn't have a fire to keep them warm, they must have gone inside. That would mean everyone would be leaving soon.

"Well, guys, what are we going to do?" Cassidy asked.

All three boys knew they'd have to decide who each would become best friends with. This was going to be very hard, but they'd been thinking about nothing else since the day Kyle had found the proof on the Internet.

Jeremy spoke first. "Well, should we let fate make the call, since fate is making *us* make a call? Draw straws?"

Draw straws. So simple. Yet the results would change their lives so much. Cassidy wanted to scream. *We'll just draw straws? There has to be a more complicated and scientific way of doing this!* But she remained silent.

Reluctantly Kyle stepped forward. "Fine," he said. He pulled four pieces of tall grass from the ground beside him. He tore two pieces into the same length and two others slightly longer. He hid the uneven ends in his palm and made sure that all of the exposed ends of grass looked the same length. "Whoever gets the same length as you becomes your new best bud."

He turned to face Cassidy. "Ladies first."

Since nobody knew who he or she wanted to have for their partner, nobody cared which straw they got. Cassidy reached forward and without hesitation, pulled a blade of grass from Kyle's hand. She held it up to the firelight.

"Okay, who will match my straw and be my friend for life?" she whispered. Biting her lip, she turned to face the boys. Firelight cast a flickering, rosy glow on her face. Her hair looked like gold threads. She opened her eyes wide to look up to the remaining straws. She didn't really mind which one of these guys she was fated to be with, but she knew that this was going to be a very big moment.

Kyle turned to the boys. "Well, who wants to draw next? This could be it, the last pull if you match Cass, or . . . " He held the remaining straws up in the firelight. Jeremy turned to face Sukh. He shrugged and shook his head, indicating that he didn't mind if Sukh picked next. All held their breath until Sukh reached up. He paused, touched one straw, paused again, then reached for another. He held it up high enough for them all to see it and then compared it to Cassidy's straw.

It didn't match.

Everyone let out their breath, Sukh and Cassidy because of the suspense, but Kyle for another reason. He still had a chance!

Kyle's heart was pounding. He loved all his friends. He grew up with them. They were always there for him and he'd always like to be there for them. But he couldn't live without Cassidy, and he'd never told her or anyone. On the day of the snowmobile accident he knew that he'd fallen in love with her. He knew that, had they never gone through the ice that day, he probably would have told her a long time ago. But for some reason he'd decided that it would be unlucky, unwise, fateful, star-crossed, or . . . whatever, if he were to tell her.

And somehow, no matter what happened with the next pick, he had to appear happy with the straw that was left. Could he do it? He held the last two straws out to Jeremy. Not trusting his voice for fear it would crack under the stress, he merely pushed his hand forward, the straws so close to Jeremy's face they almost went up his nose.

Jeremy pulled his head back out of harm's way. "What's with you, man?" he asked, but without waiting for an answer he reached for a straw. He tried to pull it from Kyle's grasp, but Kyle gripped them both so tightly that Jeremy had to hold onto Kyle's wrist and tug. Jeremy looked at Kyle, and as though he were talking to a child, he said, "Easy, fella," he said. "I know this is tough, but . . ." Then he pulled. The straw was free from Kyle's grip but now was trapped in Jeremy's hand. Jeremy held the straw up to the light. Immediately Cassidy and Sukh held theirs to the firelight, one on either side of Jeremy's.

Jeremy's straw matched Sukh's.

Sukh and Jeremy let out an unenthusiastic cheer. They would have given the same response no matter which of the friends they were matched with, the feeling of the loss of the others weighed so heavily. Both boys held up their right hands to begin a high-five, but instead turned it into a clasp.

Because of their response, nobody noticed Kyle release his breath, or the tears of relief in his eyes. Cassidy walked past Jeremy, patting him on the back as she continued over to Kyle. She stood before him, her eyes downcast. She was glad to be with Kyle, even knowing how sad it would be to say goodbye to the others. Without a word, Kyle hugged her to him. She responded by reaching her arms under his and holding the back of his shoulders.

Voices from the other side of the house interrupted their thoughts. The Locketts were leaving, which meant the party was about to break up. They were down to their last few minutes together. How could they say *goodbye?*

Sukh turned to face Kyle. "Hey, Kyle, I'll never forget you, man." He reached out his right hand to shake Kyle's. As Kyle shook it, Sukh reached around with his left hand and pulled Kyle to him. Sukh tried hard to look into Kyle's eyes, but knew that would bring tears to his own, so he looked up. Then he broke away and moved over to Cassidy as Jeremy came to Kyle and did the same thing.

Kyle tried to break the tension by saying, "You know, we can always phone each other, or chat online. This isn't goodbye-and-get-out-of-my-life."

Jeremy responded with a fake chuckle, "Yeah, you're right."

More laughter and goodbyes came from the driveway. A car door opened and shut. Then another. The sound of an ignition turning over and a well-tuned motor catching was loud inside the night forest.

Sukh stood before Cassidy. Her head was down. He tipped her chin up and saw the tears streaming down her cheeks. "Awww, Cass," he said and hugged her. Then he put each of his hands on her cheeks, cupping her face, and looked into her eyes. She had to look straight up to see his face; he was growing so tall. She looked at the dark hair that covered his upper lip and suddenly realized how mature he looked. She closed her eyes to ingrain this memory in her mind forever. Then he leaned down and kissed her on the forehead.

Cassidy felt so loved by that simple gesture. This big, tall, handsome, young man made her feel like a little child again with that tender kiss. It made her feel safe and secure and young again. Young, like before their accident. She opened her eyes and saw Sukh's watery eyes. He was crying, too. Then he hugged her one more time and moved off the gazebo to wait for Jeremy.

Kyle, tears streaming unashamedly down his cheeks, sat down on the edge of the railing that encased the gazebo as Jeremy moved away to give his regards to Cassidy. Cassidy tried to wipe the tears from her cheeks as she turned to face Jeremy. He put one hand on each of her shoulders and just looked at her face for a very long moment. His eyes were dry. His face, at first so serious, suddenly changed as his mouth curled into a crooked grin. Kyle watched him. Sukh watched him.

Cassidy began to smile. "What?" she asked.

A car drove up the winding driveway to the road. Car lights flashed through the trees. More voices said goodbye on the driveway. More car doors opened and closed. The boys could hear their names being spoken by their parents. It was time to go!

Jeremy, a silly smile still on his face, answered Cassidy's query by shaking his head. He cupped Cassidy's face just as Sukh had done. He bent down to place a tender kiss on her forehead, just as Sukh had done. Then, tipping her face higher, he placed his lips on hers. Her eyes flew wide open.

Her first kiss! And from Jeremy! Cassidy could feel his lips purse together and draw hers gently closer to his. His lips were warm and dry. They felt so gentle and tender touching hers, so nice and . . . she shivered. His lips parted slightly, his eyes closed. Cassidy's eyes closed involuntarily as she allowed her body to lean into his. She lifted her arms to clasp her hands behind his neck. A very quiet moan escaped her, hardly heard by Jeremy and not noticed at all by Sukh and Kyle. She, too, parted her lips as she felt his tongue sweetly touch hers. She caught her breath. This felt so nice, so right and yet so . . . weird. Oh, Jeremy! Her heart began to race. She was afraid Jeremy could feel her heartbeat through her chest. Her legs were tingling. "Breathe!" she thought to herself. Why did she feel so wonderfully strange?

And just as surprisingly as it began, it ended. Jeremy pulled his lips away and turned his head to whisper in her ear. "Goodbye, Beautiful!"

Then he faced the other two boys. His smile had faded. He raised his index finger to his forehead and pointed toward Kyle in a lazy salute as he stepped off the gazebo. Kyle sat flabbergasted on the railing, too shocked by what he had just witnessed. He cleared his throat. He didn't know if he felt jealousy or sorrow. He simply nodded to Jeremy, who waved his arm for Sukh to come. Sukh, a huge grin splitting his face, gave one exaggerated wave to Cassidy and Kyle and walked with Jeremy to meet their parents.

And they never looked back.

22
Cassidy and Kyle

CASSIDY DISMOUNTED PAINTBRUSH AND LED THE horse down the trail to the pond beside the big tree. Kyle's motocross bike was already there. He'd asked her to meet him, telling her he'd check with Sukh and Jeremy by e-mail, to make sure the other two wouldn't be coming to their favourite meeting place. Kyle said some chance meetings of all four were inevitable, but if they could avoid one, they would. Cassidy didn't care. She almost hoped for a chance meeting so she could see Sukh and Jeremy again. She hadn't seen them in a month, even at school, except at a glance from across the crowded gym. She thought about them every day.

When she got to the pond, Kyle was nowhere to be seen. She glanced around to find a place to tie Paintbrush's tether so she could look for him. As she guided the horse closer to the charred tree, Paintbrush balked. She neighed, pulled back on the rope, and wouldn't go forward. She pranced from side to side and tossed her head, refusing to move closer to the tree.

"What's the matter?" asked Cassidy. She looked up at the damaged branches and charred trunk and wondered if it freaked out her horse. "It's okay, girl." She patted Paintbrush's head, scratching between her eyes. "It's just a tree. A creepy-looking one, maybe, but it can't hurt you."

As long as Cassidy wasn't pulling her forward, Paintbrush was calm. She twitched her tail and tossed her mane, but stopped prancing. But when Cassidy pulled the rope forward the horse began sidestepping and snorting. Something was upsetting her. Cassidy slowly panned the forest, wondering if Paintbrush sensed or smelled a large animal. Nothing moved.

That's when she noticed the silence. Not a bird chirped. Not a branch swayed. Not a squirrel chattered at her, angry she was infringing on its territory. It was too quiet. The air was too still. What was wrong with the forest? The hairs on Cassidy's skin stood up. Goosebumps dotted her arms. She didn't want to miss a sound, so she dared not make a sound. As if on cue, Paintbrush, too, stopped moving and stood silent.

A moment passed. Cassidy wondered again where Kyle was. *He had to be here because his bike was here. But where?* Violent scenarios began to form in her head. He could have been attacked by an animal: a cougar . . . a bear . . . a wolf. Some crazed bushman could have assaulted him. She looked around the ground for signs of a struggle. No broken undergrowth. No blood. Nothing. It was as if he'd never made it this far down the path.

She wanted to call his name, but silence seemed safer. Her breath was slow and shallow. She refused to move. How long should she stay here, she wondered. *How long do I wait like a helpless victim?* She felt so vulnerable. *Fight or flight? Do something*! She felt so foolish. There was absolutely no evidence of any threat, yet she sensed something sinister. She slowly looked up the ugly, old tree for some sign of evil. It looked no more disturbing than usual.

Paintbrush turned her head back, behind them, and seemed to look through the trees at something. Cassidy slowly looked back to follow the vision of her horse just as the snap of a twig on the ground punctured the silence. She whirled her head to her other side to see something dark move from behind a tree.

It was Kyle, zipping up his fly.

Cassidy groaned as her knees buckled beneath her. She slowly sank to the ground as she took a deep breath of relief. Kneeling, she took more long deep breaths as Kyle rushed over to her.

"What's the matter?" he asked. He knelt to her and held her hand with both of his. His brow creased as he tried to look into her eyes.

Cassidy took two more deep breaths. "Where were you?" she asked him, harshly. She was on the edge of tears.

"I was just taking a leak. What happened? Are you okay?"

"Yes," she answered. "Yes, I'm fine. I . . . I just . . . "

Kyle helped her to stand. He looked into her eyes, and saw that she was about to cry. He pulled her to him and hugged her in a tight embrace.

Relief overwhelmed her but the tears still threatened to stream down her cheeks. "I thought an animal got you. You weren't here and . . . and Paintbrush was acting so weird."

Kyle laughed. "I'm sorry I scared you, Cass. I swear, I was right behind that big bush. I even heard you talking to Paintbrush."

Cassidy sniffled. She stayed in his arms, refusing to pull away. She felt protected there. "I was so scared. Please don't do that to me again."

He chuckled. "Don't worry." He held her head against his chest, stroking her hair. "You're safe with me. I'll never let anything happen to you, Cassy. You have my word." He kissed her forehead.

The kiss startled Cassidy. She remembered Sukh's kiss on her forehead. She looked up at him. He was smiling — a big, beautiful smile lit up his handsome face. Cassidy was shocked by his good looks. She knew he was attractive, but seeing him this close made her heart lurch. She stared at his mouth, his perfect teeth, his kissable lips, then raised her gaze to meet his. The twinkle was gone from his eyes, replaced by a look of longing. Kyle's smile faded, but his eyes never left hers. His hands dropped from her shoulders to the low part of her back and held her waist. He pulled her hips closer to his and continued to stare into her eyes.

Cassidy sniffled again. She wanted to wipe her nose on the back of her hand, but her hands were frozen against Kyle's chest. Her eyes were locked with his. She wondered if he was going to kiss her just as Jeremy had. She wanted to feel that tingle again. Kyle's face lowered to hers just as she tilted her head. He closed his eyes and their lips touched. She waited for her legs to go limp. She waited to feel warmth in her groin. She waited to feel breathless as she had when Jeremy had kissed her. Kyle's kiss was wetter than Jeremy's. He felt warm, safe and . . . nice. Different from Jeremy. And it was okay, because it felt so . . . nice. That was the only word she could think of.

When he lifted his head, he continued to look into her eyes. She smiled. "That was nice, Kyle."

"Yeah. That was."

He dropped his hands from her waist and took her hands. He wouldn't let her go. "I . . . I've felt some pretty strong feelings for you for a long time, Cass."

Cassidy had never thought of Kyle as anything but a friend. She'd never thought of any of them as being more than friends — until Jeremy had kissed her last month. Since that day she'd relived the moment over and over in her head. The wonderful sensation that seemed to fill her entire body had to be repeated. Yet, she knew that it never would be by Jeremy. He was gone from her life. Who would make her feel that way again? Would it be Kyle? He didn't, not just now, but Cassidy wondered if that was because the fear that she'd felt immediately before the kiss had somehow dulled her body to physical arousal. Yes. That had to be it.

A movement behind Kyle caught her attention. She turned her head and saw Paintbrush wandering down the path, almost out of sight. She'd forgotten: she never did secure the tether.

"Paintbrush!"

Cassidy pulled her hands away from Kyle's and ran past the trees to retrieve her horse. When she caught up to her, she led her around and back to the pond. Not wanting to meet Kyle's eyes, she kept her gaze riveted to the ground. She tried to think of something meaningful to say, but nothing came to mind. When she finally looked up, she saw that Kyle was standing at the edge of the pond casually throwing small stones into the water. He reminded her of Jeremy, the last time they were here together when he skipped stones in the pond. Kyle didn't say anything, just as Jeremy had refused to speak. What was it about that pond that got everybody's tongue?

The tone had changed between them. She wondered if, from this moment on, it would always be different. She liked the kiss and hoped he would try again sometime, but now she was glad his attention was elsewhere. It was too soon. She had to have time to think about this new relationship with him. To decide how things would change. To decide if she wanted them to change.

Kyle accepted her silence. He had his own emotions to deal with. He had just kissed Cassidy Sampson! On the lips!

And it felt fantastic.

23
Sukh and Jeremy

JEREMY AWOKE TO THE SOUND OF voices that carried from the kitchen, up the stairs and through his partly-closed bedroom door. He heard a man's deep voice — his father. And the higher-pitched giggle of a woman — his mother? Jeremy bolted upright. "Mom?" he said, his mind still drifting between reality and that asleep-awake surreal world. She was here! And she was happy. Wearing only his boxers, Jeremy raced out of his room and down the stairs. His warm feet squeaked on the varnished wooden stairs, sticking to them. He almost tripped on the last stair and landed in the family room with a loud thud. He turned to face his parents in the kitchen, the smell of bacon grease hanging heavy in the air, colouring it blue.

His dad stood at the stove in his robe. At the table, wearing his dad's sweatshirt, the sleeves rolled up to reveal dainty, finger-painted nails, was Bernadette. Her hair, though usually blonde and riotous, was more unkempt than usual, probably from sleep or whatever else they did in that bedroom. Dark roots were visible in her side part, fading to brassy orange and then to dull blonde ends. Mascara, usually too heavily applied anyway, was smudged brown below her eyes. Her long legs were bare and crossed under the table. And, even though he couldn't see when she was wearing the baggy sweatshirt, Jeremy knew that her large breasts, her pride and joy from the way she almost always displayed cleavage, were unsupported by a bra this early in the morning.

Man, did he hate her.

"*Bonjour,* Jeremy," she said in her heavy French-Canadian accent. Jeremy didn't want to say anything to her. He didn't want to acknowledge her presence in his house — or should he say "This is my *dad's* house and don't you forget it!" — but he knew the consequences of ignoring her. He didn't feel like experiencing his dad's parenting, which consisted of nothing but humiliation and lecture.

So he muttered a grunt. He was about to turn and go back to his bedroom when she burst out laughing. He looked at her, confused, and saw her eyes, which were staring at his crotch. Then she looked at his dad, who also began to laugh. "Keep the door shut, Jeremy," his dad chuckled and went back to frying bacon. Jeremy looked down. The fly button of his boxers was undone and the opening was gaping. Although nobody could see everything he owned, enough flesh and pubic hair was exposed to humiliate him. His face burned red.

A minute ago he'd hated Bernadette. Now he despised her.

He turned and ran back up to his bedroom. It was still early. If he waited long enough they'd both leave for work and then he could get up for school without having to see or speak to either of them. He shut the door, climbed back into bed and waited.

He may have dozed off again, he wasn't sure, but his alarm clock jumped on to the sound of bass guitar and drums. Jeremy clicked the snooze button and lay in bed a little longer. He thought about what he'd had to endure since the night at Cassidy's, since he met Bernadette. Why did she have to be in his life? She was so awful. Her voice, her accent, her habits. What did his dad see in her? She stank of cigarettes, she drank too much cheap red wine, she smelled of way too much perfume, some French crap that made him nauseous.

He made himself think of something else. Of his homework? He didn't do it. Of Cassidy and Kyle? He never saw them anymore.

What a long few months these had been. First they had to rearrange all their transportation schedules. As it turned out, Cassidy's older brother, who was in grade twelve, drove his car in every day and the only reason why Cass took the bus was so she could be with her friends. So she and Kyle got rides to and from home now. None of their classes were with more than one of the friends, so that wasn't an issue. Jeremy had no classes with Cassidy, one with Kyle and three with Sukh. Because they all lived so far out of town, at the lake, they never went to parties together. All their lives they'd just partied with each other's families or at local barbecues. They chatted on the Internet everyday, so everyone could keep up with each other, and they always warned of any plans to go to their meeting spot, the old tree. So far, things were working out — no chance meetings — but Jeremy wondered if they could spend a lifetime this way, always avoiding each other. He wondered if any of their parents were suspicious yet.

He heard the school bus come to a halt outside his house. "Oh, well," he thought. "I'm late again." The bus honked twice. Jeremy lay silently in bed. He didn't move a muscle until he heard the brakes release and the bus start up the dirt road to collect Sukh. He quickly picked up the phone and called him. "Hey. I'm skipping school. Skip with me? The bus just left here."

Jeremy could tell that Sukh's parents were nearby. "Yeah," Sukh answered. If his parents were at work and Grampaji was home, Sukh would just come right out and say, "Sure I'll skip with you," because Grampaji still understood barely any English.

But, if his parents were home it came out more like, "I have to get up to the road to make that bus. See you later. I can't be late."

Jeremy smiled and hung up. He knew Sukh would skip. Sukh hated school more than anyone he knew. He didn't excel in any subject but didn't really try very hard, either. He hated books. Hated reading out loud in class. Hated writing and was a lousy speller. Jeremy, on the other hand, had always done well in school. It came easily to him, even without putting in much effort. He knew exactly what teachers wanted and he gave it to them, so he was always pulling A's. He gave credit to the fact that he loved to read — anything. If he picked up a magazine, he could not put it down until it was read from front to back or back to front, depending on how he picked it up. Books — non-fiction, fiction—it didn't matter; Jeremy read everything.

He put on some jeans and went downstairs. At the bottom of the stairs, he flipped on some music — Pantera — then poured himself a bowl of cereal. Sukh should be here in a minute. With no fear of his dad or the bitch coming home for hours, they should have a peaceful day. Picking up his bowl, he walked over to the computer and logged onto MSN. Cassidy was online.

Jeremy says>
hey cass

Cass says>
jeremy? what r u doing home? hasn't the bus come yet?

Jeremy says>
I'm sick coff coff*

Cass says>
u were sick last week too

Jeremy says>
how do u know? . . . checking up on me? . . .

Cass says>
no . . . lisa told me

Jeremy says>
nice 2 know that 2 chicks are interested in my well being

Cass says>
ha ha!

The kitchen door opened and Sukh walked in. He dropped his backpack on the kitchen chair and walked over to Jeremy at the computer. He began reading over Jeremy's shoulder.

Jeremy says>
sukh's sick,too . . . we're sick together

Cass says>
sure u r sick and not skipping?

Jeremy says>
o, we would never do that . . . coff coff*

Cass says>
LOL. no not u . . . what r we going 2 do this weekend? my folks are having another barbecue party . . . we can't all be here.

Jeremy says>
have no fear . . . sukh and i r going to kendra's party.

Cass says>
that skank?

Jeremy and Sukh both laughed out loud.

Jeremy says>
LOL. ooooh, catfight! meowww! hiss!

Cass says>
i hate that bitch . . . she spread a rumour about me.

Jeremy says>
before i get u 2 kitties a saucer of milk, what rumour?

Cass says>
that i sleep around.

Jeremy says>
Oh . . . LOL that's too much! who did she say u sleep around with?

Cass says>
kyle.

Jeremy says>
well u do, don't u?

Cass says>
i do not!

Jeremy says>
sorry, just assumed.

Cass says>
well u assumed wrong . . . we've only been 2gethr for a few weeks . . . i'm not sleeping with him.

"Poor Kyle," laughed Sukh, still standing behind Jeremy. "I know," agreed Jeremy.

Jeremy says>
well, u've known him for ten years!

Cass says>
I'M NOT SLEEPING WITH HIM! i'm saving myself.

Jeremy says>
saving yrself 4 who?

Cass says>
o Jeez, now you sound like kyle . . . i'm only 15! i'm just not ready, ok?

Jeremy says>
Sorrrrrrryyyyyyy!

Cass says>
shut up . . . i just hate kendra.

Jeremy says>
sleeping around has to be with more than one guy . . . who else did she say u were sleeping with?

Cass says>
never mind.

Jeremy says>
come on, Kitten . . . who else?

Cass says>
not important.

Jeremy says>
meeeooow! who else?

Cass says>
u.

Jeremy felt as though someone had punched him in the stomach. It was just a rumour and it shouldn't bother him, but it did. And he didn't know why. He froze with his fingers on the keyboard. He didn't know what to say. Sukh tapped him on the shoulder and said, "Move."

Jeremy slowly stood up and moved off the desk chair to let Sukh take his place. Sukh began pecking at the keys with his index fingers.

Jeremy says>
what about me? do u sleep around with me 2?

Then before he waited for a response, he changed the display name to Jeremy/$ukh and added,

Jeremy/$ukh says>
this is sukh.

Cass says>
sorry, i only heard that i sleep with kyle and jeremy.

Jeremy/$ukh says>
damn.

Cass says>
LOL. sorry, sukhy . . . it's not true, u no, it's just a rumour . . . i only heard it . . . and i heard kendra started it.

Jeremy/$ukh says>
yeah but i can dream can't i?

Cass says>
Ha ha . . . oops, G2G, my ride is leaving . . . luv ya both.

Cass may not reply because his or her status is set to Away.

Sukh spun around in the chair to face Jeremy.

"Well, Bud?" he asked. "What are we going to do today?"

Jeremy was staring blankly at the screen. He gave his head a shake. "I don't know. What do you want to do?" Jeremy walked into the kitchen, opened the fridge door and took out two cans of beer. He brought one over to a smiling Sukh, handed it to him and pulled on the tab of his own. They barely heard the "pop" and "fizz" over the sound of the music.

"Won't your old man notice they're missing?" asked Sukh, still smiling.

"Nah," answered Jeremy. "I'll just replace them with two still in the case. He's always asking me to go check if there are any left. He has no idea how many he drinks. Besides, I'll just tell him I saw the bitch drinking some."

Sukh laughed. "You really hate her, don't you?"

Jeremy's face reddened as he remembered that morning with Bernadette. "It's gone beyond hate, man."

Sukh stared at his friend for a moment, wondering if Jeremy would explain. He finally asked, "She seems nice enough. What does she do to you, anyway? Why do you hate her so much?"

Jeremy picked up the X-Box controls, handed one to Sukh, then jumped into a sitting position on the couch, spilling a mouthful of beer. Then he muttered, "Don't know, just do." He looked his friend in the eye and added, "And I don't want to talk about it." For two reasons, he thought. One, because he was embarrassed by what had happened that morning and two, because he really had no idea.

A couple of hours and a few beers later they both agreed they were hungry and getting bored. Jeremy walked back to his fridge, opened the door and just stared for a moment. He could find nothing worth eating. He slammed the door, and then opened the freezer. Still nothing. He reached for the jar on the top of the fridge, fished through some buttons, coins, paper clips and found a twenty-dollar bill. "Let's go into town and get some burgers and fries," he suggested. "Maybe we can get someone to bootleg some beer for us."

"It's twenty miles to town!" Sukh was incredulous. "You plan on walking that far?"

Jeremy thought for a moment. "We can take my motorcycle. We'll follow the horse trail beside the highway, and hide it in the forest closer to town. Then we can either walk or hitch a ride."

Sukh pondered the suggestion. "What if we're seen by someone we know? They might phone our folks."

Jeremy didn't care. "It's almost June. I'll just tell my dad we had the day off to study for exams. There's nobody around anyway. Everyone's either working or at school. And the summer people aren't here until July."

"So, what are we still standing here for?" asked Sukh. "Let's go."

The boys didn't realize how much they'd grown until they both tried to sit on the motorcycle. There was only one set of foot pegs, one for the driver, so Sukh's feet were dragging on the gravel road before they were out of Jeremy's driveway.

"This sucks," said Sukh. "My legs are killing me. We need two bikes."

Jeremy lowered the bike's gearshift to neutral and carefully put on the brakes. He put his foot down to balance the machine. "Fine," he said. "Let's get yours."

"No way, man. My folks are home. They think I took the bus to school this morning."

The two boys thought. "How about we go to Kyle's place and get his bike?" Jeremy suggested. "His parents both work and Kyle must be at school today."

Sukh was astounded. "Steal Kyle's bike? Have you lost your mind? He's our best friend."

Jeremy laughed. "Not steal it, you idiot. We're just borrowing it. He won't mind."

Still Sukh was wary. "Only if we have it back there before he gets home. I don't want him freakin' out when he finds it missing and calling the cops." Each boy looked at his watch.

"Yeah," answered Jeremy. "We could do it and still have two hours in town. Let's go to the Internet café."

The boys had no problem finding Kyle's motorcycle. They knew it was kept in the shed and that the door was rarely locked. And the beauty of motocross bikes is that not many of them need a key to start.

The day was warm and dry, perfect May weather, and they felt like the only ones around for miles. On the forestry road they crossed paths with two deer, a doe and a buck. The stately animals came bounding out of the trees so suddenly that Jeremy had to put on the brakes to miss them. By the time Sukh had cleared the corner the deer were gone.

Soon they were riding alongside the highway. It seemed that cutting through the woods on the forestry road and game trails with motorcycles was faster than taking a car, because in no time at all they found themselves on the outskirts of town. There was a large rock just off the trail and Jeremy and Sukh rolled both bikes behind it. Dragging branches and boughs over to cover the motorcycles, they hid the bikes from anyone who wasn't actually looking for them. They climbed up to the shoulder of the highway and headed to the Internet café where they'd get themselves some lunch and play computer games against people all over the world.

An hour later they found themselves almost out of money. "Well, so much for the beer," Sukh said.

"Yeah, I guess three bucks won't get us even one, will it?"

Jeremy watched the only other two patrons in the café. One was a kid who used to go to their school, but who was a few years older than they were. The other guy was a stranger. He looked about nineteen or twenty, had long hair and sported a thin goatee. A tiny gold cross — or maybe it was an "x" — dangled from his pierced ear. Jeremy had noticed that the older guy had been watching them play, but turned away anytime one of them made eye contact with him. Now he made his way past the empty chairs and headed directly for them.

"Hey," he said, looking at Jeremy. "Want some weed?" he whispered.

Jeremy was a little surprised. Before he could give a polite "No," Sukh answered, "All we got is three bucks. You selling dubs for three bucks?"

"You're in luck," Goatee-guy said, and reached into his pocket to pull out a tightly rolled joint that he protected from the café manager's vision. "I'm in such a generous mood today that I'll front you this chron for three bucks. Pay me the rest next time."

Jeremy coughed and looked around. He couldn't believe how this total stranger could be so brazen about selling dope to people he didn't even know. They could rat on him, or call the cops or even *be* cops for all the guy knew. Then he realized how stupid an idea that was. Undercover cops do not look like fifteen-year-old kids, even if Sukh had a moustache growing on his upper lip and was almost six feet tall. And anyone who should obviously be in school would have enough problems with authority without this guy risking being reported by them.

"What's the going rate?" asked Sukh.

"Five," said Goatee-guy.

"Yeah," said Sukh as he scooped the last coins from the table and handed them to Goatee-guy who inconspicuously slipped the joint into Sukh's hand. Jeremy watched the other, younger guy make his way toward them but noticed how he kept looking back toward the front door to the clerk at the till. What was

Sukh doing? As far as Jeremy knew Sukh had never smoked pot before. And Jeremy was still trying to get used to smoking cigarettes. Now Sukh was buying a joint? This was turning into a really weird day.

When the younger guy got closer to them Jeremy remembered who he was. He'd hung around with one of Cassidy's older brothers, but must have quit school because Jeremy didn't remember seeing him at school or anywhere in ages. When he got to the table he asked, "You guys are Cassidy Sampson's friends, aren't you?"

Again, before Jeremy could answer, Sukh took charge of the conversation and said, "Who's asking?" as he tucked the joint into his chest pocket.

"Oh, sorry, I'm Todd. I know Jeff Sampson."

Sukh looked over at Goatee-guy and expected an introduction, but when none was forthcoming, he shrugged and looked back at Jeffrey. Then, to Jeremy's astonishment, Sukh asked, "Is this kill bud?"

What would Sukh know about "kill bud"? This was amazing. Happy-go-lucky Sukh, who always seemed to just follow the crowd, was in a take-charge mood and was really taking charge.

Goatee-guy smirked. "Normally I would say that you get what you pay for, but in this case, you guys got the best deal. That bud is so kill that you should only smoke half now and the other half some other time. And you'll still get ripped."

Sukh stood, stared at Jeremy and said, "Well, I guess we'll have to go try some now, won't we? See you around." With that, he began walking toward the front of the café, weaving between tables. Jeremy followed him into the bright sunshine.

As soon as the two boys had walked to the sidewalk, they both doubled over laughing. Jeremy, in between guffaws, asked

Sukh, "Who are you and what have you done with my buddy, Sukhwinder Sangera? Where the hell did you come up with that 'Is this kill bud' stuff from?"

Sukh wiped the tears of laughter from his eyes and said, "My cousins on the Coast. They talk like that all the time. Last time I was down there, they were selling stuff to some friends of theirs and I just hung around with them."

Jeremy, still laughing, looked around the road. He did not recognize anyone's car or anyone nearby, so he said, "Here, let me see the 'dub'."

Sukh reached into his chest pocket, slipped it out and ran it under his nose. He closed his eyes and took a deep breath to smell the marijuana. Then he passed it over to Jeremy who did exactly the same thing. Both boys let out their breaths simultaneously and laughed again.

Sukh looked at his watch and said, "Oh-oh, we got to get back. We can't smoke this today. Let's save it for Kendra's party."

They followed the sidewalk to the outskirts of town and headed back to the rock that was hiding their motorcycles. As Jeremy lifted his leg to get on the bike, he thought he saw someone past the trees and down the road watching them. His first thought was that they were busted, in big trouble, and his chest tightened but then he realized that it was just Todd, crossing the street and heading to the business district.

He kicked the bike to start it and followed Sukh down the trail that led home.

24
Meow!

CASSIDY WALKED THROUGH THE HALLS, BOOKS in hand, and dodged the other students. Through the throng of other kids she was able to catch glimpses of Kyle waiting beside her locker. When she arrived in front of him, she offered him a big smile, pulled on her lock and spun the dial to open it. "I hate French," she said without really looking at him.

"J'adore le Francais."

"You only like it because you've got the hots for the teacher. I've seen the way you guys all look at her!"

"Mais non, ma petite aimie chaude," he said. *"Je t'adore."*

Cassidy chortled. She opened the door of her locker and took a breath. Sitting on her books was a small bouquet of wildflowers — lupines, Indian paintbrushes, buttercups and lilies. A piece of lined paper, torn from a notebook, rested on top. It read: "To the most beautiful girl in the world". Cassidy gasped. Her heart pounded from her chest all the way to her forehead. Her legs felt weak. Jeremy had called her "Beautiful"! It must be from Jeremy! She reached for the paper, turned it over and saw, "Love, Kyle" written on the back.

It was like a balloon popping — how quickly her euphoria changed. She struggled to keep her face from falling. Why was she so disappointed the flowers weren't from Jeremy? She felt like an idiot for even thinking they could be. Of course they were from Kyle, she told herself. She looked up at him, forced a smile on her face and said, "Awwww, that's so sweet." She kissed him on the cheek.

Kyle feigned ignorance. "What's this?" he asked in a terrible French accent. "You have a secret admirer?"

Cassidy giggled. "Not much of a secret when you leave your name on a note. Thanks, Baby." She lifted the bouquet and held them to her nose, forgetting that none of those flowers had much of a scent. Jeremy and Sukh knew her combination, too, but Cassidy was foolish to think that either of them had anything to do with this. A month ago, she would have been at a total loss as to who would have put flowers in her locker. But, now, well . . . she should have known it was Kyle. He was her boyfriend. So why did she feel so let down? She reached for her lunch bag, closed her locker and walked to the cafeteria with him, the bouquet in one hand and her lunch in the other.

As they approached the outside doors, Kyle steered her toward them. "Hey, it's sunny and warm outside. Let's eat on the lawn."

"Fine," she answered and stepped outside into the warm June sun.

They found an empty bench near some trees and began to eat. Cassidy was in a quiet mood. Kyle was content just to be near her and to watch everyone else walking, eating, and horsing around. His arm was draped over the back of the bench, and his hand rested on her farther shoulder.

Cassidy dropped her head onto his shoulder and let out a contented sigh. Kyle felt so . . . nice. Why could she still not think of a single word other than "nice" to describe him? She always felt so comfortable in his arms.

Loud laughter just beyond the trees attracted their attention. They recognized that laughter; it sounded like Sukh. Both leaned forward to see past the trees. There stood Sukh, his hands in his front jeans pockets and his head back as he laughed at a joke with some other kids in their grade. But beyond them were Jeremy and . . . Kendra.

Cassidy bristled. Jeremy stood with his arm possessively around Kendra's shoulders. Kendra's arms were around Jeremy's waist. And they were sharing a cigarette, except Kendra was too much of a loser to let go of Jeremy's waist to hold it, so Jeremy held the cigarette to her lips so she could take a drag! Cassidy had to take a long, slow breath to stop herself from walking through the trees to scratch Kendra's eyes out of their sockets.

Kyle, oblivious to Cassidy's emotional roil, said, "Hey, well look at that. Are Jeremy and Kendra an item?"

Then he looked at Cassidy.

"Oops," was all he could say.

"That stinking bitch. I hate that skank, that witch, that . . . that . . ." She couldn't think of a word nasty enough to express her feelings about Kendra. And seeing Jeremy, her Jeremy, acting — and Cassidy was sure he was *acting* — so in love with her, so familiar with her, just made her shake with anger. How could Jeremy touch Kendra? Especially after Cassidy had told him online how much she hated her. The betrayal hit her like a slap in the face.

She was so angry. Angry that Kendra could be so close to Jeremy and she couldn't. Angry that Sukh and Jeremy were sharing a joke with that bitch and not her, like it always used to be. Angry that Jeremy liked another girl. Angry that Kendra was in Jeremy's arms. Her slow breath provided no relief to the anger that was growing into a monster in her head. Without even realizing what she was doing, she jumped up from the bench and began walking in their direction. "Get your filthy, bitchy, skanky hands off Jeremy," she muttered quietly to herself.

It took Kyle a moment to remember what Cassidy had told him about Kendra's misdeed. He got up from the bench and ran after her. His long legs allowed him to reach her in no time. He'd never seen her this angry. Grabbing her by the arm, he said, "Oh, no you don't. Just settle down, Cass."

Cassidy pulled her arm from Kyle's grasp and continued to storm over beyond the trees to the small group of students, who were still oblivious to her presence. Her small feet stomped into the soft earth, cushioned by conifer needles. Her hair bounced off her shoulders with each heavy step. Again Kyle ran back to her and grabbed at her wrist, but this time he reached for both of her hands to stop her. She looked past him, shouting, "Let me go!"

Kyle lowered his voice. "Listen Cass. You know the rules. You can't go over there. Jeremy and Sukh are there. We're too close to them. Think about what you're doing."

Cassidy was forced to a stop with Kyle in front of her. "I don't care. I hate that . . . that . . . cow! Did you hear what she said about me?"

"Yes, I heard, but who cares? It's just a stupid rumour." He was amazed at the degree of her anger. "You don't even know if she really said it!"

"Oh, please," she said, rolling her eyes at his ignorance. "Everybody says she did." She continued to try to push past him.

"Cassidy! Who even cares if you do sleep with me? We've been going out for over a month! I've been in love with you for over a year. And we've known each other for over ten years. What's the big deal? You know the rumour isn't true. Hell, everyone knows it's not true. Let it go. She's just jealous of you!"

Cassidy lifted her arms up, twisted her wrists around and quickly jerked them downward, instantly releasing them from Kyle's grip — a little trick she'd learned from growing up with so many brothers. "Jealous, like hell. She didn't say I was sleeping with just you! She said I was sleeping with you and . . . and . . ." Cassidy didn't want to say it. Why did it bother her so much that the rumour was also about her and *Jeremy*?

"And Jeremy," Kyle offered. He was baffled. She looked like she was ready to kill. And risk their destiny on some big-mouthed girl like Kendra? Why was she being so irrational? He wondered if it was her time of the month, or if she knew something he didn't know. What was her problem?

She couldn't take her eyes off the kids in the smoke pit. "She's just evil and I'm going to teach her a lesson. She'll never tell that rumour to another soul." She darted past Kyle and began to run through the trees.

Kyle sighed as he watched her. Shaking his head, he bolted into a run, his long legs easily carrying him faster. He stepped in front of her, grabbed her arm and picked her up and slung her over his shoulder. Cassidy began to pummel Kyle's backside, screaming, "Let me go!"

Kyle held her tighter. "Kyle," she screamed louder. "Put me down . . . right . . . now!"

Sukh stopped talking to his friends and looked through the trees. He, too, recognized voices and signalled to Jeremy to look. At that point Kyle, with Cassidy still over his shoulder, looked up to see his friends staring at them. He smiled, gave a silent salute, then turned back to walk in the direction he'd come, Cassidy still over his shoulder, her screams muffled by the back of his shirt.

Sukh smiled. He had no idea what had just happened, but he thought it looked pretty funny. He leaned over to Jeremy and whispered, "Cassy's spittin' fire!" Sukh glanced at Kendra leaning all over Jeremy, then his white teeth showed even whiter against his dark skin as he grinned and added, "Meow!"

Jeremy watched the retreating Kyle and Cassidy. He took a long, slow drag from the half-finished cigarette, threw it on the ground and crushed it under his foot. He took his arm away from Kendra's shoulders and pushed his hands into his jeans' front pockets. He didn't know what had just happened either, but he wondered if it had anything to do with his little e-chat with Cassidy a week ago. She was pissed about something.

His stomach grew tight. Kendra meant almost nothing to him. Cassidy meant . . . He didn't know what she meant to him anymore. He was torn between not giving a damn about her and wanting to protect her forever. He had a funny feeling he'd just hurt her. Really hurt her. His stomach grew tighter.

For the first time in his life, he actually thanked God when the bell rang and they had to go back into the school for afternoon classes.

25
Business Dealings

SUKH AND JEREMY LOOKED AROUND THE Internet café for signs of Goatee-guy. School was still in session so the place was almost empty. Just a few young men and one girl sat in a small group beside the dark wall. The two friends had skipped school again, but it was Sukh's idea this time. He'd skipped more than a few days already this month so school was harder than ever. He knew he should try to catch up, but it was easier to miss more than face the humiliation of asking anybody for help. No report cards had come home yet, so his parents still lived in blissful ignorance. He knew there'd be hell to pay later, but he was willing to enjoy today and worry about tomorrow, well . . . tomorrow.

They'd shared the joint at Kendra's party. Her parents were out that night and a few of the kids had stood outside in her backyard to smoke it. Everyone agreed that it was indeed kill bud, the best any of them had tried before, so the boys promised they'd find their "connection" and get some for next time. Many of the kids pitched in money and asked for some for the summer. So here they were, *dealers,* with Jeremy's and Kyle's motorcycles stashed away in the forest, looking for the man who would provide them with more pot. And there he was, leaning against the back wall, talking to Todd. As the boys moved toward him, he looked away from Todd and nodded to them, but made no move toward them. The boys continued to weave between the tables as Jeremy nudged Sukh and whispered, "You do the talking." Sukh nodded as Jeremy stepped in behind him, slowing down slightly.

"Hey, Todd," Sukh said. He would have greeted Goatee-guy if he knew his name, but he didn't think that the nickname they had given him would be very well received, so he simply flipped his head slightly back in acknowledgement. As he got closer, he lowered his voice and spoke, "Hey, I'm hoping to score some more of that chronic bud from you. Any chance?"

Every time Sukh spoke to these guys Jeremy wanted to laugh. Where did he get this language? Jeremy had never heard him talk like that outside this café and it both amused and frightened him. They'd spent almost every day of their lives together, yet he was amazed by the transformation of his best friend when he fell into this manner he must have learned from spending time with his cousins on the Coast.

Goatee-guy glanced at Todd, nodded, and turned back to Sukh. "Maybe. You got money?" Then on second thought, he added, "More than last time?"

"Yeah," said Sukh. He reached into his pocket and pulled out some twenty-dollar bills with a few other bills hidden between them.

Goatee-guy looked up at the front desk to make sure the clerk wasn't looking. He nodded toward the hallway where the washrooms were. Sukh began walking in that direction. Goatee-guy looked up at Todd, lifted his eyebrows, then followed Sukh. Immediately Todd began backing away from them and headed toward the small group of people at one of the other tables.

Jeremy first started walking behind Sukh and Goatee-guy, but felt left out. He tried to listen to the conversation, but they spoke in such hushed tones that he missed too much. He turned and walked back out of the hallway just in time to see Todd dash out the front entrance. Where was he going in such a hurry? He looked around at the other people playing computer games. Was it his imagination, or did they seem a little too interested in what they were doing? Something was different. Nobody was talking anymore. Or maybe he was feeling a little guarded because of what he and Sukh were doing. Buying and selling drugs! Whoa, had he changed.

"Jer!"

He turned back to Sukh. It was time to leave.

When they were outside the café, Sukh said, "We have to go down the back alley and meet him in an hour. Let's get some food."

They walked to the nearest fast-food restaurant, bought a couple of burgers and still had more than half an hour to wait, so they walked toward the high school. It was lunchtime and their friends would be outside. If they got caught, they'd have to pretend they'd just taken the morning off, missed the bus, whatever. They walked over to the smoking pit — the area just off of school grounds where teachers had no jurisdiction and no rules applied. There were at least a dozen kids from their own grade in the pit. Kendra was standing there with two other girls. When she saw Jeremy her face broke into a wide smile and she walked over to him.

"Hey, Jeremy," she purred, "You missed French this morning." Her smile turned into a melodramatic pout. "And I missed you," she added in a playful French accent.

Oh, brother, Jeremy thought. It reminded him of Bernadette; he now hated all things French. But out loud he said only, "I hate French."

He took her hand, and without removing her cigarette, lifted it to his mouth and took a drag , knowing she'd love the physical contact. She rested her other elbow on his shoulder and leaned her body against his. Jeremy slipped his left hand around her waist and pulled her closer. After exhaling the smoke, he nuzzled his lips against the back of her neck; a soft moan escaped her.

Sukh stepped between Kendra's two friends, put one arm around each of their waists and whispered something that made them both giggle. Neither of them pulled away, allowing Sukh to pull them closer. Jeremy was suddenly struck by how handsome girls must find Sukh with his dark eyes, dark skin and perpetual smile. And he looked way older than fifteen.

The bass of somebody's loud music beat a rhythm in each of their chests. Everyone in the pit watched a small, low-rider pick-up truck, decked out with shiny wire rims, chromed exhaust pipes and a sleek black tarp over the box come to a stop behind Sukh and the girls. A heavily tinted passenger's window rolled down to show the passenger's intimidating face. It was Goatee-guy. The driver of the pick-up looked even scarier: he had long hair tied into a ponytail, his eyebrow was pierced and he wore only a denim vest to show off numerous tattoos which covered his arm from his hand to a well-muscled bicep. Jeremy wondered why he'd never before noticed this truck or this stranger in their small town.

He pulled his arm from around Kendra's waist, shrugged out from under her elbow and followed Sukh, who'd let go of the two girls and was walking toward the pickup. Most of the students were backing away from the truck and were surprised to see Sukh and Jeremy walking toward it. Everyone was curious about the relationship between their friends and these two strangers. After a few moments of straining their ears to hear the conversation, the students decided the strangers weren't as threatening as they looked and began to move a little closer to the pick-up, relishing their closeness to its occupants.

"Yeah, we'll be there," was all they could hear. Sukh and Jeremy nodded. The truck began to creep forward just as the school bell rang. The others turned to walk toward the school but they kept watching the sleek truck inching its way down the road.

Kendra walked over to Jeremy and put her hand possessively on his back. "Are you coming to Math?" she asked.

Jeremy looked at Sukh and smiled. "Naw, not today. See you tomorrow."

Kendra pouted again. "Who were those guys?"

"Never mind," he answered. Then he added, "Nothing to worry your pretty little head over."

She began to walk to the school but kept her eyes on Jeremy. Just as she reached the doors she raised her hand, kissed it and blew it to Jeremy.

As he smiled and waved at Kendra, Jeremy heard Sukh chuckle. He raised his eyes to the classroom windows above the door. Someone was watching them, but the glare off the glass obscured the person's identity. Sukh had turned away and was tugging on Jeremy's shirt. Finally they both began to walk back through the deserted smoking pit toward town to meet their connection.

When they got to the sidewalk, Jeremy looked back at the window. The glare was gone. He could see and he froze in his tracks. His heart leapt. It was Cassidy. She wasn't smiling; she looked thoughtful. Jeremy wondered if she was mad at him. He smiled, but she didn't respond in kind. He waved. No response. Finally he lifted his hand and blew her a kiss.

She turned away. Jeremy wondered why lately he always felt like someone was punching him in the stomach.

26
Cassidy's Angst

CASSIDY HAD FELT PRESSURE IN HER sinuses all day. If she allowed her thoughts to drift, she found tears in her eyes, so thinking safe thoughts — math homework, exams, "I hate French," Paintbrush — helped her get through the remainder of the afternoon. What was it about Jeremy that had her emotions running amok? Was it that she felt she'd lost a friend? But she felt she'd lost Sukh, too. Was it that she couldn't get out of her thoughts a crying Jeremy from their first day of kindergarten? Even though she didn't really remember the day, her flashback played over and over in her head like a video. That frightened and lonely little boy sitting on the floor, sobbing. Her heart sank just thinking about him. Did she feel she should be watching over him, keeping him in line, picking his girlfriends for him? She sighed. She wasn't his mother.

Maybe that was it. He needed a mother. Cassidy surprised herself with the sudden rage that welled up inside her thinking about Jeremy's mother. How could she have left him? If she'd been here, would things be different?

Her teeth hurt. She forced her jaw to stop clenching. Boy, did Kendra act very familiar with Jeremy. And what an awful choice she was for him. Cassidy wondered how far they'd gone together.

Had they gone all the way? Were they sleeping together? Stop thinking about it! Stop it! She knew Jeremy had kissed Kendra. And Jeremy kissed so incredibly. Cassidy's legs began to tingle just thinking about that one and only kiss from him. She wished it hadn't come on so suddenly, that she could have been prepared for it somehow. Cassidy bit her lip to stop the tears. She would never feel Jeremy's kiss again.

Get over it!

She shook her head — *math homework, exams, "I hate French," Paintbrush . . .*

27
Guilt

By the time Sukh and Jeremy returned to the forest on the edge of town, the dismissal bell was ringing back at school. By the time students were opening their lockers for the last time that day, they realized that Kyle's motocross bike was no longer hidden behind the rock. It had been stolen.

By the time Sukh and Jeremy realized they were in deep, deep trouble, their two closest friends were getting in the car with Cassidy's brother and were on their way home. And by the time they got back to Jeremy's house by doubling on one bike, Sukh's legs were burning with muscle fatigue. His shoes were ripped and ragged from dragging on the rocky roads. Jeremy's back and shoulders were sore from the way he had to sit up very straight, with his back arched, to allow Sukh room on the seat. His crotch was sore from constantly banging against the gas tank.

And they were very worried.

Sukh had carried the plastic sandwich bag containing the marijuana tightly against his ribs, held in place by his shirt tucked into his pants. Occasionally he'd get a whiff of the strong aroma that reminded him of a skunk after it sprays. The smell was sometimes so powerful that he was sure Jeremy was getting wind of it, too. He wondered if his parents would be able to smell it when he got home. Man, was this worth stealing a bike?

Jeremy seemed to read Sukh's thoughts. "We didn't steal it, you know, Sukh. Somebody else did. We just borrowed it. Kyle would have let us use it if we'd asked him. I know he would."

Sukh didn't respond.

"Should we tell him?"

Sukh still didn't respond.

Jeremy waited a few more moments, then yelled, "Answer me, will you?"

"We don't tell him. We don't tell anyone."

Then they made a pact, their first two-man pact, they wouldn't skip out of school anymore. At least not in grade ten. It was June anyway. In a few weeks school would be out for the summer. They could last a few more weeks.

28
The Slippery Slope

THEY DID LAST A FEW MORE weeks, attending every class religiously. They made it to the last day of school and felt that a celebration was in order.

Kyle says>
ya it was trashed . . . first the creeps ran it ragged then doused it with gas and torched it . . . then they left it on some old trail in the woods on the other side of town . . . cops found it yesterday . . . three weeks after they stole it

Cass says>
only a nut would torch a perfectly good bike

Jeremy/Sukh says>
who do u think did it?

Kyle says>
the cops figure joy-riding kids

Cass says>
i hope they get the creeps . . . just the thought of someone

helping themselves to your stuff on your own property
makes me burn

Jeremy/Sukh says>
any chance of catching them?

Kyle says>
cops say that unless they brag about it they almost never get caught . . . bright side is these kinds of guys almost always brag about it

Jeremy breathed a sigh of relief. He and Sukh would never brag about taking it. "We can never talk about this again, Sukh."

Sukh nodded his head. "I know. I know. I just feel so . . ."

"So do I. Would I like to get my hands on the snakes who took that bike."

They both agreed that ultimately Kyle was the victim, but that they were "middlemen" victims, too. The bike had been stolen from *them*, whether it was theirs or not. Their celebratory mood was changing.

Jeremy/Sukh says>
talk to u later . . . got things to do . . . going to a party later

Kyle says>
have fun . . . sounds like a lot of kids r going 2 be there

Jeremy/Sukh says>
u 2 aren't going r u? 'cuz if u r, then we won't go

Kyle says>
nope . . . we r not exactly friends with the host

Jeremy/Sukh may not reply because his or her status is set to Away.

Cass says>
do u think that whoever stole yr bike goes to our school?

Kyle says>
probably . . . but whoever did it must have skipped school . . . it happened during the day . . . cops are looking into it

Cass says>
how r they looking into it?

Kyle says>
they r checking with the school for students with unexplained absences . . . then they'll have some names that they can start checking

Jeremy looked at the small plastic bag of dope: there were only a tiny stem and a few seeds left. He cursed himself for letting it run out before he could get more. In the last few weeks, he and Sukh had smoked some in the pit during lunch hour, at Jeremy's house before his dad came home, and out at the old tree. The rest they'd delivered to their classmates who had put in orders.

Sukh moaned. "If we have no weed left, what are we going to take to Kendra's party?"

"I don't know. How about some beer?"

"And where are we going to get beer? Is there some in your fridge?"

Jeremy checked the refrigerator — nothing. And the case on the back porch was empty. He checked for money on the top of the refrigerator. Just a few coins were left. "Man," he said, "what are we going to do? It's the last day of school, the party of the year and we have to go empty handed."

Sukh said, "We can't go empty handed. That sucks! Not on the last day of school! What a yawner this is going to be if we have to go sober."

Jeremy thought. "What about at your place?"

Sukh shook his head. "Naw, not since Naniji's funeral. We almost never have booze."

A few moments went by. "Wait a minute," said Sukh. "Remember that time a few years ago when we went for a snowmobile ride on the other side of the lake, up the hills by Poplar Bluff? Remember that old cabin that didn't have any locks on the door? Didn't we find a couple of half empty bottles of booze—some brandy or something?"

"Yeah," said Jeremy.

"Well, let's head over there. The Summer People aren't going to be here yet, not until next week. Let's see if we can find some liquor over there!"

Jeremy smiled. "Well, it's not like we have any other choice, do we?"

That old cabin had no liquor in it, but in the one beside it they found a small bottle with a couple of mouthfuls of dark rum. Both boys took a swig and emptied the bottle. They then set off down the road looking for another cabin. It was easy to tell if the cabins were empty for the season: summer chairs were stacked on porches, boats were pulled up and left upside down on the shore, grass was growing long.

Unfortunately, the first two cabins were the only ones with unlocked doors. The rest were sealed up tight. After checking out the third locked cabin, the boys noticed one window with curtains slightly open. Peering warily in, they noticed a small bar under a kitchen counter. They couldn't tell if they were full, but they could see the necks of at least five bottles of various liquors.

Now, how would they get in?

"We could kick the door in," suggested Jeremy.

"No, we can't," said Sukh. "That's breaking and entering."

"But didn't we already break and enter when we got the rum from the old cabin?" asked Jeremy.

"No, that wasn't 'breaking'. That was only 'entering'. And that's just a misdemeanour. 'Breaking *and* entering' is a criminal offence."

"How the hell do you know so much about it?" asked Jeremy.

Sukh smiled. He looked at Jeremy and began, "I have . . . "

"Cousins, I know." Then he added, laughing, "Why they let your people in this country, I'll never know."

Sukh continued smiling and answered, "Careful, my friend, now you're sounding racist."

Jeremy shook his head. "Okay, smart-ass, if we pick the lock and don't break anything, is it still called 'breaking and entering'?"

"Well, now, I don't know. How about we try that? I just happen to have my Swiss army knife on me and . . . would you look at that? It just happens to have a pin on it." Sukh opened the bright red knife. It had many attachments: a screwdriver, three different knife blades, a bottle opener, a can opener, a tiny pair of scissors and a thin, metal pin that looked like a skinny allen wrench.

Jeremy laughed. "You mean you know how to pick a lock, too? Jeez, Sukhy, you're scaring me. What other sorts of crimes do you and your cousins commit?"

"I could tell you, but then I'd have to kill you," he answered, laughing.

Sukh stuck the pin in a doorknob so old it wobbled in his hand. As he tinkered with the lock, Jeremy noticed, every so often, Sukh's bracelet peaking out from under his cuff. He wondered if Sukh was thinking about sin right now.

Jeremy shook his head very slowly. He remembered something Oma Lockett had once told him: that locks were meant to keep honest people out, because dishonest people could always get in. But the pang of guilt was instantly replaced by triumph: Sukh had the door open in a few moments. They held their breath and pushed the door open, a loud squeak from the old hinges penetrating the silence. Inside, the musty smell of winter still hung onto the wooden walls. An old couch, too old and stained for either boy to ever consider sitting on it, lay against the far wall. The counters were just pieces of plywood nailed together. In between two pieces of wood rested an old laundry sink that drained outside through a small hole in the wall. Half-burned candles stood in holders on an old coffee table in front of the couch. A couple of campers' lanterns hung from ceiling rafters.

Three of the bottles were half-filled with wine that smelled like it had already turned to vinegar. Two of the bottles were vodka, but the first was already more than two-thirds empty. The second bottle was full.

"Jackpot!" said Jeremy.

Fishing through one of the makeshift cupboards, Sukh found two clean shot glasses. He opened the bottle, filled the glasses to the brim and held one out to Jeremy. They tapped their glasses together and Sukh said, "A toast . . . to partners in crime."

"Here, here!" answered Jeremy. They lifted the glasses to their lips. In a show of bravado, they tipped the glasses back and downed the contents without taking a breath. But as soon as the liquor was gone, both boys began to cough and sputter, the fiery liquid scorching their throats and knocking the wind out of their lungs.

"Whew! That stings," whispered Sukh.

Jeremy coughed some more. Tears sprang to his eyes as he tried again to take a breath and smile. "My virgin lips," he sputtered, and laughed.

When he was able to breathe without coughing, he looked at Sukh and said, "Well, my friend, it looks like we're set for the party. Let's go!"

Sukh put the vodka bottle in his backpack and pulled the drawstrings tight. They closed and locked the cabin door, then walked out to their motorcycles. It was almost dinnertime, but the sun still sat high in the sky. It was solstice, the longest day of the year, and both boys knew that, being so far north, they still had hours of daylight in which to get through the forest and back into town. How they were going to get home, they still hadn't planned, but that was something they'd deal with later.

For now, they hopped on their motorbikes and began the slippery descent to the trail along the lakeshore that led to the highway and to Kendra's place.

29
Daring

Kyle says>
meet me at the old tree at 5:00

Cass says>
what up?

Kyle says>
it's a surprise!

Cass says>
i love surprises

Kyle says>
well, not for u . . . it's a surprise 4 me

Cass says>
so why can't u tell me what up?

Kyle says>
just meet me at the old tree . . . kiss kiss

Cass says>
hug hug

Kyle may not reply because his or her status is set to Away.

Cass may not reply because his or her status is set to Away.

Paintbrush nibbled on the buttercups at the pond while Cassidy threw stones into the water. She thought about the time she'd watched Jeremy throw stones, the day they'd discovered the truth about their accident. It was the last time she'd felt truly happy and carefree with her best friends.

First Jeremy, then Kyle, and now here she was, throwing stones in this pond. She forced herself to stop, wiped her hands on her jeans and looked around. She stared at the reflection of the tattered tree, the omen that seemed to carry so many secrets. She adjusted her gaze to follow the long shadow created by the afternoon sun; the tiny ripples on the water made the shadow move as though it were alive. It reminded Cassidy of a giant hand stretched across the pond ready to pull an unsuspecting victim underwater. No wonder Paintbrush had been so spooked the last time she was here with Kyle.

She shivered. Where was Kyle? It was already a few minutes after five. She had no idea how he'd get here. His motorcycle was gone. It was too far to walk. He didn't have a horse. She looked around to the branch where she'd tried to do pull-ups that day with Sukh. Could she do one now, she wondered? As she walked toward the tree, a dim crackling sound, like a chainsaw, echoed in the distance. If she hadn't known better, she would have guessed it was Kyle's motorcycle.

It sounded to Cassidy like a motorcycle was coming up the forestry road. By the high-pitched whine, it sounded like a motocross bike. Kyle was the only one on the lake (except for some of the Summer People) who ever rode a two-stroke motocross because everyone on the lake hated the sound of them. She pulled the tethers on Paintbrush and began to walk toward the forestry road to see who was on the motorcycle.

She waited for a few moments at the side of the road, but because of the sharp bend in the gravel path her vision in both directions was limited. All she could see were trees. She heard the motorcycle gearing down, which meant the driver was going to stop nearby. She waited.

A rider rounded the bend. He was dressed in full leathers, complete with elbow pads, kneepads and a helmet to match both the suit and the bike. The rider's face was completely covered by the visor. Cassidy suddenly felt very vulnerable sitting out here all alone in the middle of the forest.

The motorcycle stopped in front of her. The rider unstrapped the helmet and removed it, exposing a gorgeous smile and thick blonde hair. It was Kyle.

"Kyle! Where did you get this set-up?"

His smile widened. "Pretty nice, eh?"

Cassidy looked the red, white and blue bike up and down. She touched the matching leather on his arm. "Very nice."

"My folks felt so bad that my bike was stolen. I had some money from my summer job last year and my dad has a friend on the Coast whose son grew out of this gear and bike, so he bought it off him for a good price. The kid got free stuff from a sponsor! He's supposed to be pro-motocross. I have no money left, but look at this stuff! It's incredible!"

All Cassidy could do was nod. It was indeed incredible.

"Here," said Kyle. "Take Paintbrush back to the old tree. Tether her and I'll take you for a ride." He leaned forward to reveal his old helmet strapped on the seat behind him.

Because she didn't want to leave Paintbrush for long, they didn't go far. Kyle drove fast. Cassidy held him tightly round his waist and squeezed her thighs together to grip Kyle's hips. He went faster.

Cassidy began to fear Kyle's speed. She remembered her brother telling her stories about motorcycle accident victims on gravel, how the doctors had to use wire brushes to scrape all the grit out of the wounds. He told her patients could hear the screams from three floors up. She leaned forward and asked Kyle to slow down. He laughed and went faster. Gradually he slowed the bike to downshift into low gear, then turned off the road, leaning low to the ground onto a tiny trail that Cassidy knew led to the gravel pits. There were hills there. Lots of them.

"Slow down, Kyle!" she yelled.

"It's okay, Cass. I know what I'm doing."

They approached a hill made of dirt and gravel. Kyle gunned the machine to get more speed for some good air.

Cassidy screamed. The motorcycle was airborne. "No, Kyle!"

She held on for dear life. She closed her eyes and tried to bury her face behind Kyle's helmet. Somehow the motorcycle landed, first the rear wheel, then the front wheel. Kyle turned the handlebars to bring the bike to a skidding stop. He really did know how to handle the bike, but Cassidy was livid. She got off as quickly as she could and unstrapped her helmet. She hurled the helmet into the nearest pit and turned to face Kyle.

Kyle watched the helmet sail down to the gravel floor of the crater. *What the hell did she do that for?* His first instinct was to insist that she retrieve it, but when he looked back to meet her eyes, he knew there was no hope. Her eyes were wide, her teeth were set and her chest was heaving with barely controlled rage. For just a few seconds she managed to control her anger, but then she began swinging with closed fists. She hit his shoulder, his arm, his back.

"Don't you . . . ever . . . do that . . . to me . . . again!" she screamed at him in between hits.

Kyle tried to laugh to diffuse her anger. "Settle down, girl. I knew what I was doing." He tried dodging the hits, but that only fuelled her rage. She finally stopped when he ducked his head and her knuckles connected with his helmet. She shrieked and began to flick her hand to shake the pain away.

"Haven't you learned your stupid lesson, you idiot? We were almost killed last year!" she screamed at him. Her hands and knuckles were red.

Kyle kicked the stand down, and with the speed of a cat was off the bike. He caught Cassidy's arms before she could swing again and held them in his strong grip.

"It's okay, Cass. I know what I'm doing!" he yelled.

Cassidy's frustration grew when she could no longer hit him. She wanted to cry, her hand hurt so much, but she preferred that he see her anger rather than her pain. "Don't you ever do that to me again. If you don't care if you live or die, don't drag me with you. I don't want to die."

Kyle released his breath and looked down. When he was certain she wasn't going to hit him again, he let go of her arms and put his hands on his hips. "I'm not going to die, Cassy, and neither are you. Look around. Are Sukh and Jeremy here? Or Catrina and Jamieson? No! We won't die if they're not here."

Cassidy took a deep breath. Tears of frustration began to fall down her cheeks. After a few moments she looked at him, "How can you be so sure? We don't even know who Catrina is. Or . . . or who Jamieson is. Are you positive we understood that right?"

He nodded. "Yeah, Cass," he said. "I'm more positive about that than anything in my life. More positive than that the sun will rise every day and set every evening. We will not die if we are not with Sukh and Jeremy," he continued, his voice calming. "I know that. And you can count on it, too."

"Okay, maybe we won't die, Kyle. But we can become quadriplegics. Or we can break our legs or become horribly disfigured, you know. Or we could be maimed or burned."

"Okay, Cass. You're right. We could." He walked toward the pit where she'd thrown the helmet. Without hesitating, he jumped into the soft sandy gravel on the side. He sank to his knees and strained to pull his legs out so he could walk. Cassidy went to the edge of the pit and watched him struggle to grab the helmet.

"I'm walking back," she called.

"No, you're not. It'll take you an hour to walk back to the tree. I'll double you."

"No way, Kyle. You're insane on that bike." She turned away and began the trek to the old tree.

Kyle grabbed the helmet and ran up the side of the pit. When he reached the top he spotted Cassidy partway down the trail. "Cassidy!" he shouted.

She raised her hand in a wave, but didn't look back at him.

Kyle secured the helmet on the seat of his bike, kicked up the stand and started the motor. He gunned the machine, spitting rocks and gravel behind him. The front wheel popped off the ground as he leaned his body forward and did a perfect wheelie. He raced after his girlfriend.

Cassidy wouldn't look at him when he came up beside her. "Come on Cass. Get on the bike. I promise I won't go fast."

She kept walking.

"Please, Cass. I'll drive very slowly . . . and safely."

Cassidy stumbled over a root. She maintained her balance and kept walking, ignoring him.

"You're right, Cassidy. I don't want to be maimed or paralysed. You're right. It could happen. I'll ride more carefully. Now, get on."

Cassidy kept walking.

Kyle took one last try. "Look, Paintbrush is tethered all alone by the pond. A wolf or cougar or bear could get her. Get on the damned bike and we'll go to her. Please."

Cassidy stopped. Paintbrush! She'd forgotten all about her. "Promise to go real slow."

"Promise!" He crossed his heart with his fingers.

As they rode cautiously down the road toward Paintbrush, Cassidy stretched her bruised knuckles and closed them back into a fist. They were starting to swell. She wondered if they were broken. Sighing quietly, she laid her head against Kyle's back. She trusted him. But she trusted Jeremy and Sukh, too. Did they truly believe they'd all die together? She missed them so much and she wondered if she would ever be happy again.

30
Defiance

AFTERWARD, JEREMY AND SUKH REMEMBERED NOTHING about Kendra's party. They didn't remember throwing up. They didn't remember passing out on the side of the highway. They didn't remember Opa Lockett finding them and taking home. They both woke up with splitting headaches, dry mouths and queasy stomachs. They were both grounded for life. They both vowed to themselves that they'd never drink alcohol again.

And they were very happy to learn that Opa Locket had found their motorcycles where they usually left them behind the rock on the outskirts of town, because they didn't remember telling him they were there.

Kyle says>
how's your head?

Jeremy says>
how do u know?

Kyle says>
everyone knows . . . u 2 were the hit of Kendra's party

Jeremy says>
i feel like crap

Kyle says>
LOL . . . sukh says the same thing

Jeremy says>
stop yelling . . . my head hurts

Kyle says>
ha ha ha . . . i feel fine . . . i got a new bike . . . thanks to the creep that stole my old one . . . it's real dope

Jeremy's first response to Kyle's information was that he was going to puke again. He took a deep breath and closed his eyes. The wave of nausea disappeared as he considered that Kyle losing his bike was a good thing. Kyle wouldn't have got a new one if it hadn't been stolen. Before he could take a second deep breath, the nausea returned. He ran to the toilet and began heaving. There was nothing left in his stomach, so he got a taste of bile. So this was what everyone meant by "dry heaves." *I'm going to die,* he thought. *And my head, ohhhh. And why does that clock tick so loud?* He stood up, absentmindedly flushed the toilet and returned to the computer.

Kyle says>
r u there?

Jeremy says>
barely

$ukh is online.

$ukh says>
my folks say they don't want me hanging around with you for a while

Jeremy says>
i don't want me hanging around with me for a while . . . what did u tell them? it was my fault?

$ukh says>
of course . . . what else would I say?

Kyle says>
where'd u guys get the booze from, anyway?

$ukh says>
secret

Jeremy says>
let me just say this . . . sukh is not who we think he is

$ukh says>
ha ha ha

"*Bon matin*, Jeremy!"

Jeremy groaned. Bernadette. Why was she here? Before he could force politeness from his mouth he said, "What are you doing here?"

"Your father asked me to keep an eye on you today. He has to work."

Jeremy's back stiffened. He didn't know if it was because he was angry that his dad hired a babysitter for him, or because her accent was so . . . grating. But here she was.

She continued in her sing-song, irritating French voice. "You were very . . . ill, last night. He was very worried about you."

Jeremy could not think of a thing to say.

"Where did you get the booze?"

He thought of a number of rude comments, none of which would reveal the truth, but said nothing.

"Your father is going to want to know," she said.

Jeremy typed.

Jeremy says>
sukh, rescue me . . . SHE's here and I have to get out

Sukh says>
i'm grounded . . . aren't u?

Jeremy says>
i don't know, i don't remember anything but I will die if I have to stay here with HER

Jeremy heard a match struck. He turned just in time to see Bernadette touch a lit match to a cigarette in her mouth. He watched her lips purse around the filter. She pulled the cigarette away, released a huge plume of smoke into the kitchen and shook the match until the flame was extinguished.

"What are you doing? You can't smoke in here!" he yelled.

She took another long drag off the cigarette and again exhaled, this time in his direction. "Why not? Your father never said I couldn't. I just smoke outside out of respect for him."

How dare she! "Well, I don't want you smoking in here."

Bernadette chuckled. "You don't? Why should I respect you? You don't respect me."

He knew she was right, but that didn't give her the right to smoke here. He knew his dad wouldn't appreciate it. He got up and walked over to the phone. He punched in the numbers to his dad's business and was relieved that his dad answered the phone.

"Dad, Bernadette is smoking in the house," he said, and suddenly felt like a tattling child.

"So?" his dad asked. "You have some serious questions to answer, young man. Where did you get the liquor from?"

Jeremy ignored his dad's question. "Are you going to just let her smoke in here?"

"It's my house. She can do as she damn well pleases." Unfortunately, his dad said the last sentence so loudly that Bernadette heard it from across the room. She laughed out loud.

Jeremy looked at her. She sat at the table dressed in her robe and what appeared to be nothing else. Her legs and feet were bare. As usual Jeremy could see cleavage.

When Bernadette noticed the venom in Jeremy's look, she pulled her robe tightly against her chest, all cleavage disappearing under the terry cloth collar.

He spoke slowly and deliberately. "But I don't want her smoking in here when I'm home."

Jeremy's dad spoke in an angry whisper. "You are in no position to make demands on me or Bernadette. Your behaviour last night was disgusting. I don't care if she wants to burn the damn house down, you will be polite to her. I have a customer, so I'll talk to you tonight. And by the way, you're grounded!"

Jeremy heard a click.

He looked over at Bernadette again. She had the most irritating smirk on her face. Jeremy didn't know if he should pretend to say goodbye to his father or if he should just hang up. He slammed down the receiver.

Without saying another word, he grabbed his jacket from the hook by the door and stormed out of the house. He could hear her hollering, "You can't go anywhere! You're grounded!"

He shook his head and walked down the road to Sukh's house. The blood was pounding in his head. It throbbed with pain. At least he didn't feel like throwing up anymore.

When he got to Sukh's house, he was in luck. Sukh's parents weren't home and Sukh was outside doing some chores for

Grampaji. Talking Sukh into breaking rules was easier than skipping stones. A few moments later, both boys were walking down the dirt road toward the highway.

"Where are we going, anyway?" Sukh finally asked. "We have no money and no wheels."

"I don't know or care. I had to get out of that house." Jeremy stopped walking. He put both hands up to the sides of his head. "You have no idea how much I hate that woman."

Sukh nodded. Normally, he would smile and wonder what the big deal was but his head hurt and his stomach hurt. So today he would sympathize with Jeremy and his feelings about Bernadette.

When they got to the highway, Jeremy asked, "Which way?"

Sukh looked up the highway toward town. He turned and looked down the highway toward the corner store. "Let's go this way," answered Sukh.

They hadn't walked for more than a few minutes when a car slowed down beside them. Both boys turned to see an older, mid-sized sedan pull up. The car stopped and the boys opened the passenger door to see Todd in the driver's seat. He was alone.

"Hey, you guys. Want a ride?"

Both boys looked at each other and shrugged. "Sure," they said to him and got into the car.

"Where you headed?" Todd asked.

Sukh and Jeremy said nothing. After a long moment, Jeremy said, "Nowhere. How about you?"

Todd smiled. "Let's go out to a clearing up around the next bend. I have something for you guys."

The something was a big fat joint. They sat on an old, sun-bleached log staring at the tiny white flowers that would be wild strawberries in a few weeks. Tiny red vines connected one to the next and covered the clearing. Tall trees surrounded the meadow, separating them from the highway. Occasionally they heard a logging truck on the road but they were too far away to hear anything smaller.

Time seemed to stop as Jeremy and Sukh shared the joint. They tried sharing it with Todd, but every time they passed it to him, he declined. After they'd both had a few hits, Sukh offered to snuff out the joint on a rock.

"My stomach still isn't right," said Sukh.

"Mine, neither," added Jeremy.

Todd said, "Hear there was some party in town last night. You guys go?"

Sukh smiled. "How do you think we got these headaches?"

"Yeah? Any babes? That Cassidy Sampson sure turned out to be quite a looker. She there?"

Sukh's smile faded. "No. No, she didn't go."

Todd pulled out another joint and began smoking it alone. Jeremy took a deep breath. The smell of the smoke was different from the first joint. Todd must be smoking something more than just some weed.

"Too bad, man. I'd like to get a piece of her. I had my eye on her since she was just a little thing, when I used to hang around Jeff. I knew then she had potential."

Jeremy and Sukh winced. This guy was strange.

"Well," said Sukh, "too bad she's taken. She's got a boyfriend. Kyle Aspen."

Todd took a hit and laughed. "Haven't you heard? Boyfriends are like goaltenders — they only stop half the guys from scoring."

That did it. "Well, Todd," said Jeremy, "we hate to smoke and run, but we gotta get home. It's a long walk back, you know."

Todd nodded and walked toward the car, but Sukh called, "No, don't worry. We don't need a ride."

Todd laughed over his shoulder and continued to walk to the car. "That's okay, guys. But you can't leave before the show."

With the joint hanging out of his mouth, he opened the trunk, reached in and pulled out a small jerry can of gasoline and a stack of newspapers. Before Jeremy and Sukh could ask what the show was going to be, Todd threw the newspapers into the backseat of the car and dumped the contents of the jerry can onto the papers.

"What are you doing?" asked Sukh, shocked.

Jeremy wanted to get out of there. This guy was acting very weird.

Todd stood beside the car, faced the two boys and, with a stupid grin on his face, tossed the smoking joint into the backseat. He casually stepped away from the car and headed toward them. Immediately, the gas exploded with a loud *whump*!

Jeremy and Sukh, astonished, ran to the edge of the clearing. "What the hell are you doing? Have you lost your mind?"

Flames licked out of the open windows. Black smoke from burning upholstery and floor mats billowed out.

Todd laughed. Over the roar of the flames, he hollered to them, "Relax, you guys. It's not my car."

"Well, whose car is it?" yelled Jeremy.

Todd shrugged. "Don't know."

Sukh and Jeremy said together, "You stole a car!"

Sukh looked at Jeremy. "He stole a car. He's nuts. He stole a freakin' car!" He then turned to face Todd and screamed louder. "You stole a freakin' car — and you torched it! You're insane, man. Insane!"

Jeremy was speechless. He could only stare at Todd. A small explosion erupted from the car; they jumped and ducked their heads under their arms. The flames were so hot they couldn't even face the burning car. A larger explosion followed and pieces of burning debris rained down on the ground near them. Huge plumes of black smoke now rose high into the air. Jeremy tapped Sukh.

"Let's get the hell out of here."

Sukh nodded. Both boys backed away to the entrance of the clearing, took one last glance back at Todd standing in a trance and then broke into a run toward the highway.

31
Invincibility

Kyle hit the kill switch and listened for the engine to purr, sputter and stop. Instantly forest sounds assailed his ears, as if someone had changed the radio station from engine growl to the sounds of nature. Wind rustled the poplar leaves. They flashed silver in the sunlight as the swirling air turned the leaves over. Somewhere above him a squirrel chattered. A male grouse, its chest puffed and pounding, called *thump, thump, thump* to a mate somewhere behind him. And the slowly moving water of the Hayfield River below the cliff splashed, trickled and babbled on its meander through rocks and grass.

Kyle removed his helmet, but didn't get off the motorcycle. He looked across the river to the opposite cliff that seemed to be the exact same height as this one. He'd never been on that side of the river, on that cliff face before. Nobody had. This side was where the snowmobile trail came out of the forest to the spectacular view of the Cariboo hills. This was the side that faced west and the stunning red sky of low winter sunsets. This was the side where they'd roasted hot dogs in the winter.

He looked around. He saw the blackened, charred wood from the huge bonfire they all helped make last winter. There was still a partially burned paper cup, its edge scorched, that had held hot wine or hot chocolate, or maybe some of Opa's brandy. A bottle cap lay on the ground beside it. He remembered eating samosas right over there while he and Cassidy and Sukh's mom sat on that log. That tree right there, the one with the broken branch, had been laden with snow, and Jeremy and Sukh had kicked it and laughed when all the snow fell past Kyle's collar and down his back. And right about there was where Kyle had tackled Sukh and rubbed his face in snow, but Jeremy had managed to run behind Bear to use his huge body as a shield from Kyle's snowball. Kyle remembered pegging one that Jeremy had ducked just in time, but Bear got straight on his ear. He remembered thinking how Bear must have got his nickname when he growled and chased Kyle through the trees until Kyle stumbled. He didn't have snow just down his back when Bear got through with him. It was in his pants, his underwear, his boots and his ears. Everyone had laughed when he came back from the forest, looking as if he had just survived an avalanche but following a very smug and satisfied Bear.

He found himself smiling. They'd gone on those long snowmobile rides with the entire neighbourhood for years. Sometimes there were more than twenty machines following the leader through the forest, like boxcars following a train engine. Opa was usually the leader. Not that no one else could do it, but it was a sign of respect, Kyle figured. As long as he was alive and well, Opa Lockett would always lead the machines on the Sunday afternoon snowmobile rides. Kyle's smile faded as he realized they'd never be here together again. Never, ever again.

Kyle took a deep breath and glanced across to the other cliff. It wasn't that far, really. Bear always talked about one day bringing a chainsaw to this place and felling a tree across from one cliff to the other to use as a bridge. Then they could all go to the other side. When Donna, his wife, asked him why he thought they should go to the other side, he was silent. Everyone laughed as Bear tried to think of one good reason for going there.

Kyle could think of one reason. A good reason. Because it was there. It beckoned him, challenged him, laughed at him. *It's really not that far,* he thought again. He looked again at the log he'd sat on last winter. If he moved it to the edge of the cliff and dug up some dirt in front of and behind it, he could use it as a ramp. If he started way back at the edge of the forest and hit fourth gear just before the log, he could get enough air to . . . He looked back to the other cliff. He could do it!

Kyle lowered the kickstand and got off the bike. He moved the log to the edge of the cliff. Finding a wide piece of bark he could use as a shovel, he began making piles of loose, sandy soil both in front of and behind the log. He stamped the ground to pack it tight and continued until he had a smooth ramp. He stood on top of the log and looked across to the other cliff again. He visualized the motorcycle arcing over the river and landing safely on the other side. Then he visualized what would happen if it didn't make it. He looked down at the little river. He guessed it was two, maybe three stories to the ground. Large boulders, some old and dead trees looked dangerous, but the soft green river grass and the short willowy bushes that lined the river seemed harmless.

Besides, he thought, *I'm invincible. Without Cassidy, Jeremy and Sukh, nothing can happen.* He thought about what Sukh had said that day at Jeremy's, when he found the paper with those names on it. They tried to think about how they could prove their theory of dying together was true. "Are you going to jump off a bridge and see if you die?" The words echoed over and over in his head. "Are you going to jump off a bridge and see if you die?"

"Not a bridge," he said aloud. "A cliff!"

Kyle lifted his helmet to put it on, but stopped before he pulled it into position. He wondered why he needed a helmet. He was invincible, right? If he truly believed that, he didn't need the helmet. He had to believe or he wouldn't make it to the other side. "You can do this," he thought. Then another thought entered his head. Cassidy yelling at him the other day: "We can become paraplegics or horribly disfigured." Or get permanent brain damage, or lie in a coma for forty years. *Hmm, maybe I should use the helmet.*

Kyle grabbed the strap and buckle and pulled the helmet over his head. But just to show that he truly believed in his fate, he didn't bother to cinch up the strap. He straddled his bike, kicked his heel on the starter and revved the accelerator. Forest sounds instantly gave way to the motor's whine. He turned the bike and rode toward the trees, finding a nice opening perpendicular to his ramp. He could do this.

Kyle was glad Cassidy wasn't here. She'd freak if she knew. He smiled: she'd try to beat the crap out of him before she'd let him chance getting hurt in a fall down this cliff. Sukh and Jeremy would love to see this, though. They could witness for themselves the proof that they were invincible. He wished they could be here. He wished they could cheer him on, be his conscience, instil him with confidence. That could never happen, though. If they were here, then it might not work and he could . . . he thought again about the boulders and dead trees sticking out of the river. No, never again. His smile faded as he felt his chest tighten and tears sting his eyes. They couldn't be friends anymore. Those days were gone.

He shook his head, cleared his thoughts and focused on the motorcycle, the ramp, and the cliff on the other side of the river. "I can do this! I can do this!" he chanted. He thought about his Alien God. "Let me do this," he prayed.

Kyle released the clutch at the same time that he turned the accelerator. The bike lurched into a wheelie. Second gear came so fast that the tires kicked a patch of dirt into the air. Clutch, shift to third gear. The ramp was rushing closer. The edge of the cliff was closing in. Clutch, shift to fourth gear. No, too close to the ramp! Not enough speed. Kyle turned the handlebars to the right just as he was about to hit the ramp. The bike veered toward the border of the cliff, riding parallel to its edge. The heavy rear wheel, supporting the weight of the rider, the motor and the bulk of the bike, loosened gravel and stone that fell to the Hayfield River below. But Kyle, a skilled rider, managed to keep the bike under control and pulled himself away from the edge, back to the grass — and safety.

His heart pounded furiously. His breathing was shallow as he rode back to the forest. *Need more distance to get more speed,* he thought. Leaving the bike idling, he moved an old dead log out of the way to give himself a little more distance through the opening. *Let's do it!*

First gear, pop the clutch. Forward. Second gear, through the forest onto the grass. He passed the dirt patch where he'd hit second before, but he was already clutching and shifting third gear. *Here comes the ramp! No fear!* Clutch, shift, fourth gear. *Yes.* He was hitting top speed on the bike and he still wasn't at the ramp. *Do it! No fear! Go! Go!* The front wheel hit the packed dirt at the foot of the ramp and changed the entire angle of the motorcycle.

He was looking into the sky before he realized he was past the log and the edge of the cliff. *I'm flying! Good air! Great air! I'm doing it!* The edge of the far cliff was coming. He had to keep the front wheel up to land safely, but he was losing speed. If the rear wheel didn't land first on solid ground, he may lose his contest with fate! The balance was so precarious! The front wheel would make it, but . . . but . . .

The rear wheel landed on soil, as close to the cliff's edge as possible. Rocks and dirt slipped down the edge, but the

momentum carried Kyle forward. His landing was not as graceful as he'd hoped. He'd over-compensated on his balance, keeping his weight too far toward the back of the bike. When it landed, the bike popped into a wheelie and then flipped right over so Kyle found himself lying on his back skidding along the soft earth, the motorcycle skidding along with him. The wind was knocked from his lungs and his leg stung from the hot tailpipe burning through his jeans and into his flesh. But he'd done it! He was on the other side!

Kyle shoved his bike off of him and stood to look at the other side of the Hayfield River. He had done it! He was invincible! He wanted to scream for joy, but air still hadn't found his lungs. Instead, he raised two closed fists as high into the air as the taut muscles of his body would allow and looked into the sky. He laughed out loud. *Thank you, my Alien God! I proved it! Cassidy, Sukh, Jeremy and I are indestructible!*

He stood facing the other cliff for a very long time before he decided he should head back. He glanced at his motorbike, lying on its side in the soft earth. A glint of metal on the ground beside the wheel intrigued him. How did a piece of metal get there? No human had been on this bluff before, he was sure of it. Yet here was a piece of metal, very small — the size and smoothness of a large coin — but more square-shaped. Was it man-made? Natural? Then he smiled.

Aliens. It had to be from aliens, a sign from his Alien God. With the smile still on his face, he pocketed the piece of metal and considered his next challenge. He had no idea how he'd get home from this side of the river. He'd have to follow the water as far as he could to find a low spot to cross. It could take hours, but he really didn't care.

Today, he'd cheated fate.

32

More Secrets

Kyle says>
u should have been there!!!! i cleared the entire gorge and landed on the other side . . . barely a scratch on me

Jeremy says>
that's dope

Kyle says>
we're invincible man

Jeremy says>
sounds like it

Sukh says>
what'd cass do?

Kyle says>
she wasn't there . . . i won't even tell her about it . . . i'm not stupid

Sukh says>
LOL . . . she would've killed u

Jeremy says>
that would be the ultimate test of our invincibility man . . . 2 see if cass could kill u

Kyle says>
LOL . . . she couldn't . . . i'm — we all r — indestructible.

Jeremy says>
LOL . . . she could maim u

Sukh says>
Ya . . . ha ha ha . . . she could decapitate u . . . and if u couldn't die then u'd be the only headless teenager walking around school . . . ha ha ha

Jeremy says>
good one sukh . . . or she could dismember u . . . then u couldn't ride the motorcycle anymore

Kyle says>
now that would kill me . . . she was ready to kill kendra last month

Jeremy says>
is that when we were in the smoking pit?

Kyle says>
ya . . . she was furious! i've seen her pissed before but she was downright dangerous!

Sukh says>
that was funny . . . u looked f'ing hilarious carrying her over your shoulder like that

Jeremy says>
why was she so mad?

Kyle says>
dunno . . . something about some rumour kendra was spreading . . . i didn't see what the big deal was . . . girls!

Sukh says>
Ha ha ha ha

Kyle says>
how long r u at the coast with your cousins sukh?

Sukh says>
dunno

Kyle says>
what do u do down there anyway?

Sukh says>
dunno

Jeremy says>
he could tell u but then he'd have to kill u

Kyle says>
LOL . . . no really . . . what do u do all summer down there?

Sukh says>
what jeremy said

Kyle says>
he didn't say nothing

Sukh says>
like j said

Jeremy says>
he won't tell u cuz whatever he's up to it's no good

Sukh says>
LOL . . . what he said

Kyle says>
i might be coming down to the coast for a motocross race next week . . . to mission hills, near abbotsford . . . since cass and jer will b up here in the cariboo, do u wanna come see me race?

Sukh says>
that would b dope man . . . but isn't that against the rules? i thought we could only b with our partner—the one we drew straws for

Kyle says>
since when do u care about rules? what do u think j?

Jeremy says>
hell i don't care . . . if me and cass r both up here what could possibly happen to kill all of us?

Kyle says>
well sukh what do u think? j says it's ok

Sukh says>
dope . . . i'll see u next week . . . G2G . . . later man

Sukh may not reply because his or her status is set to Away.

Kyle says>
so j, i hear you're in foster care? what up?

Jeremy says>
it's just temporary . . . it was that or juvenile detention . . . my old man wanted it . . . says i'm too hot 2 handle now and juvie would be worse . . . courts agreed . . . for awhile anyway.

Kyle says>
how is it? i hear you're way up at the next town

Jeremy says>
it's ok. if i hitchhike i can be in town in an hour and at my old man's in one and a half

Kyle says>
is it better than living with your dad?

Jeremy says>
it's better than living with bernadette

Kyle says>
she was over here with your old man the other day for dinner . . . i know u don't like her but she sure has a sexy french accent

Jeremy says>
U THINK IT'S SEXY?

Kyle says>
kind of . . . don't u? just a little?

Jeremy says>
i'd rather have sex with my grandmother

Kyle says>
that's disgusting

Jeremy says>
so is bernadette . . . G2G . . . have fun on the coast

Jeremy may not reply because his or her status is set to Away.

33
True Confessions

KYLE WAS GONE MOST OF THE summer. If he wasn't *competing* in motocross events, he was leaving town to *see* a motocross event. He was good. Very good. Cassidy knew she'd been in good hands when he took her for a ride, but since the bus accident she was tired of pain and wanted to avoid it at all costs. Was she just growing up? She didn't know. She was scared for Kyle. He knew he couldn't die, but it seemed that with each new trick he learned on the bike he was showing the world, had to *prove*, that he wouldn't die.

Sukh was on the Coast for the summer. Rumour had it that since he'd had so many visits from the police in June, his parents were going to make him go to school on the Coast, where his cousins went. She hadn't heard much from him since he left, but through the occasional times she was able to chat with Jeremy online she'd managed to keep up on anything new with Sukh.

Jeremy. He was getting into just as much trouble with the police. She'd heard that he and Sukh were being considered for charges of car theft, damage to property, and drug possession. Apparently there wasn't enough evidence to charge and convict, but her parents were glad she hadn't been hanging around them lately.

Cassidy sighed. She wished she *had* been hanging around Jeremy lately. At the moment, he was living too far away in his new foster home. She'd heard his dad tell her parents that he thought it would be best, since Jeremy was getting out of control.

Cassidy missed Jeremy the most. She could finally admit it to herself. She loved Kyle and missed him. She loved Sukh and missed him. She loved Jeremy and really, really missed him. And she was miserable. She took a summer job in town, working at a drive-in restaurant. All day long she served soft ice cream, milkshakes and French fries to her school friends. Some afternoons she stayed in town after work to visit with some girls, but she missed the boys the most.

Today was her day off. She slept until noon, put on a bikini and lay on the wharf to read a book and soak up some sun. The book bored her quickly so she closed it, tossed it in her beach bag and searched the bag for something more exciting. Her fingers touched something cold and round — a candy? She gripped the item and pulled her hand free.

It wasn't a candy, but a marble — clear almost to its centre, where bright blue swirls and dots lay inert inside the glass. She lay on her back and wondered how the marble had gotten in her bag. She continued to look deep into the centre of the marble, marvelling at the shape of the swirls, wondering how the marble was made and how the swirls got trapped in there. She rolled the marble in between her fingers, enjoying the cold but solid feel of it. Finally, she grasped it in her palm and looked up to the blue sky.

Bored, she turned her head to look at one shore of the lake. She suddenly noticed that if she turned her head slightly she could see past the waters of the lake to the trees on the northern horizon. But if she turned her head back she could see all the way around to the trees that bordered the southern horizon, with no mountain in between. She looked back to the north and realized that, from this perspective, the sky appeared spherical, as if she were inside a glass ball, like the swirl in the marble, looking out to the universe beyond — to God, her universe and beyond.

The thought reminded her of the night she and the guys had talked about their spiritual beliefs. She hadn't thought about that night in a long time. She couldn't. And she didn't want to think about it now, either. But she'd think about it again, she promised herself as she tossed the marble back into her bag. A growl in her stomach signalled hunger and she welcomed it, giving her the excuse she needed to abandon the wharf and go in for lunch.

While she was inside, she checked to see who was online. Jeremy. Immediately she signed in:

Cass says>
What? What should I say?
hey
Think of something else to say.

Jeremy says>
hey beautiful!

Cassidy melted. Her face broke out in a smile that she couldn't control. Her heart started beating so loudly she could hear it in her ears.

Cass says>
i'll bet u say that to all the girls

Jeremy says>
no just 2

She felt her chest tighten. *Me and that cow, Kendra?* she wondered. She just had to ask.

Cass says>
me and who else?

Jeremy says>
u and the only other beautiful little filly in the world

Cass waited. Was he going to tell her who else? Was it Kendra? She waited long enough and typed:

Cass says>
who?

Jeremy says>
paintbrush . . . who else?

She laughed, relieved and amused. She didn't know if she should believe him, but she felt better.

Cass says>
what up?

Jeremy says>
i'm moving

Her grin faded.

Cass says>
moving where?

Jeremy says>
the coast . . . my mom's . . . i leave tomorrow

Cass says>
the coast? your mom's? u don't even know your mom

Jeremy says>
courts recommended it

Cassidy groaned. This couldn't be happening.

Jeremy says>
i want 2 talk 2 u about it . . . not online . . . can u meet me?

She considered. Jeremy had been off limits to her since the night they drew straws and she drew Kyle. But, there was no chance they'd meet up with Kyle and Sukh. The rules were that they should avoid all chances of being together, but under the circumstances there was no chance that all four of them could be in the same place. Not with Sukh and Kyle out of town.

Cass says>
i dunno . . . should we?

Jeremy says>
it's ok . . . kyle and sukh know . . . they're going 2 meet on the coast

Cass says>
well then sure . . . where?

Jeremy says>
the old tree . . . in an hour?

Cass says>
c u.

Cassidy raced around her house trying to find something to wear. She found a tank top and a pair of jeans that were clean.

For some reason she got a lot of compliments in this top. Must be the colour. It was a very bright pink. She ran to the bathroom, brushed her hair, applied some sheer lip-gloss, a little eyeliner and mascara. She ran outside to saddle up Paintbrush. She was going to see Jeremy! She didn't want to think about the fact that he was leaving tomorrow, probably forever. She was going to see him *today*. She couldn't help smiling.

Small clouds of locusts and tiny purple butterflies rose into the air as Paintbrush trotted and disturbed their resting places on the small rocks and flowers that lined the dusty road. It was sunny and hot, the air heavy with forest smell. The heat was intense. Normally Cassidy would not want to be out here at this time of day. She looked up. Giant billowy clouds lay to the west, but above her was the clear, blue Cariboo sky.

As she came around a bend she noticed someone walking far ahead on the side of the road. Since the lumber companies had taken the trees a few years ago and it really led nowhere, only people on all-terrain vehicles, motorcycles and horses used it. As she approached the lone figure, she realized it was Jeremy. Her heart again began to beat quickly. She trotted up to him and he turned to face her, a huge smile on his face.

"You're walking? Where are you coming from?"

Jeremy couldn't take his eyes off her. "Town. I had to hitchhike to get to the main road. Then I had to walk from there."

Cassidy was surprised. "But it must be five miles from the road."

Jeremy smiled wider. "To see you again, I'd walk five hundred miles." He winked at her.

Cassidy blushed. She'd swum almost naked with Jeremy in the past. She'd had sleepovers with him and the other boys. They'd shared every secret in their lives together and here she was, blushing. She blushed redder just thinking about the absurdity of it.

"Well, get up here on Paintbrush with me. It's so dusty. Let's get to the pond."

Jeremy climbed on top of the horse. He positioned himself behind Cassidy, on the back of the saddle. He rested one hand on her waist and the other on his thigh.

Cassidy's breathing turned shallow. She could feel Jeremy's hand on her waist. She felt hotter as she felt his chest against her back. He tipped his head down and whispered in her ear. "This feels good." Then he made a gentle growling sound. Did he lick her ear? Or did he kiss it? She couldn't tell. She could have imagined the touch, it was so gentle.

As Paintbrush continued walking to the pond, Cassidy leaned forward to stop herself from leaning against Jeremy. She couldn't understand why she was suddenly so aware of his physical contact. She had never cared about it before, remembering wrestling matches with him and the guys countless times before. She loved the feel of him behind her but it just seemed so . . . sexual. And that was what made her uncomfortable now. She felt a tingle of excitement and wondered if Jeremy was feeling it, too. But, by the way he continued casually talking, she sensed he wasn't feeling the same thing.

When they finally arrived at the pond, Jeremy slid off first, turned and reached his hands up to help Cassidy down. As she slid down the horse, she was forced to face him. He didn't back up to give her space. He stared at her. Their faces were inches apart. His hands were still on her waist. He had the most mysterious little grin on his face. A long moment passed.

Cassidy wondered if he was going to kiss her like that first kiss, so long ago. Feeling uncomfortable in the silence, she looked down and stepped past him to gather Paintbrush's tethers. She walked away, leading the horse to a tree surrounded by soft, green grass.

By the time she faced Jeremy again, he was sitting on a log near the water. His shirt was off, revealing a tanned back and shoulders. He was in the process of taking off his socks and skate shoes. One foot was already dangling in the water up to the hem of his jeans.

"Man, am I going to miss this place," he said. "You know, I think of this here as being the root of all of our problems. It was this place that Kyle showed us on the day of the accident. And then it was here we discovered our destinies. It can be really creepy here . . ." his voice drifted as he looked up at the disfigured tree. "Yet, it's the most beautiful place in the world. I'm drawn to it." His gaze returned to Cassidy.

Cassidy sat down beside him. "I know what you mean. It's so weird here." She looked up at the tree. The tiniest shiver moved through her body as she continued. "That tree. It just seems so . . . I don't know . . . so all-knowing. It just sits there unmoving, yet I can't help thinking that when there's nobody here it has a life of its own. I should be creeped out about it, but I love coming here." She looked back to Jeremy. "So, why are you going to your mother's?"

Jeremy shrugged. "I have to. I don't want to." He looked out toward the pond, picking up a tiny stick and flinging it into the water. He clasped his arms around his knees. "Well, that's not really true. I wanted to get away from my Dad's place." He shook his head as he looked down, an insincere chuckle escaping his mouth. "I hate his new girlfriend and she's there all the time. But I don't want to go to the Coast. I don't think I do, anyway." He waited a long moment and said, "Maybe if I looked at it as an adventure."

Cassidy felt for him. His confusion seemed to match hers. "Who says you have to go? The courts? What's up with that?"

Jeremy slid off the log, sat in the sand and leaned against it. "Sukh and I have done some pretty stupid things lately," he said. He hesitated. "Now, don't get me wrong. We didn't do everything they're accusing us of doing. But we did some dumb stuff. And we were with the wrong person at the wrong time."

Cassidy hoped that if Kendra was the wrong person that he had finally come to his senses about her. "Who were you with?"

Jeremy smiled. "Actually, it was with a friend of your brother's. Todd MacLean."

"Todd MacLean!" Cassidy faced him. "He's no friend of my brother's. He's bad news all around. Why in God's name would you hang around with that freak?"

"Don't ask me. And don't you think I know that now? Sukh and I were just walking along the highway when that nut offered us a ride in a stolen car. How the hell could we know it was stolen? We barely knew him. We didn't even know if he had a driver's license, which he didn't. He took us to some clearing up the road and torched the car." Jeremy's tone became more contemplative. "He was freaky, man. He just stood there like he was in some trance, staring at the car burning. Sukh and I bugged out of there so fast. But the idiot waited until the cops came and told them we did it."

He faced Cassidy, held one of her hands and said, "I swear we didn't do it, Cass."

Cassidy looked into Jeremy's eyes. Of course she believed him. How could she not? He would never do anything like that. She was shocked by what he'd been through, but a thought was niggling at her brain. "You don't think Todd was the one who stole Kyle's bike, do you?"

Jeremy winced. "Why do you ask?"

"Well, because it was torched, too," she answered. "Don't criminals usually use the same m.o., the method of operandi, or whatever you call it?"

"Maybe. I don't know about that." He changed the subject. "But now everyone thinks that because I've been making some bad decisions lately I should go and live with my mom, who I've barely spoken to in years. I wanted to stay with the Locketts. They even offered to take me, but there's so much red tape between the government, the courts, juvenile detention. I kept hearing 'family' and the next thing I know, the judge says I have to go to my mom's."

Cassidy's heart was breaking. *You can't leave*. "Well, what bad decisions have you made?"

Jeremy released her hand. "Just stuff. Skipping school." He waited, probably to see how she'd respond. "Buying some dope," he added. Still she said nothing. "We got hammered one day because we stole some liquor from some old cabins up on Poplar Bluff."

"You *what*? You broke into cabins? Jeremy . . . if you guys want to ruin your brains with dope, that's your business. But breaking into cabins — that's everybody's business. How could you?"

He looked down, acknowledging his fall from grace.

"Well, we didn't *break* into them. Not really. Sukh picked the locks." Then to take the heat off himself, Jeremy added, "You think you know Sukh? You don't know Sukh. I love him like a brother, man, but I think he's done some real nasty stuff on the Coast with his cousins. And the biggest irony of it all is that his parents think he's better off with those delinquents." He shook his head. "Now that's some *adults* making a 'bad decision'."

Cassidy was quiet. She was surprised to hear Jeremy's revelations. But instead of being disappointed in him, she found that, for some reason she could not comprehend, he appeared even sexier than ever to her. Now she knew why all the girls in school swooned when he so much as looked their way. He was a bad boy and she wondered why so many of the girls, including she, loved to think that they could love the bad boys. *But bad boys get sent away,* she thought. First Sukh did and now Jeremy would.

He picked up her hand again. "I'm gonna miss you, you know."

Not as much as I'm going to miss you. She touched her other hand to hold his and leaned against his shoulder. She sighed.

"Man, it's hot today. And muggy. Look at me. I'm sweating like a mo' fo'." He ran his hands through his curly brown hair. Rivulets of sweat were streaming down his neck and forehead. He continued, "I think we're going to get a Cariboo thunderstorm. Did you see those big clouds when we were riding in?"

Cassidy nodded.

Jeremy stood up. He undid the top of his jeans and unzipped the fly. Without a glance in her direction, he slipped out of his jeans and dove into the water in only his boxers. When he broke the surface in the middle of the pond, he turned onto his back and faced her, "Come on, Cassidy. Last one in is a loser." He began chanting: "Cassy is a loser! Cassy is a loser!"

Cassidy laughed at the reminder of their childhood. She hadn't swum with the boys in her panties since she got her first bra, so long ago. She shook her head.

He pressed. "Come on in, Cass. I can see you sweating, too."

Cassidy gasped with a smile on her face. She stood up. "Women don't sweat!" she called to him. "For your information," she began as she started to unbutton her jeans and kicked off her shoes, "horses sweat." She removed her jeans as she continued.

"Men perspire. And women . . ." she said as she pulled off her tank top to reveal a lacy white bra, " . . . glow."

Jeremy gasped. Without smiling, he said breathlessly, "You're glowing, alright."

Cassidy stepped into the water and swam over to him. He stood in the middle of the pond where the water was up to his chest, waiting for her. When she got close enough, he reached his arms around her waist and pulled her into his embrace. Then he began to kiss her.

Cassidy moaned in surrender. Oooooh, how she loved this. His lips, his tongue, his breath. She loved it all. She wasn't surprised, but she was confused. She was dating Kyle. She kissed Kyle all the time, but why did those kisses never feel like this? She loved Kyle, but for some reason, this felt so right. She tried telling herself that it was only a goodbye kiss. It was not ever going to happen again. It couldn't possibly hurt Kyle because Kyle had seen her kiss Jeremy before. They were just friends, damn it. But, but, but . . . why did her kisses with Kyle never feel like *this?*

Jeremy stopped kissing her and they stared into each other's eyes. She was aware of how handsome he looked and how passionately he looked at her. Right into her eyes. He made her feel that he was so in love with her.

He still held her, but he had such an unreadable look in his eyes. "I'm going to remember this for the rest of my life," he whispered.

Again Cassidy sighed. She looked at a rivulet of water making its way down his chest. She touched it, then raised her eyes to look into his again, saying nothing. She was ecstatic that he would remember this always because she knew she would too. A distant rumble in the distance broke their trance. They both looked in the direction the thunder had come from. It was still very far away.

He smiled. "Told you. There's going to be a thunderstorm."

He released Cassidy, gently gripped one of her hands and began to walk toward the shore, pulling her along with him. Silently, he opened his shirt and laid it on the grass in the sunshine. He pulled her to it and indicated that she should lie down and dry off. Reaching for his jeans, he stretched them out as flat as he could and placed them down on the grass beside his shirt. Then he lay down beside her, on his side, one hand lovingly pulling her against his body. He kissed her again, first on her lips, then down to her neck and behind her ear. She giggled, tensing her neck. "That tickles," she whispered.

She reached her hand behind his neck, her fingers playing with his curls. She wanted him to touch her — everywhere.

"Oh, Cass," he whispered. "You feel so good." His hand moved from her waist up to her shoulder. He pulled his body closer to hers, pressing her hips against his own. He gently touched her bra strap and lowered it from her shoulder to her arm as he kissed her again.

Within a moment, darkness covered the pond. A large black thundercloud had moved over the clearing. It blocked out the sun, stirred the trees and chilled the late summer air. Jeremy raised his head to look around, his lips still slightly parted from her kiss. Something landed on the ground beside them. First one and then another. Hailstones. Tiny little plops disturbed the calm waters of the pond. Jeremy felt a sting on his back, then another and another as the ice pellets assaulted his exposed flesh. He tried to shield Cassidy from the battering but realized that they had to get to cover. The ground was quickly turning white from the frozen raindrops, as big as marbles. Cassidy jumped up to put her clothes on as Jeremy shook out his shirt and pulled it over his head. As more stones pelted at them from the black cloud, he tied his shoes together and threw them over his shoulder, then slipped on his jeans. In seconds they were dressed and ran over to where Paintbrush was tethered. Jeremy untied the straps and helped Cassidy up onto her horse. He put his foot in the stirrup and joined her in the saddle as he guided the horse toward the path that led to the road.

"Should we stay in the forest for cover or try to make it home?" Cassidy asked. In answer to her question, a bright flash lit up the sky. Within seconds, thunder pounded the forest and beat at their chests.

Cassidy flinched. Jeremy's arms tightened around her as he looked back at the old dead tree. He thought about how lightning had struck it more than a year ago and it had virtually exploded. The forest was not a safe place to be in a storm. But, at the same time he thought, lightning never struck the same place twice. The hailstones were getting larger and hammering the ground around them. If nothing else, they had to get out of the hail. Cassidy had a tank top on. She'd freeze. And he was still barefoot.

"Let's wait it out over there," Jeremy said pointing to the trail through the forest. Cassidy gently squeezed her heels together to direct the horse toward the dense spruces and firs. She patted Paintbrush's neck, soothing her with calm words, but the horse was undisturbed by nature's din. Under the cover of the trees, they waited.

The hailstones were trapped among the fir boughs, and those that fell through landed gently on the soft ground. The air was still chilled, but Cassidy leaned against Jeremy to absorb his body heat. He kept his arms around her to protect her bare arms. Paintbrush shivered occasionally, but Cassidy assumed that was caused more by the electrically charged air than by the cold. Neither of them had to speak. Their physical contact was comfort enough.

Two more flashes of light and cracking thunder and the hail stopped. Cassidy looked up through the canopy of trees and noticed a tiny patch of blue sky. It took only a few minutes for the storm to start and stop, but they both knew there were more thunderclouds around. They should get started home. She nudged Paintbrush forward. Jeremy rested his head on her shoulder as they made their way down the dirt road.

"You are so beautiful, you know. And you smell — " he took a deep breath, " — so fine. And you belong in my arms." He nuzzled the back of her neck with tiny little kisses.

Cassidy laughed. "That tickles, Jeremy." But she didn't want him to stop.

"I've known you forever and I never realized how ticklish you are."

"Yeah? Well, my brothers used to tickle me all the time. They thought it was funny. I thought it was cruel."

"Cruel? You think this is cruel?" He nuzzled her neck more forcefully.

She laughed. "When they did it. But there's something about the way you do it. It's . . . wow."

"You've got an amazing body, you know. "

Cassidy leaned to the side and tried to face Jeremy. "This is a new side to you, being so flattering. Is that something Kendra taught you?"

As soon as she said it, she regretted it. She did *not* want to sound like a jealous cow. If she brought up Kendra, Jeremy might bring up Kyle and she didn't want to discuss her relationship with Kyle because at this point, she didn't know what that relationship was. She felt very happy right now, and she couldn't remember once feeling this good being with Kyle. But Jeremy was leaving soon and Kyle would always be with her.

Jeremy laughed out loud. "Kendra? She didn't teach me anything. She's nice enough. She's attractive, but . . ."

He did not finish what he was going to say. Cassidy wished he would clarify his relationship with her, but asking him to continue would have segued into exactly what she didn't want to talk about. The only bright spot about him leaving was that at least Kendra wouldn't be able to get her clingy arms around him anymore.

Cassidy changed the subject by offering to take him back to his dad's house. He insisted he could walk from her place.

When they got to the edge of her property, Cassidy was disappointed to see one of her brothers outside gathering things that had to be put undercover before the approaching storm. They dismounted. Feeling very uncomfortable about someone in her family seeing her embracing Jeremy, Cassidy simply said "Goodbye."

Jeremy stood in front of her for the longest moment, just looking at her. He didn't want this moment to end. Ever. She couldn't take her eyes off of his face, reading every feature, burning it into her head. He didn't touch her, not with her brother nearby, but simply whispered to her, "I love you, Cassidy Sampson." He gently kissed her on the forehead, turned and walked down the road.

As he walked away, tears began to stream down Cassidy's cheeks. *Why do I always feel like crying lately?* she asked herself. She knew he wouldn't look back, but she watched him until just before he cleared the last bend. When he was about to disappear from her sight, possibly forever, she whispered, "I love you more, Jeremy Kendall."

She waited a long time after Jeremy had disappeared before she turned and led Paintbrush to the barn.

34
No Good

SUKH SIGNED OFF THE CHAT LINE, grabbed his jacket from the hook on the wall and walked down the stairs to see if Jaspal was ready to go. He'd been told they were going to meet someone at noon and it was almost that time now. Downstairs he found his auntie making *roti,* the thin pancakes, like crepes, they ate every day. He picked one up, rolled it into a tube and dipped it into the lentil *daal* beside the stove. As he ate it, she smiled at him and gestured for him to take another. Sukh smiled back and shook his head. In Punjabi he told her that he, Jaspal and Jaswinder were going for lunch and would be back later.

His voice attracted the attention of two young children, a boy wearing a white cloth on his hair and a little girl still in diapers who'd been sitting on the floor watching television. When the little boy heard Sukh's voice, he ran into the kitchen and wrapped his arms around Sukh's legs, laughing and calling his name.

Sukh chuckled and, in Punjabi, said, "Whoa, Auntie. Do you hear a mosquito? I hear an annoying mosquito and feel . . . one . . . on . . . my leg." He made an exaggerated swat at the little boy, who squealed with laughter and held his leg tighter. Sukh rolled to the ground in a wrestling fall and pulled him on top of his chest. As the little girl toddled near him, he grabbed her and pulled her on top of the boy as she squealed with laughter. All three rolled on the floor, giggling and laughing, as Sukh's aunt smiled and made roti.

"Sukh! Let's go!" Jaspal was hanging up the phone as he called to him from the kitchen door.

"No, no, no!" Speaking in Punjabi, little Raman begged Sukh to stay with him.

Sukh held the little fellow with two hands and placed him on the floor beside him. In one move, he was in a standing position and told Raman and his sister that he had to go, but he'd read them a book when he came home.

As Sukh followed Jaspal to the door, Jaspal chuckled and said, "You're always reading them books. Who reads so many books?"

Sukh just shrugged. "They like it."

Jaswinder was already sitting in his polished, 2007 red Mustang — his muscle car. He revved the five-litre engine to make the dual exhaust roar. The driveway was wet, indicating that he'd just washed it for the second time that day. Sukh had to smile. "How many times can you wash a car in one day?" he asked as he got in his cousin's car.

Jaspal smirked. "It must have rained. If it rains, he washes it twice. Sometimes three times. It all depends on how many times it rains in one day."

Jaswinder pulled onto the road and said, "At least it's better than that piece of crap you drive Jaspal. You're just jealous."

Jaspal whistled and smiled. "Hell, yes!"

It took only a few minutes to drive to the restaurant where the meeting was scheduled to take place. Indian music was piped quietly into the seating area. There were a few booths around the perimeter of the restaurant and tables in the middle. Jaspal indicated a booth beside the window that looked out onto the street. Sukh was the first to sit down; Jaswinder and Jas sat across from him.

"Is your connection here yet?" asked Sukh.

Jaspal looked around at the tables. Only a few were occupied. "No," he answered. "I told him to meet us at one o'clock. Then we have time to eat."

"Well, then what the hell are we still sitting here for?" asked Sukh. He got up and walked over to the buffet table just as the waiter was bringing a bowl of naan. Sukh was hungry and didn't care that Jas and Jas stayed in the booth to talk quietly. He helped himself to a heaping plate of basmati rice seasoned with fresh coriander and cumin, some curried paneer vegetables and his favourite, butter chicken. To help balance the spice, he added some fresh vegetables and herbed yoghurt, then returned to sit with his cousins.

Immediately their whispering ceased, but not before Sukh heard Jaspal say, "Yeah, but he still owes me money and he'll pay for threatening me." Whatever they'd been discussing, Sukh realized, he wasn't in on it. And he knew better than to ask. His role was to be an extra body — a big one. He was the intimidator, even if he was just a teenager. So he began to eat.

After a few moments of silence, Sukh, with a full mouth, asked, "Well, aren't you guys going to eat?"

Jas laughed. "It looks like you're eating enough for all of us."

"You know that when you walked through those doors, there was a hidden sensor that weighed you in. When you leave they weigh you again. You pay by the extra pound on the way out," Jas added.

Sukh stopped chewing and looked at the front doors. "No way. Really?"

Both his cousins laughed, attracting the attention of the other diners for a moment. "Man, are you a mark!"

Sukh sat up as straight as he could. "Well, at least I'm a big mark. I could take you down, man!"

Jaswinder laughed again. "You sure could. You're bloody huge. Eat some more! I need you for protection."

It wasn't until Sukh went for his second helping of food that his cousins decided to join him. As they returned with full plates, they were all startled to find a light-skinned man sitting in their booth, in Sukh's seat. Sukh didn't recognize him. He wasn't very large, but he looked . . . mean. He wore dark sweat pants and a baseball cap with a skater logo on the front. His grey bubble jacket looked out of place on the summer's day, but was undone at the front. Dark blonde, neatly trimmed sideburns joined a thin moustache and goatee, enhancing the look of nastiness. His feet were up on the seat where Jas had been sitting, his back against the wall and his legs stretched out along the seat. His blue eyes met a menacing glare from Sukh, which made His Nastiness reluctantly put his feet on the ground, but not before he gestured with a sneer. No introductions were made, which was fine with Sukh. He figured that after today he'd probably never see him again.

This man was not a big talker and Sukh noticed how Jaswinder seemed to intentionally remain silent for a long time before speaking. He appeared to be choosing his words carefully, but Sukh wondered if it was a tactic he used to instil fear and distrust in this connection.

It seemed that everyone he met through his cousins always made him feel some level of fear. It used to bother Sukh, being used to the openly, friendly people of the Cariboo. He felt sorry for his cousins sometimes, knowing they trusted only each other, whereas Sukh could put his faith not only in his family but also in so many of his neighbours and especially his three best friends. He knew none of them — neither Jeremy, Cassidy nor Kyle — would ever betray him. He could put his life in their hands at any moment and they'd come through. He smiled ever so subtly at this thought, a slight stab of pain in his chest at the memory of their separation. He suddenly missed seeing Jeremy every day. And Cassidy — beautiful Cassidy. He was happy just looking at her. Oh well, he'd see Kyle again next week! He was really looking forward to that.

Tipping his head in a subtle shrug, he began eating and tried paying attention to a conversation too stilted and full of code words to follow. Sukh assumed that whatever words didn't make sense were symbols for other things. Illegal things.

Sukh noticed that his cousins still hadn't touched their food. And His Nastiness did not appear to be in any hurry to leave. Sukh reached for a piece of naan, tore off a strip and dipped it into the butter chicken sauce. He put it into his mouth and again wondered if his cousins were going to eat. He was just about to dip again when Jaswinder reached his hand into his jacket's inside pocket. As he made this apparently unexpected move, His Nastiness jumped and reached inside his own pocket, a look of fear on his face for just an instant before it changed to nasty again. Jaswinder froze with his right hand in his jacket; his left hand rose in a gesture of surrender, and he said, "Easy, man."

The man released a breath in a show of relaxation, but didn't remove his hand from inside his jacket. Jaswinder pulled out an envelope and tossed it calmly onto the table, a stack of twenty dollar bills spilling out of it. "Count it," he said.

The man forced a smile and said, "I trust you." He gathered the bills, tucked them back into the envelope and put them in his inside jacket pocket.

Sukh doubted his sincerity very much, wondering why His Nastiness would trust *them* when Sukh wouldn't trust *him*, even at a police station.

Jaswinder held out his hand in anticipation of receiving something for his money. Before responding, His Nastiness looked carefully around. Since everything appeared to be in order, he reached into another pocket and pulled out a small felt bag. Sukh recognized the bright purple bag with the gold drawstrings; they usually came containing bottles of Crown Royal, but whatever was inside it right now was too small to be a liquor bottle. Jas reached to take the bag, but His Nastiness seemed to grip it for a moment too long. Sukh noticed his cousin's eyes narrow. Jaspal sat up straight, anticipating a problem. Sukh took a deep breath, wondering if there was going to be trouble. His Nastiness smiled, released the bag and said, "Enjoy!" Then he turned to face Sukh and said, "Let me out."

Sukh watched his cousin silently weigh the bag in his hand. He looked at Sukh and nodded. Sukh disliked the man's attitude and wanted to take his sweet time, but decided he didn't want to antagonize His Nastiness. The tension at the table was thick enough. He turned and stood up so the man could slide out of the booth. Without looking back, the stranger left the restaurant and the three cousins were alone at the table.

The purple bag was nowhere to be seen and Sukh assumed Jaswinder had tucked it into his jacket. Jaspal stood up, reached for his wallet and placed two twenty-dollar bills on the table. Then he said, "Let's go."

Immediately Sukh's cousins stood to leave. Sukh was surprised at their hurry and wondered again why they hadn't eaten. He took one more piece of naan, dipped it into his plate and followed them out to the car. As soon as they were safely in the privacy of the car, Jaspal said, "Let me see it."

Jas started his car and said, "In a minute. I want to get away from here first."

Sukh looked outside. Nothing seemed out of place, but Jaswinder appeared cautious. They left the parking lot and drove along the main road in silence for a few minutes. Jaspal kept checking the side mirror and Jaswinder kept checking his rear view mirror. Sukh's curiosity about the contents of the purple bag was growing. Whatever was in that felt bag was remarkable enough to destroy his cousins' appetites. He wanted to ask what it was, but knew better than to show any impatience. Since he'd begun living with his cousins, he'd learned that they expected behaviour that was cool and aloof.

Finally, they pulled into a small parking lot in a neighbourhood park. A late summer rain was falling and the grass was littered with brown and red leaves. Swings and slides sat empty of children and filling with rainwater. Nobody was around. Jaspal turned the CD player down. Leaving the car running, Jaswinder put the transmission into neutral and turned to face Jaspal. With a smile on his face, he reached into his pocket to remove the purple bag.

While Jaswinder loosened the drawstring, Jaspal held out his hand. With a tip of the bag something heavy fell into Jaspal's hand. He let out a contented sigh. Jaswinder's face was alive with delight as he looked at whatever it was gleaming in the dull daylight. Sukh, already leaning forward from the back seat, tried to look over their shoulders to finally see what had cheered them so dramatically. All he could see was a flash of metal until Jaswinder touched something on the object and it clicked.

As he raised it in the air to have a better look, Sukh gasped. Cradled carefully in his cousin's hand was something Sukh had never seen before.

It was a handgun.

35
The Coast

By November, Jeremy knew he didn't like living on the Coast. It almost never stopped raining. If it wasn't raining, it was cloudy and . . . dreary.

On the rare sunny day, the city was beautiful. The North Shore mountains loomed up on the skyline from almost everywhere he stood in Vancouver. The ocean spread from one beach to another, under bridges, around Stanley Park, into False Creek, past the Point Grey cliffs. Jeremy could see across Georgia Strait to the Gulf Islands and to Vancouver Island. The forests that bordered the Lower Mainland were thicker than the ones in the Cariboo, more lush, with tall cedar trees that drank up the rain and ferns that lined the forest floor. It was a beautiful city, he knew, but it wasn't for him. He couldn't believe that only a six-hour-drive away, there was an entirely different world. The one he came from. The one he wanted back.

His mother had changed. She was skinnier, and looked older and haggard. She reminded him of a woman who had seen some hard living, and partied hard, too. She was always looking for a good time. She had a full-time job as a waitress in a dive of a restaurant near Hastings Street. Occasionally she worked nights, but usually she worked days. Lots of times she called in sick. She often seemed to be nursing a hangover.

At first she tried hard to give Jeremy the idea that she was a very respectable person. She was home every night, playing "mother" for this teenager who'd suddenly appeared in her life. Gradually, however, she started going out evenings, more and more every week. One day she brought a man home to meet her son. He reminded Jeremy of an older Goatee-guy. His name was Collin. Jeremy neither liked nor disliked him. Collin was neither polite nor impolite. He was indifferent to Jeremy, as if he didn't exist.

They lived in a small apartment and Jeremy went to what he considered an inner-city school. The kids, almost every one new to Canada, all seemed to hang around in gangs. There were Asians, from China, Hong Kong, India, Vietnam and Korea. There were some Russians and some Poles. Kids like Jeremy, born in British Columbia, were rare.

Jeremy kept to himself for the first little while. He made a few trips out to Surrey to see Sukh, and Sukh came into the city a few times to spend the day with Jeremy, but mostly Jeremy kept out of trouble and did his school work.

By Christmas, Jeremy knew that he hated Vancouver. The grass was green. *Green* at Christmas time! There should be snow on the ground. The lakes and ponds should be frozen. And the sky should be blue, not grey. There were no long snowmobile rides with friends and family. No winter bonfires and wiener roasts in the middle of the forest. No hot wine for the adults and hot chocolate for the kids. People here *bought* their Christmas trees!

One day, during Christmas Break, Jeremy decided to catch a bus downtown. He disembarked at Granville Street and walked along the crowded sidewalks. There were lots of young people here.

Some had hair dyed black and wore black lipstick, black leather and boots. Others had pierced and tattooed . . . everything. And still others appeared to be living there, right on the street. They sat on sleeping bags, kept little signs in front of them asking for money and didn't appear to be in any hurry to go anywhere. Some of the stores in this part of town surprised Jeremy. Some were very respectable, but others sold pornography, sex toys and kinky clothing.

Jeremy stopped walking. He thought he'd heard someone call his name. Turning around, he looked back at the many people walking behind him. He heard it again. Someone *was* calling his name. He looked across the street. There was a small group of kids waving at him. He recognized two of the girls and one of the boys. They were in his new school and had been in some of his classes. One of the girls sat right in front of him in Math. She was waving at him. He waved back, then crossed the street to talk to them.

"Hey, Mandy, right?"

She was a very pretty girl. Her long hair was dyed reddish-brown colour and was twisted and pinned up at the back. She wore black eyeliner, but it didn't look overdone on her. Jeremy had always found her intriguing, but hadn't tried very hard to make friends yet. A few times she'd made polite conversation with him, but only before class. The conversations had always been forced to an unnatural end when the bell rang.

"Yeah, how are you?" she asked.

"Meh," he answered. "Okay, I guess."

"We're going to get some CDs with our Christmas money. What are you buying?" she asked.

"Nothing really. I'm new here. I thought I'd just do some sightseeing. You know, play tourist."

The group began walking toward the nearest music store; Jeremy and Mandy hung back.

"So where are you from?" she asked. She had a very nice smile.

"The Cariboo. Ever been there?"

"No," she answered. "I've never been anywhere. Once I went to the Island, but that's about it. Where do you live?"

"In an apartment. With my mom. How about you?"

Her smile faded. "I live with my mom during the week. My dad on weekends. It sucks. He's always hounding me to come to his place. But on weekends, I just want to hang with my friends. He lives in Burnaby, in the lamest neighbourhood."

Jeremy thought about his childhood after his mom left. He never had been pulled back and forth between parents. He'd always wanted to see his mom, but he guessed now that it might not have been that easy or that much fun. "I lived with my dad all my life . . . well, until recently."

"You don't like your dad?" she asked.

Of course he liked his dad. What kind of a question was that? Now that he was living with his mother, Jeremy realized how much his dad had sacrificed to raise him. His mother had bailed on her responsibilities, but his dad stayed with him. If it wasn't for Bernadette, everything would have been fine. "Yeah, I like him enough," he said. "I hate his girlfriend, though."

Mandy laughed. "Wait until she's his wife. It's like they say about women becoming bitches when they get married. They become hags to the stepchildren, too. I know. In fact, all of the kids we're walking with have divorced parents."

One of the other girls had hung back and was listening to them. "I like my stepmom," she said. "More than I like my real mom. My real mom's messed on drugs and stuff. I can only see her with a social worker there. And the guys she's with all the time?" She made a retching sound. "Well, let's just say I wouldn't want to be alone in a room with any of them."

Jeremy told them both how much he missed his friends and even his dad. He didn't know why he was being so open with them, but decided it must have been because he was starved for company. He told them how much he hated his dad's new girlfriend and was relieved when he got to leave, but that now he wasn't so sure. Mandy, too, was candid with him and told him about how her family was messed up. Her brother was in jail and her sister was living on the street somewhere.

The other kids had gone into the store, but Jeremy and Mandy stayed out on the sidewalk. "We're all rejects," she said. "That's why we go to that stupid school. If we had normal lives, we sure as hell wouldn't be living where we do and going to school with those losers." She laughed, a high-pitched and abrupt laugh that made Jeremy wonder how long it would be before he found it irritating. He didn't really know who she was talking about, but he laughed along with her.

Time went by quickly for Jeremy, talking outside with this pretty girl. After a while, the others came out to join them and showed Mandy what they'd bought. She squealed with delight over one of the CDs, and claimed that she hadn't been able to find a copy before Christmas. It was a band Jeremy had never heard of. Some local alternative band. Mandy claimed she knew the bass player. Jeremy acted impressed, but secretly he couldn't have cared less.

While they were standing on the sidewalk, a young, dark-skinned man wearing a ball cap low over his eyes approached one of the boys next to Jeremy and whispered, "Ice? Wanna buy some meth?"

Jeremy didn't respond. He remembered hearing about crystal methamphetamines in his counselling class back home. At the time, he thought he'd never be stupid enough to try it, but he wanted to see what his new friends would do. Nobody at home had ever tried anything like it, he was sure. Unless maybe that idiot Todd MacLean. Jeremy wondered if Goatee-guy could even get any of it.

Mandy shook her head, but one of the guys and a couple of the girls stepped aside and began talking quietly to the stranger. Jeremy noticed that money was exchanged and assumed that Mandy's friends had bought some.

Before the meth guy left their group he adjusted his hat, made eye contact with Jeremy, then turned and disappeared into the crowds of people. Jeremy gasped. He thought he knew the young man, but couldn't recall from where or how. Mandy looked at him and asked, "What's the matter with you?"

Jeremy stepped up on his toes to try to get one more glimpse, but meth guy was gone. "I just thought I knew that guy, but I don't remember how. Did you recognize him?" he asked.

Mandy shrugged. "I don't recognize one Hindu from another. They all look the same to me."

Jeremy was uncomfortable with her bigotry. He said nothing to her and continued to look in the direction meth guy had left. He thought of Sukh, his parents, and Grampaji and how different they all were from each other.

Suddenly it occurred to Jeremy who the guy was. He was one of Sukh's cousins who he'd met at Naniji's funeral. One of the Jas's. And he was selling crystal meth? Jeremy had a sudden fear for Sukh. Would he be involved in this, too? Is that what his cousins did for a living? A meth lab? Whoa, this was really serious stuff! Jeremy tried again to see where Jas had gone, but there was no way. The streets were too crowded. He glanced around to see if he could see Sukh, but he didn't recognize anyone.

Mandy tapped him on the shoulder. "Hey, do you do crystal?" she asked.

Jeremy turned back to her and shook his head. "Naw."

"It's delightfully wicked, you know," Mandy said, and winked at him. "I think you might like it. Keeps you going for hours, if you know what I mean."

Jeremy pretended he knew what she meant and winked back. He was going to have to have a little talk with Sukh. Find out what the hell he was up to. And maybe find out what "delightfully wicked" was like.

The small group stopped walking when they came to a bus stop. Mandy reached for Jeremy's hand, held it in front of her and said, "We're going to a little party tonight. Do you want to come?"

Jeremy could think of nothing else he would do other than sit at home in front of the television wondering when his mom and Collin were coming home. "Sounds like a plan," he said.

"Good," she said. "I think we're going to meet at the school around eight o'clock. In front of the flagpole. We'll all go from there."

Jeremy looked up and down the road for their bus. On this street, there was almost always one going by, but the one Mandy said they needed to take was nowhere in sight. Her friends were idly chatting when Mandy reached into her jacket pocket and pulled out a joint. She showed it to Jeremy and asked, "You smoke?"

Jeremy looked around the crowded street. "Here?" he asked.

She laughed and lit it up. Immediately all her friends crowded around. Everyone, including Jeremy, took a couple of hits off it before Mandy took the last and stubbed it out with her foot. No one in the crowds seemed to notice or care that they were smoking pot. When their bus arrived and they boarded, Mandy sat next to him. She held his hand and began nuzzling his neck, kissing it gently. "You're cute, you know." She giggled. He was a little surprised at her boldness, but didn't want to pull away. He was even more surprised when she held his hand against her breast and whispered in his ear, "You want a little piece of this tonight?"

Jeremy felt like his hand had just touched a hot stove. His first response was to pull away, but he realized the stupidity in that. If she was offering, who was he to refuse? The public be damned, he thought. By the time they got to their stop, Mandy and Jeremy were making out on the bus. Mandy's friends tapped her on the head, giggling, to indicate that it was time to disembark. At first, Jeremy didn't know where he was. Then he recognized the block his apartment was on. He stepped off the bus holding Mandy's hand. His clothing was dishevelled. Her lip-gloss was smeared both on his lips and around her mouth. He gave her one more long kiss before she whispered to him, "See you at eight."

He nodded and she walked away with her friends. He turned and walked toward his apartment building.

By the time he got off the elevator he could hear the yelling. Something smashed. He opened the apartment door just in time to see Collin take the back of his hand and strike it across his mother's face. She fell sideways, bouncing off the coffee table on to the couch. A bottle of vodka was lying on the table, pouring its contents on the carpet. One glass lay smashed on the floor.

Before he took the key out of the lock, Jeremy yelled, "Hey!"

Collin stopped and faced him. "Leave her alone!" Jeremy yelled.

The anger on Collin's face was frightening. He first took a step toward Jeremy, then turned and went back to his mother.

He picked her up with one hand by the front of her blouse and was about to strike her again when Jeremy flew across the room and grabbed Collin's hand with both of his. "Leave her alone!" he yelled again.

"Stay out of this, kid," Collin hollered. "It doesn't concern you!" He tried to shake Jeremy off of his arm.

When Jeremy refused to let go, Collin released his mother, turned his left hand into a fist, swung it around and clocked Jeremy over his right eye. Immediately Jeremy saw tiny little lights floating around his head. He felt immense pain as his legs buckled and he sank to the floor.

Then he saw only darkness and felt relief from the sickening pain.

36
Ashley

"Hi, Kyle!"

Cassidy turned to face the very feminine, flirtatious voice that had just addressed her boyfriend. An attractive, dark haired girl waved at Kyle, who sat astride his motorcycle. He blushed, answered, "Hi, Ashley!" and averted his attention to the mud on the ground. Ashley's smile froze when she looked at Cassidy, who smiled back. Eyebrows raised, Cassidy turned back to face Kyle, wondering why he was blushing.

"Who's that?" she asked.

"Ashley?" he answered too quickly. "Just a girl."

Cassidy stood beside Kyle and his bike, rubbing her hands together to warm them. "Duh!" she responded patronizingly. "I can see she's a girl. Who *is* she?"

His gaze still riveted on the mud, he answered, "She's Mark's sister. You know, Mark, number thirty-six." He lifted his head to search the other riders for number thirty-six. "Over there." He nodded in the direction of a young man astride a black, white and red motorcycle. He went back to staring at the fascinating mud.

Cassidy had met Mark earlier that morning. He was one of the contestants in Kyle's races. He was good, but so far Kyle was better. In fact, Kyle was definitely the contender to beat in this first annual Christmas motocross event, The Chris Cross, in Mission. Kyle had heard about the new event while he was at a race in Kamloops in the fall. It was down on the Coast and ordinarily his parents wouldn't have been able to attend; the Christmas holiday was his dad's busiest time at work. Luckily, though, Mr. Lockett and Bear had a volunteer firemen's training session near Mission and offered to take Kyle for a few days. There was room in Bear's truck and it was still Winter Break from school, so Cassidy was invited to come watch. She hadn't been to the Coast in years and planned to go, after the race, to the huge shopping mall near the track, much bigger than anything in their small town.

But this girl, or more specifically Kyle's *reaction* to this girl, interested her. Kyle had spent many weekends away at events. If this girl had been with her brother before, could something have gone on between them, Cassidy wondered. Kyle sure was acting suspicious. He was finding the mud far too interesting, avoiding eye contact with her. And Ashley was attractive. Very attractive. Cassidy turned back to see where the girl had gone and was astonished that she hadn't moved. She was standing in the same spot, her eyes riveted on Kyle.

Cassidy nudged Kyle. "She's staring at you," she whispered.

Kyle looked back at Ashley. His face turned a deeper shade of red as he put on his helmet and visor. His gloved hands struggled with the ring that held the strap in place. Cassidy tapped his fumbling fingers away and tightened the strap for him. Even with her standing face to face with him, he wouldn't make eye contact with her.

Oh my! How much more obvious could he look? Kyle was actually squirming. It was almost funny. She wanted to get to the bottom of this. Putting her hand on Kyle's, she asked, "Did something happen between you two?"

"What are you talking about?" Kyle looked stricken; he forced his eyes wide and faced her.

The crackling of the public address system interrupted their conversation. Kyle's event was about to begin and the riders were to report to the starting line. The huge and obvious sigh of relief that escaped him convinced Cassidy he was hiding something. She tried to look into his eyes for the truth, but even through the visor he avoided her gaze. Later, she thought; we'll talk about this later.

"Kiss for luck!" she called. She blew him a kiss as he stood up and pushed down sharply with his heel on the kickstart. Instantly, the rattle of the engine pressed on their eardrums. Light grey exhaust assailed Cassidy's nostrils. Kyle revved the accelerator and took off to join the other racers.

Glancing back to see if Ashley was still there, Cassidy wasn't surprised that the dark-haired girl had watched Kyle leave. Then Ashley turned to stare — more like glare — at her. *I think* I *should be glaring at* you, *girl,* Cassidy thought as she walked to find a seat in the grandstand. But as she sat and waited for the race to begin, she wondered why she wasn't angry. She should be mad, jealous, resentful! But she felt none of those things. Cassidy looked across the stands at Ashley. She wondered if the girl would root for Kyle to win or would cheer for her brother. As she watched her, Ashley lifted her hand to her lips and blew a kiss at one of the racers. Cassidy's eyes opened wide. Was that for her brother? Not likely. Cassidy looked at the group of riders. Kyle was facing the stands. Ashley had just blown a kiss at Kyle!

Now she was convinced that something had happened during the summer. Kyle never mentioned an Ashley until just now. Yet here was Ashley, blowing him a kiss. Something had surely happened last summer and she could hardly wait to confront Kyle about it. Cassidy tapped her foot on the floor to ease her impatience and discontent. She had every right to be angry. She should be livid . . . why didn't she feel livid?

She sighed. She'd gone ballistic when she saw Jeremy with Kendra, and Jeremy wasn't even her boyfriend. Why did she feel nothing when she was almost sure Kyle had kissed Ashley — maybe even more than kissed her? Why did she feel . . . indifferent? The only thing that made her angry was the fact that Kyle had kept a secret from her — a secret about another girl.

Oh, but she should talk. Hadn't she kept the fact from Kyle that she and Jeremy had spent that afternoon at the pond? She could justify it by saying it was a goodbye kiss, but in reality it had been a kiss of passion, a kiss she'd wanted to go further. While she lay on the ground with Jeremy that day, she had wanted to go all the way. To give her entire self to Jeremy. She had realized later that she was saving herself for *Jeremy*. She had been just as deceitful to Kyle as he must have been to her. Guilt started to press on her conscience. Shame made her blush. But anger? No anger.

It was a cold engine start. Cassidy watched Kyle's hands on his helmet, waiting for the starter pistol to crack, then in an instant he kick started his machine. Then he and twenty other racers bolted for the coveted "holeshot." As usual Kyle got it, the lead spot on the narrow track.

Cassidy held her breath as she watched him. Only she knew why Kyle was so fearless: because he eluded death. And he always would unless Sukh and Jeremy were with them. During every race, Cassidy wondered what reckless move he would make. He already had the nickname "Suicide Aspen". His reputation was growing among the contenders. Some of them thought he must have a high pain threshold. Others felt he'd become too good too fast to know any better and that his time would come.

Only Cassidy knew the truth. He thought he was invincible . . . because he was. Every time Cassidy thought about it, she wondered again if Sukh, Kyle and Jeremy were right. Were they really invincible when they were apart? Kyle tried to prove it every day. Cassidy never tried proving it once. Just the thought of it creeped her out. She reached into her jeans' pocket and pulled out the marble she'd found in her bag last summer; she was never without it anymore. She crossed her fingers, looked up to the sky and made a silent prayer to her Atomic Structure God, who she'd nicknamed Atom. As she fingered the marble she prayed to Him, as she'd done regularly ever since the last day the friends had been altogether at her house.

They were well into the race and Kyle had a good lead, at first. Rain throughout the afternoon had soaked the track, turning it into a slippery mess. Twice Kyle had almost lost his balance trying to keep the wheels from slipping into a rut and sliding down the edge of a hill. It had cost him a good lead. His thoughts kept wandering and he found it difficult to force them back to the race. *Not today,* he thought. *Not now. Don't think about Ashley and Cassidy sitting in the same stands.* Fear gnawed at his heart. Why did Ashley blow him a kiss? Cassidy might have seen. He'd just tell her it had been meant for someone else. How did he get himself into this mess? Cassidy was the love of his life. But Ashley was so hot . . . and she was so much like him. She was fun, reckless, free-spirited. Cassidy was so fearful. *Don't think about it. Not now.*

The next hill had a sharp turn, Kyle knew, and a steep grade down its backside. He couldn't miss the top. Slipping down that hill would cost him the race. He'd never be able to pull the bike up in time to be a contender. Out of the corner of his right eye he saw the front wheel of another bike pulling up beside him. *Can't play it safe now.* He revved the accelerator.

He needed to get farther ahead of this rider to make the sharp right turn in the track on the other side of the hill. The bike beside him revved harder. Both bikes sped neck and neck to the top of the hill. "They don't call me Suicide Aspen for nothing," Kyle said quietly. He thought again of Ashley. She was the one who'd given him the nickname, that night last summer when they lay outside under the stars. He gave the accelerator a bigger turn and the bike pulled ahead.

Too fast. He knew almost instantly there would be no way he could clear the mound and make the sharp turn. At the crest of the hill, his front wheel turned too late. The back wheel, supporting most of the weight, pulled him down to the basin of the knoll. *Damn!* He missed the turn and was now off the track. At least he had managed to keep the bike upright. He'd lost valuable seconds, but was still in good position to continue. Kyle looked up to see who'd tried to pull up beside him and now had the lead. Mark. But he, too, had tried to go too fast up the hill, trying to keep up with Kyle. His bike had missed the turn entirely and was coming right down into the same valley Kyle was in! Right at him!

Kyle was about to be T-boned, but the front wheel wasn't going to hit his bike — it was going to hit his leg! He had no chance to lift his leg to safety before he felt the full weight of the motorbike, the rider and the force of the motorcycle's speed collide with the side of his right leg.

Unbelievable pain! The wind had been pounded out of his lungs. He fell to the side, his bike falling on top of him and the other bike and rider on top of that. He tried to put down his hand to brace his fall, but as soon as he touched the dirt he felt his wrist crack. Further agony.

He closed his eyes, hoping to miss what was happening. Wait until the dust settles, he thought. Go with the movement. By the time he stopped moving, his face and mouth were buried in the dirt. He lifted his head, spat out mud and looked around. His wrist was killing him. His knee was worse. He wanted to throw up; the pain was excruciating.

Mark was able to stand without difficulty. He was apologizing. He tried to lift his own bike off the tangle first, then tried lifting Kyle's. That movement alone was enough to elicit a scream of pain from Kyle. Race officials came running. Crashes were common at these races, but agonized screams from contestants were not. The first man to reach him asked where it hurt but Kyle couldn't talk. He wanted to say, "Everywhere!" but he knew he'd have to be more specific. It hurt to breathe. He felt a sharp, jabbing pain in his side in addition to the pain from his knee and wrist. Finally he did whisper, "Everywhere."

From the unnatural angle at which his leg was bent and twisted, the official knew Kyle's injuries were serious. He waved for help and spoke into his walkie-talkie. The first aid attendants were to bring the stretcher. Kyle would have to be transported to a hospital.

Cassidy had stood up as soon as Kyle was hit. She watched him go down and knew immediately that this was serious. So did the spectators. A collective moan echoed through the grandstand. She followed the first aid attendants as far as they'd let her and stood at the ropes waiting for Kyle to come out of the cordoned-off area. They were taking a long time to move him. How badly was he hurt? She tried to see if Kyle was moving, but too many people blocked her view. Twice she tried to duck underneath the ropes and twice an official stepped in front of her and blocked her. Ashley was standing beside her, but Cassidy was too frantic to talk. She wished Mr. Lockett and Bear were there, but they were hours from coming back. How could she get in touch with them? She was so scared for Kyle. She was so scared for herself. Her feelings swung from fear to anger to fear within seconds. *Why, Kyle? Why did you do it?* Her thoughts kept going back to the summer, when Kyle got his new bike. When he took her for the ride. When he scared her. How badly she wanted to tell him now, "I knew it! Just because we can't die doesn't mean we can't get hurt!"

By the time they were able to get Kyle to the ambulance, Cassidy was sobbing. She didn't know what to do. She told an official that she had to stay with him, that she and Kyle weren't from around here, that their parents were hundreds of miles away and their guardians weren't expected back for a while yet. The official took some information from her and spoke to the ambulance drivers, who reluctantly allowed her to go to the hospital with them.

The last thing Cassidy heard before she climbed into the ambulance was the concerned voice on the loud speaker. If Ken Lockett was on the premises, would he please report to the officiating area?

37
Rosary

JEREMY AWOKE TO A ROOM DARK except for the glowing computer monitor. It took him a few moments to realize where he was and a few more to realize what had happened. His forehead above his right eye hurt. His stomach hurt. He felt like vomiting. He took two deep breaths and felt he might black out again. Someone had laid him on the couch and thrown a blanket over him, but he was sure he was alone in the apartment's living room. His first thought was his mother. Was she okay? Then he realized that it wouldn't have been Collin who covered him with a blanket.

He tried to stand. Dizziness overcame him and he sat back down, a low moan escaping his mouth. He *was* going to vomit. Again he tried to stand and, disregarding his dizziness, wove his way to the bathroom where he emptied his stomach into the toilet. He moaned again and washed his mouth out in the sink. In the mirror above the sink he saw the huge red and purple bruise, with a deep cut, on his eyebrow. Someone had cleaned most of the blood off, but he noticed there was still some dried blood on his chin.

"How are you?"

Jeremy whirled around to face his mother in the bathroom doorway.

Before he could answer, she said, "Collin is very sorry. He just lost his temper."

Jeremy repeated what she said silently to himself, trying to understand. Aloud he said, "Collin is very sorry? He just lost his temper? That's all you have to say?"

She leaned against the door, hugging herself. She said nothing. Jeremy could see that she too had a bruise, on her cheek. That's when he remembered the creep had hit them both.

"Where the hell is he?" Jeremy asked.

"In bed. Sleeping it off," she answered.

Jeremy was incredulous. "He's here? You didn't throw him out? What the hell is the matter with you?"

She turned away and walked into the dark living room. She didn't turn on a light, but sat on a chair near the window and looked out to the dark street. Slowly Jeremy followed her. He stood beside her. "Why do you live like this?"

She continued to look outside. "Like what?"

Jeremy crouched down to be at eye level with her. "Like this! With a guy who hits you."

"You make it sound like he does it all the time. He doesn't," she said.

Jeremy wanted to shake his head, but was scared any movement would cause him throbbing pain. He tried to recognize this woman, his mother, this stranger. Wasn't once enough? "Has he done this before?"

She didn't answer him. She continued to look out the window.

Jeremy looked past her to the streets below. It couldn't be very late: pedestrians were still coming home from work or going to the small local markets. He put his hand on her lap. It was the only physical connection he'd made with his mother since she left him and his dad so many years ago. He wanted her to know he cared for her. That somebody did.

She looked at Jeremy's hand on her lap. Very slowly she touched it with her hand and even more slowly, she held it. But she said nothing.

"You don't have to put up with this crap, Mom," he told her.

She smiled. "You sound like he does this all the time. He really doesn't, you know."

Jeremy sighed. "Why don't you call the police?" he asked.

"The police?" She looked at him with wide eyes and shook her head. "Oh, no. Not the police."

"Why not the police?" Jeremy wanted to do something. He didn't want Collin here anymore. Not if he couldn't trust him.

"I . . . I just don't think it's such a big deal. He was really mad at me. You know, I don't really blame him." She squeezed his hand tighter.

Jeremy squeezed her hand back. "What could you do to make him that angry?" he asked.

She sighed. He could tell she wasn't going to tell him. Was it because she hadn't really made him angry, that Collin had just flown off the handle, or was it because she was genuinely ashamed of whatever she'd done?

"Never mind," she answered.

He still didn't want Collin living there. "Well he hit me, too, and I didn't do anything to make him mad. *I* should call the police. He assaulted me."

She looked at him. "Now, don't you be going and doing that," she said, annoyed. "It was really no big deal."

Jeremy was taken aback. If she knew what his head felt like, she wouldn't be saying it was no big deal. His bruise and cut hurt like hell. "It *is* a big deal. We could charge him with assault and he wouldn't be able to hurt you or me again."

His mother stood and faced him with her finger pointed into his face. Sternly she said, "Do not call the police about this, Jeremy. I mean it. I do not want Collin getting any hassle from the police. Let it go."

Suddenly, like a slap in the face Jeremy realized how little she cared for her own son. It didn't matter that Collin had hurt him. He could have killed him. This man had knocked him out, but that did not seem to matter to his mother. Instead of calling an ambulance when she saw her son unconscious, she had decided to tuck her precious Collin into bed. *He's sleeping it off! What kind of a mother would allow her own child, her only child, to be harmed by a man?* The revelation hurt. Really hurt. She had left them so long ago and, while Jeremy had pined for her return, he now realized that he had wasted too much time wanting her back. What kind of a mother was she?

He had to get out of there. Away from her and that bully, Collin. What would Collin do next? Should he wait and find out? Forget it. He walked toward the door. As he reached for his jacket he heard her call, "Jeremy, it's not a big deal. I can handle this. Lots of men lose their temper and hit the closest person to them. It doesn't mean they hate them." Desperately, she called out one more time: "Lots of men do it!"

After he opened the door, he turned back and looked at her. "Dad never did. You left a life with me and Dad for a better one, I thought. And now you're telling me we made you so unhappy that you think *this* is better? We weren't bad. It's just you . . . you're pathetic."

He slammed the door behind him.

The streets were dark and wet. A light drizzle sprayed Jeremy's face, cooling the bruise on his forehead, but making the cut sting. He didn't know where to go. He missed home and his dad. He missed Sukh, Kyle and Cassidy. He'd never felt so alone. So lost. He looked up the street at the people in dark coats trying to dodge him. He turned and looked down the street. Then he began to walk, slowly.

People with a place to go streamed past him. Seeing them made him feel even lonelier. A car horn blasted beside him as he tried to cross a side street on a red light. It made Jeremy jump, but he kept walking. He didn't know where he was going until he came to a small old church, its parking lot full of cars. The carved wooden sign above the front steps said St. Luke's Roman Catholic Church. Without a pause, Jeremy walked up the steps, two at a time, and walked through the front doors.

The smell of incense, years and years of it permeating the walls, assailed his nostrils. It reminded him of the little church in the Cariboo. Parishioners, their backs to Jeremy, were standing and reciting the "Our Father" with the priest. He looked at the dark pews at the back of the church and noticed an old woman kneeling alone, whispering prayers with her rosary. Turning, Jeremy knew the Holy Water would be near the entrance and, finding the small cup attached to the wall, he touched his right hand to the water and made the sign of the cross. Then he walked to the end of the old woman's pew and knelt to genuflect. She moved in toward the middle without looking at him. Kneeling beside her, he put his head into his folded hands, careful to avoid the bruise on his forehead.

Then he finally allowed himself to weep.

Silent tears wet his eyes and fingers, the only indication of his pain being the sniffling sounds he made as his nose began to run. He listened to the priest, now at the end of the mass, request that parishioners "Go in peace." He heard the recessional hymn and listened to the quiet rustling of gowns as priest and altar boys slowly walked past him. He didn't notice when the church became quiet. He didn't notice that he'd stopped crying.

What startled him was the smell of wax as the candles, one by one, were snuffed out.

He lifted his head to see the priest, wearing dark pants, black shirt and white collar, walking past the altar. Jeremy knew the priest wouldn't hurry him out of this sanctuary. Even though he hadn't prayed and he'd missed most of the service, he did feel peace. He could go now. He made one more sign of the cross, stood and noticed something lying beside him on the pew. It was the rosary the old woman had been holding, praying with, when he sat down. Jeremy picked it up and looked around the old church to see if the woman was still there. She was gone. Instantly, memories of Opa and Oma Lockett flooded his head. He couldn't know for sure whether or not the old woman wanted him to have the rosary, but he assumed she had. He wouldn't give it to the priest for the lost and found box. He slipped the rosary into his pocket, rubbed the denim to make sure it was secure, and left the church.

Outside, the drizzle had turned to rain. He walked back up the road from where he'd come. He realized then that he was homeless. He had no refuge in this wilderness, the city. If he were in the Cariboo forest, he could survive. He could hunt, fish, build a shelter. But here in the city? This was a whole new jungle, one that Jeremy was sure he couldn't survive in alone.

Not wanting to go too far without knowing where he'd end up, he stopped in front of a public phone and leaned against it. He searched his pockets for some loose change, then dialled the operator to help him make a long distance call.

After three rings, an answering machine picked up. He listened to Mrs. Lockett's grandmother-voice telling him, in her German accent, that no one was home right now, but to leave a name and number. He had no number, not anymore, but he still had a name. Fighting back tears, he said: "Hi . . . Oma. This is Jeremy."

He tried to think of what he could say. *I hurt and I need a hug?* No. *I miss my dad and I want to come home . . . but not if Bernadette is still there?* No. *My mom is pathetic and I finally realized it?* No. He needed someone to love him right now. He needed his friends, who'd all but forsaken him since they'd discovered their destinies. Damn their destiny. *Why can't we be like everybody else and never know who we're going to be with on our last day?*

More tears welled up in his eyes. He looked up to face the rain that began to spill from the sky. Crying seemed so much easier to do in the rain. "Why aren't you there, Oma?" he asked the answering machine. He wanted to — had to — talk to Opa . . . tell him about his life since the snowmobile accident . . . something he promised his friends he'd never do. But there was nobody there for him. He hung up the phone.

Jeremy looked at the clock on the wall of a grocery store. It was only seven o'clock. He picked up the phone again and made a local call. The person who answered couldn't speak English and reminded him of Grampaji. He asked to speak to Sukhwinder. Jeremy wondered what Sukh's name was in Punjabi because whoever answered the phone acted as though he had no idea who Jeremy wanted. Finally, after first talking to one of the Jas's, he got Sukh.

"Hey, Bud!" Sukh sounded sincerely happy to hear from him.

"Hey," said Jeremy. "Want to go to a party tonight?"

"You know me," he answered, "I'm always in for a party. Where?"

"Here, in Vancouver. Can you get a ride?" Jeremy waited while Sukh called to someone. Jeremy heard a muffled conversation.

"Yeah, but I have to do a little something around midnight. Is that okay?"

Jeremy released a sigh of relief. "You can do anything you want around midnight, my friend." He told Sukh how to get to the school flagpole and to be there at eight o'clock. Then he hung up the phone, walked to the nearest store for cigarettes and went to the school to wait for Mandy and her gang.

He sat on the ground under a covered door, leaning against the school. By the time Sukh got there, five butts lay on the ground beside him. A small security light glowed above him. His eye was swollen but not shut, and a dark purple half-moon coloured his lower lid. He was happy to see Sukh and hugged him. Sukh's first question was, "What the hell happened to you?"

Jeremy touched his forehead. The cut, still oozing a little blood, felt sticky. He probably should have gotten some stitches. Jeremy just laughed and said, "You should see the other guy." He had shared so much with his greatest friend, but he just couldn't bring himself to tell Sukh what had happened. And he knew Sukh wouldn't pry.

Changing the subject, he asked, "So, how's your new school? Any hotties?"

Sukh followed the cues and said, "What school?"

Jeremy groaned with a smile on his face. "You're not going to school? What the hell's wrong with you, man? C'mon Sukh, you got to go to school."

Even in the dark, Jeremy could see Sukh's big smile. "Who says I got to go to school? My mom and dad have gone to India for three months so they aren't here to make me, and my uncles and aunts don't know better. They think I'm going, but I'm not. I don't think any of my cousins finished school — well, except for Jaskirat. He's at university now, going to be a doctor. And

Raveena. And, I guess, Gurinderpal, too. Okay, just two of the Jas' didn't finish."

Jeremy could hear young voices getting closer. It must be Mandy and her friends. "What do you do all day?" he asked Sukh.

Sukh winked at him. "I could tell you, but then . . . "

" . . . you'd have to . . . I know." They both laughed.

Mandy stepped off the sidewalk, walked over to Jeremy and gave him a long, lingering kiss. It wasn't until after she stopped that she noticed his forehead and eye. "Oooooh," she said. "What happened, Jeremy? Did you get in a fight?"

Jeremy laughed weakly. "Me? I'm a lover, not a fighter." He pulled her back to him and gave her a gentle kiss on her forehead. "Haven't you noticed that about me, yet?" He looked at Sukh and winked. Then he introduced them. Mandy was polite enough, but Jeremy sensed she was tense. He didn't care what she felt about his best friend with the brown skin. Tonight, he needed to have Sukh around.

By the time they got to the party, Sukh had fit right in with the little crowd. Loud music blared halfway down the street from the little house in east Vancouver. Kids were everywhere: standing on the front stoop, smoking in the front yard, inside every room in the house. Jeremy recognized a number of people from his school. There were some very attractive girls who gave Sukh the once over and smiled invitingly at him. Sukh was glad to be there.

Just before midnight, Sukh walked up to Jeremy with his arms around two of the prettiest girls in the house and said he was going, but he'd be back. He kissed both girls and left. Jeremy acknowledged his departure, feeling lost and lonely, then turned his attention back to Mandy, who'd spent most of the night sitting on his lap making out with him.

He had no life that he could speak of, no family, no home, and his head hurt like hell, so he smoked and drank and swallowed anything that was offered him by Mandy and her friends. Half the things he was sure he'd never heard of. But he didn't care. Even if he wanted to kill himself, he knew it would be impossible. Sukh, Cassidy and Kyle weren't there. He was invincible. Kyle proved it. Kyle, his old buddy, proved they couldn't die unless the four of them were together. He could take any drug in the world and not overdose. How frustrating to feel like killing yourself, but not be able to.

At one point, another girl more wasted than he was sat beside him and flirted with him. Jeremy didn't remember this girl from school. She looked wild: tattoos all over her neck and a pierced tongue and nose. She had a cute face, even though she wore tons of makeup mostly around her eyes. Her pierced nose reminded him of Cassidy. *Cassidy*. His heart lurched. How he missed his Cassidy. What would she think of him now? Would she be disappointed in him? Of course she would. Again. *Oh, Cassidy, I'm sorry.*

He got up and found it difficult to stand. He had succeeded in getting wasted, stoned, polluted. Mandy stood and leaned into him possessively. She looked back at the girl with the tattoos and made a face at her. "He's mine, bitch."

Jeremy whistled. "Easy, Mandy," he slurred. "There's enough of me for both of you." He tried to walk as straight as possible and find the washroom. He didn't really have to go, but he needed to get off the couch. The next thing he knew he was lying down on a bed in a dark bedroom. He thought of his forehead and was surprised at how much better it felt. Must be the drugs he'd smoked. He wondered what they were.

Someone was pulling off his shirt. Someone else was giggling. Someone was sitting on him, straddling him. He felt lips touching his. Someone was undoing the button of his jeans. Lips were touching his chest. He thought of Cassidy, when they'd kissed in the pond; when she'd traced the drop of water down his chest. He thought about how much he wanted her then. How much he wanted her now. He thought about how good he felt — this felt. He was lying beside Cassidy at the secret spot. He was looking into her eyes. He was kissing her. Holding her. Whispering to her. She felt so good. He felt so good. This . . . felt . . . so . . . good. He thought he was going to explode.

Then, nothing.

38
More Business

EVEN IN THE CAR, SUKH WAS freezing. What was it with this city, he wondered? It was not even below zero outside and yet it always felt so cold. No matter how many clothes he wore the dampness went right through him and chilled him to his bones.

It was dark under the bridge beside the Fraser River. Jaspal was in the driver's seat and Jaswinder always got the passenger seat. Rookies got the backseat, they joked to him. He didn't mind the back, but he minded the cold.

"Could you please turn up the heat?" he asked.

"Man, cousin, you are a wimp. I thought it gets to be, like, negative forty degrees where you come from. How come you can't handle this?" said Jaspal.

Jaswinder laughed.

"How long we got to wait?" asked Sukh. "It's almost two in the morning."

Jaspal's smile faded. "We wait until they come."

Jaswinder turned down the CD for the next song. Ordinarily they liked to play their music booming loud but tonight they didn't want to attract attention.

Sukh rested his head on the back of the seat. He was tired and bored. This was getting to be boring business. He wished he was back at the party with Jeremy. Now, that was fun. Lots of hot girls. Lots of people his own age. That was the one thing he missed about not going to school anymore. All the kids. Oh well, at least he was making money. He looked up and down the road to see if a car was coming. Nothing. Maybe he could fall asleep for just a second.

He might have drifted off for a few moments, but he sat up straight when Jaswinder turned off the CD player and said, "Here comes someone."

Sure enough, Sukh could see headlights moving slowly down the street. The car came to a stop in an empty lot a few hundred feet in front of their car. Sukh switched on the police scanner and held it close to his ear. Immediately, Jaspal and Jaswinder opened their doors and walked out to meet the occupants of the vehicle. Sukh's instructions were to stay in the car. His job was to watch and listen to the scanner for any trouble, but he couldn't participate in any transactions and he wasn't necessarily supposed to hear their conversation. The less he knew, the less the cops or . . . whoever . . . could interrogate him. He didn't much care. He would sit back and think about the party he was missing and hope that those two gorgeous girls were still there when he got back.

He reached forward and turned the CD player back on but quietly so as not to interfere with any dialogue from the scanner. Anything was better than watching four people talking when you couldn't hear what they were saying. A few minutes went by. Sukh noticed that his cousins' body language, and their acquaintances', was getting tense. He could hear the occasional shout; their hands were gesticulating wildly. He sat up and cracked his window slightly to try to hear something. Nothing but a few swear words.

Finally his cousins turned and walked with long, angry strides toward the car. The two men they'd been talking to got in their own car, slammed the doors and peeled out angrily.

When his cousins opened the car doors, Sukh was forced to listen to numerous epithets in both English and Punjabi. Something was obviously wrong, but he knew better than to ask. Odds were that they wouldn't tell him, or they'd get even angrier trying to explain to him what happened. If he gave them some time to cool off he might be able to go back to the party.

As they drove along the city streets, his cousins quieted. "Now what?" Jaspal asked.

Jaswinder looked at him, shrugged and suggested, "We give them a few hours. They've got our cell number. They'll call."

Sukh groaned. A few hours? "Well . . . then . . . " he ventured, "can I go back to the party?"

Jaspal looked at Jaswinder. "I don't see why not. What else is there to do?" He glanced back at Sukh and said sternly, "You just better be ready to go when we honk!"

Whatever you want, Sukh thought. "Yeah, sure."

By the time they got back to the house party, the front yard was empty. They dropped him off and promised to return shortly, but reminded him to be ready when they honked. Sukh walked into the living room and found that most of the kids still there were pretty tanked. He smelled all types of smoke. Liquor was spilled on the carpet. One girl was throwing up in the toilet. The two girls that he'd met earlier were nowhere to be seen and he couldn't see Jeremy.

He began opening doors. In one bedroom he found a group of people smoking something from a bong. In another he saw somebody about to inject something into his arm. The third room was dark. By the hallway light, Sukh could see a pile of clothes on the floor and a few bodies on the bed. He wondered if one of the girls was Mandy. It kind of looked like her. Who was the guy? He almost looked dead — very grey anyway, or was he green? The room was too dark. He switched on a lamp.

If it weren't for the nasty bruise on the guy's head, Sukh never would have realized that the naked guy sleeping between two naked chicks was his best friend Jeremy.

39
Iniquity

From far away, he could hear voices. Someone was shaking him. *Sukh?* He could hear Sukh's voice. He opened his eyes. He squinted; the light was too bright. Sukh's face was over him. Jeremy could feel someone lying next to him. He sat up. He was naked. There were two girls, also naked, one on each side of him. Who were they? Mandy? Tattoo Girl? What had he done?

He shook his head and felt the throbbing, searing pain in his forehead. He looked at Sukh. "Where's Cassidy?" Jeremy asked.

"Cassidy? Where do you think she is? She's up north, man." Sukh wasn't smiling.

Jeremy groaned and held his head. He fell back onto the bed, gripping his fingertips to his forehead. He squeezed his eyes tight to block out the light and still the pain.

Sukh shook his shoulder. "Come on, man. Look at you. Who are these chicks?" Jeremy wouldn't open his eyes. He couldn't talk. He hurt too much.

Sukh shook him again. "Jeremy, what did you take?"

Jeremy didn't say anything. What did he take? How the hell should he know? He felt better before. Now he was in agony.

He wanted to feel good again. "I don't know," he muttered. His throat was hoarse. Must be from all the smoke.

Sukh was shaking his head. He leaned very close to Jeremy and said, "In the business, we have a saying: Users are losers. And they don't make any money. Stay off the shit, Jeremy!" A car horn sounded outside, two short blasts and one long one. Sukh stood up to look out the bedroom window. He turned back to Jeremy and said, "I've got to go. Get home, Jeremy. I love ya, man!" And he was gone.

Jeremy sat up again. He opened his eyes and noticed, really noticed, that he was naked. Where were his clothes? The bedroom door opened and in walked one of Mandy's friends carrying a bong. She knelt on the bed and held it to Jeremy, flicking her lighter. Was that what made him feel better before? He took one more long blast and fell back onto the bed. Then he closed his eyes.

And did not remember anything else.

40
Bang!

SUKH STEPPED OUT OF THE HOUSE. He didn't want to leave Jeremy looking like that, but he didn't even want to think about what his cousins would do to him if he wasn't ready to go right away. The car was waiting across the street. He had to go.

His long legs took the three stairs in one step. One last glance at the house was all he could offer his best friend. *Bye, Jeremy, and please go home where you're safe,* he thought. *You look like crap.* Sukh promised himself that he'd phone Jeremy in the morning, just to make sure he got home okay.

The house was on a quiet street; at this time of the night, traffic was nonexistent. "Let's go!" Jaspal called to him.

Sukh ran the short distance and was just reaching for the door handle when he heard a vehicle approaching from behind him. A car? He was sure he hadn't seen any headlights when he crossed the road. Why did he hear a car?

He glanced to his left. Sure enough, with the help of the streetlights he saw a small car heading toward them with its headlights off. Sukh was lifting the handle of the driver's side back door when he heard a loud "Pop!" He turned to see where it came from. At the same instant that he saw a small white car drive past him a searing pain ran through his back and ribs.

Somebody in the back seat of the little white car was holding what looked like a sawed off shotgun, an alley sweeper, and was pointing it directly at him and his cousins.

"Duck!" Jaspal called to him as they attempted to lie down in the car seats.

Duck? Where am I supposed to duck? Another popping sound. *That doesn't sound like a gun,* he thought. It sounded like a toy. He felt a stabbing pain in the back of his leg. Reaching for his hamstring, he collapsed to the pavement. What was hurting his leg and back so badly? Had he been shot? He couldn't believe it! Something on his pant leg felt sticky and wet. Blood? It must be blood! He'd been shot. Twice. *Oh, please no.*

His cousin called to him, "Get in the car! Sukh, get in the car!"

On his knees he tried to pull the back door open, noticing three tiny new holes in the car's rear quarter panel. As he tried to lift his body onto the seat, he heard the white car speed off. Jaswinder pulled Sukh's arm to try to get him in swiftly. Sukh screamed. "No!" he yelled. "Leave me alone!"

A few people from the party house came out onto the lawn. He tried again to get into the backseat, but instead slipped into a sitting position on the pavement. There was no way. He leaned against Jaspal's car. It was no use. It hurt too much for him to get inside. Jaswinder jumped out and came running around the car to see Sukh while Jaspal called 911. He heard Jaspal's frantic voice ordering an ambulance.

"Oh, my God!" screamed Jaswinder when he saw the blood on Sukh's hand. He took off his jacket and draped it over Sukh's shoulders. Then he tried to put him into a prone position. "Hold on, Cousin. An ambulance is on its way."

Sukh lay on his side on the cold, wet pavement. He was shivering. *This can't be happening,* he thought. He could feel grit on his cheek and moved his hand to separate his head from the blacktop. His bracelet, now as cold as the ground, pressed against his cheek. He thought about how cold he'd felt in the car earlier. That was nothing compared to the chills he felt now. This damned city! It was always so wet and cold.

A siren. He could hear a siren. More sirens. From two different directions. He could see the reflections on the wet pavement of blinking blue and red lights. The police. The police? He wanted an ambulance. *Please tell me there's an ambulance coming,* he thought.

He knew he couldn't die. Cassidy and Kyle weren't here. He wanted to tell his frenetic cousins not to worry. He wasn't going to die. It was impossible for him to die. He opened his mouth to speak, but the pain was too great to talk. He closed his mouth. He closed his eyes. *Just for a minute,* he thought. *I'll sleep just for a minute. By the time I wake up, maybe the ambulance will be here.* He did not want to feel pain any more.

He just wanted . . . a little . . . sleep.

41
Emergency

THE EMERGENCY BAY DOORS OPENED JUST as the ambulance attendants approached with Kyle's gurney. Cassidy ran behind, carrying his helmet. She'd stopped crying hours ago at the first hospital Kyle was taken to. The doctors there recommended that Kyle go to Children's Hospital, an hour's ride away, where they were more prepared to set Kyle's leg because surgery was recommended. Mr. Lockett and Bear still hadn't caught up to them, and with each passing moment Cassidy felt more overwhelmed by her responsibilities.

One of the attendants directed her toward the admitting desk so she could give as much information as possible without Kyle's medical card. He was taken through two doors, out of her sight. She asked the woman behind the desk if she could phone Kyle's parents. They told her they would. She walked back to try to get through the doors through which Kyle had just disappeared, but a nurse there asked her to stay in the waiting room. She sat down and tried to take a deep breath to still her shaking hands.

Minutes ticked by. She wondered if she could see Kyle. A nurse came through the emergency area and Cassidy asked her if she could go in. The nurse suggested she wait; Kyle was going to get x-rays. She asked Cassidy if there was a parent or guardian nearby who could come to the hospital. Cassidy told her about Mr. Lockett and Bear, but they hadn't arrived yet.

She sat down again. More minutes ticked by. She got up and began walking around the waiting area. A number of people waited. There was a young mother holding a toddler on her lap. The little girl had cheeks as red as cherries and was sucking on a pacifier. Her nose was running and her eyes looked heavy. A man stood beside the pop machine. He was holding a newspaper open; Cassidy noticed that he was just flipping pages. A couple who appeared to be the same age as her parents sat together, holding hands. The woman was clenching a tissue and looked as though she'd been crying.

Cassidy searched her pockets for money and tried phoning her parents. No answer. She didn't trust her voice to leave a message, so she hung up. She didn't want to worry them until she knew more. She wished Mr. Lockett and Bear would hurry.

She began to chew her fingernails, something she hadn't done in years. In the distance she could hear the wail of an ambulance siren; it made her uncomfortable. It meant someone else was injured or sick or worse. That sound meant that someone's life had taken a turn for the worse, like Kyle's. That someone's life may be forever altered. Cassidy didn't want to think about it. She walked to the pop machine and considered choosing a drink. The siren sounded very close and went silent. It made her want to cry again. She took another deep breath and decided on a cola.

She couldn't stay in this room doing nothing. She had to move around. Get outside. Check the parking lot for Mr. Lockett and Bear. Anything but stay in this place. She went through the first set of doors she found, walked down a hall and went through another set. By the time she'd finished her drink, she still hadn't found the parking lot.

Suddenly a set of doors opened, letting in a rush of cold air. Two paramedics came through first, one on each side of a gurney. Cassidy could see the jet-black hair of a teenager lying on his side. Some of the sheets on the gurney were stained with fresh blood. Cassidy's stomach turned. She felt nauseous. The sight of blood suddenly made her feel sick. A woman with a clipboard asked, "Is this the gunshot victim?"

The first paramedic nodded and headed through a set of doors that Cassidy hadn't gone through yet. The sliding doors swallowed the victim and the paramedics. Cassidy knew this was not the way to the parking lot and knew she didn't want to be here, either. She turned and headed back to the waiting room just as two young Indo-Canadian men with sideburns and neatly-trimmed goatees rushed in. Their eyes were wide and full of fear. Cassidy stared. Why did they seem so familiar to her? They ran to the admitting desk and spoke frantically to the woman. She asked them questions about the injured teen.

Cassidy walked over and sat in the chair closest to the admitting desk. Who were those men? Why did she think she knew them? She overheard the woman asking their relationship to the victim, a question she'd asked Cassidy earlier. When she asked them to spell the victim's name, Cassidy's heart froze.

"S-U-K-H-W-I-N-D-E-R."

Cassidy screamed, "SUKH!"

Everyone, — the Indo-Canadian men, the admitting clerk, the people in the waiting room, the paramedics — within range of Cassidy's voice turned to look at her. She ran over to Jaspal and Jaswinder, grabbed their jacket sleeves and asked in a desperate voice, "Is that Sukh Sangera?"

Jaswinder nodded.

Jaspal stared at Cassidy, furrowed his brow. "How do you know?"

"You're . . . you're his cousins, aren't you?" Her eyes were frantic. She wouldn't let go of their jackets.

Both Jaswinder and Jaspal nodded. Jaspal looked at the frantic blonde girl and remembered. "You're the girl from the lake, aren't you? You were with Sukh in the snowmobile accident."

Cassidy nodded. She started crying again. "What happened?" She looked from one of them to the other. She shook their sleeves impatiently. "Tell me what happened to Sukh!"

Jaspal and Jaswinder looked at the floor. Guilt silenced them. Their actions had put their young cousin here. They knew the shooter had meant to kill them and not Sukh. They couldn't voice their thoughts yet, neither to each other nor to this girl.

Cassidy let go of their jackets. She remembered the woman with the clipboard asking about a shooting victim. "He was shot?" Cassidy asked.

Jaswinder and Jaspal nodded.

Cassidy turned away from them. She wanted to see Sukh. She had to see Sukh! This could *not* be happening. She ran back through the doors she'd wandered through, back to where she saw Sukh's gurney come in. She could hear the woman at the desk calling, "Young lady! Young lady, don't go in there!"

On the other side of the doors Cassidy could see curtained bays with beds and gurneys. She recognized the attendants who had pushed Sukh's gurney. They were talking to a nurse. Sukh still lay on his side, his back toward Cass. She ran to him, crying. "Sukh! Oh, Sukh."

Before anyone could stop her, she was at his side, facing him. He looked at her through dark eyes filled with pain and smiled, "Hey, Cassy. You *are* here. Jeremy was right!"

Cassidy could hear the pain and fear in his voice. She was confused by his comment, but she was more concerned about him. "Oh, Sukhy. What happened?"

Pain wiped away his smile. "I hurt, Cassy," was all she could get from him. She brushed the dark hair from his sweaty forehead.

"Who shot you?" she asked him.

Sukh tried to take a deep breath. He tried to give her his best smile. His forehead furrowed but he managed to say, "I could tell you, but then I'd have to kill you." He tried to laugh.

A doctor rushed over. He told Cassidy to leave. When she made no effort to go, he called to a paramedic and stepped between Cassidy and the gurney. He lifted the sheet off Sukh's back but stood in Cassidy's way. While he looked the injuries over, he began talking. "Hello, Sukhwinder. My name is Doctor Jenson. I'm going to take a look, okay?" She watched Sukh grimace.

Cassidy felt a tug at her arm. A paramedic was guiding her out of the area. She wanted to kiss Sukh on his forehead but it was too late. She wondered where Jeremy was and what Sukh meant by the comment, "Jeremy was right." If Jeremy were here, it meant that they'd all be together. That shouldn't happen, especially if two of them were so gravely injured.

As she was led away, she heard Sukh gasp and moan. The doctor had touched one of his wounds. Cassidy saw another doctor rush past her. "You'll be okay, Sukhy," she called, "I love you!"

Glancing to her left and right, she hoped to get a glimpse of Kyle, but he was nowhere to be seen. As she was led back toward the waiting room, tears stung her eyes. She said another silent prayer that Sukh would be okay. She hoped to see Mr. Lockett's or Bear's familiar face but, as she stepped through the next set of doors, she froze. Another gurney stood at the entrance. An ashen face rested against the pillow. Cassidy recognized the dark curls, the handsome face, the slim build. His eyes were closed.

He had a large bruise on his forehead. A tiny red slash glinted in the light. *Jeremy.*

She spoke his name in an anguished voice. "Jeremy, no." She couldn't believe it. They were all here together. They couldn't be together! She yanked her arm out of the paramedic's grip and rushed to him. His face was too pale. His lips were too blue. The bump on his forehead was purple. He wasn't responding. He didn't look at her. She touched his face.

"Jeremy," she called again. Tears streamed down her cheeks. Her voice was shaking with sobs. But Jeremy laid there, his eyes still closed. He smelled of smoke. He had no shirt on. What had happened to him? "Jeremy!" she screamed. The paramedic behind her called to someone to help him get control of this girl. She was making a scene, she knew, but she didn't care.

She tried to put her arms around Jeremy's shoulders, tried to hug him. Someone tried to stop her, but she yanked her arm away. She tried to lift Jeremy in her arms, but he was too heavy. She wanted him to lift his arms and hug her back, but his arms lay unmoving at his sides. "What's wrong with him?" she asked in an anguished voice. "Jeremy, wake up!"

Two nurses and a security guard ran in and forcibly pulled Cassidy away from the unconscious boy. She tried to pull her arms free but they were too strong. One of them said firmly, "Miss, Miss. You have to leave here."

She gave up trying to fight and allowed them to lead her toward the waiting room. Cassidy could hear the other nurse ask the ambulance attendant, "Is this the head injury?"

Cassidy looked back in time to see the attendant nod before the doors closed behind her and she was left with strangers. When they got back to the waiting room, they sat her down in a chair.

"Is he dead?" wailed Cassidy.

"No, honey," the nurse told her, still holding her down in the chair. "We have to get him some help, though. You have to stay here. Or you're going to be forced to leave the hospital."

Cassidy's breathing shallowed. They were all in the same place. Jeremy was dying. Sukh was dying. Kyle was dying. She wondered if she should leave the hospital, to stay apart, to cheat fate. The lights in the waiting room seemed to dim. She put her hands to her temples and rubbed them. She squeezed her eyes shut for a second and opened them. The room seemed to be turning. Oh, no! Please don't let me faint again, she begged her God. She had to know if Catrina and Jamieson were here! Breathless and frantic she asked the nurse, "Are there any patients here named Catrina Elsa Birgman or Jamieson Frank Otters?"

The woman looked at her as if she thought Cassidy had lost her mind. She let go of Cassidy's shoulders and motioned to the security guard to stay close by. Cassidy felt the blood drain from her head, from her neck. The room was still turning.

At that moment, the doors opened and a haggard Ken Lockett walked in. The blast of cold air attracted Cassidy's attention. She turned to look but that movement made the room spin faster. She tried to steady herself. She took a deep breath and called, "Opa!" She tried to get up, but her legs wouldn't move. They felt heavy, so heavy. The room still felt like it was moving and Opa seemed so far away. The lights dimmed again. Cassidy wondered why everyone was staring at her. Didn't they feel the world coming apart? Her head felt so light, but her legs still felt so heavy.

By the time Ken got to her, she was sliding to the ground. He caught her. Someone screamed; someone shouted that she was hyperventilating. Before Cassidy had a chance to pass out completely, someone held a small paper bag over her mouth. Opa was telling her to take deep breaths while he held her small frame in his arms. Cassidy took deep breaths into the bag and the room stopped spinning. She took more breaths and her legs felt lighter. She took one very long and steady breath and she began to cry. Opa wouldn't let go of her and held her in a hug. Bear was beside them, his large hand touching her head, so gently. She cried so hard she couldn't talk to them. Opa held her, rocking her from side to side and holding her head against his chest.

After a few moments she pulled her head off his chest to look at them.

"Jeremy, Sukh and Kyle are all here and they're all dying. And . . . " Her cheeks were soaked with tears. Her nose was running. Her eyes were red. She paused for a long moment before she continued.

"And that means I'm going to die, too!"

42
Miracle Teens

The Miracle Teens were in the news again: the "unbelievable story of tragedy and survival!" The "supernatural bond of the four star-crossed teens that continuously brought them to the brink of death"; "the ill-fated teenagers who escaped death together not once, but twice!" Skeptics believed the teens had somehow set up their accidents. Some believed they were just accident-prone. Was it coincidence? Was it happenstance? Was it contrived? The media wanted to know. And the headlines read "only the teens know for sure".

But now Opa Lockett and Bear knew. Cassidy had told them; she had to. After the hospital attendant had shown Cassidy and her guardians into a private room and after someone suggested sedating Cassidy but she refused, she told them everything. Everything she knew and how she understood it. She told them about the book or the pages or the . . . whatever it was, and about their names and the other names, and how Joseph Smith and Ann Johnson and Adam Schuler had died at the same time they were in the frozen lake. She told them the names of the people who were going to die with them, Catrina and Jamieson, and how they all agreed they'd have to stay apart to cheat fate and how it didn't seem to be working because they were all together now and that they were all going to die now, anyway . . . she left nothing out.

They had hours to talk, hours for Opa and Bear to sort through Cassidy's account of what led them to the night before, while they waited for Grampaji, Kyle's parents and Jeremy's dad to fight the treacherous winter driving conditions through the Fraser Canyon.

By the time she'd finished talking, she was remarkably calm. Her eyes were dry, but still stung from the tears she'd shed for so long. Bear agreed to stay with her while Opa went to look for information on Kyle, Sukh and especially Jeremy, the little boy he'd helped raise and who now needed him.

More hours went by. Jeremy's dad came in to sit with Cassidy. He looked very tired. He'd driven everyone down from the Cariboo, fighting snow, fog and rain. Jeremy was still unconscious. Shortly after, Grampaji and Mr. and Mrs. Aspen came in. Kyle and Sukh were out of surgery but still in recovery. They weren't awake, but they were alive. Cassidy kept wondering when they were going to die. She wondered why she felt fine, just scared and tired. How could she die when she felt perfectly fine?

Finally the doctors determined that Sukh would survive his gunshot wounds. He had some tissue and liver damage, but the beauty of the liver, they were told, was that it had the ability to regenerate itself. No other major arteries or organs were touched. His leg would have an ugly scar for the rest of his life, but, the doctor joked, he'd have quite a story to tell his grandchildren, if he improved the crowd he hung around with so he could live to *have* grandchildren.

Kyle had surgery to put a pin in his leg. In a year's time he'd have to come back down to the Coast and have the pin removed. He was fortunate that the best doctor to fix juvenile shattered bones happened to be in the hospital when he arrived. Otherwise, he might have lost the leg. His wrist was broken and cast and the cracked rib would heal on its own. He wouldn't be riding motorcycles for a very long while, he was told. Kyle snickered and told the doctor that he was right. It was winter: snowmobile season. The doctor rolled his eyes and tapped him on the top of his head with a clipboard.

Jeremy was the luckiest. The doctor had told him jokingly that, luckily for him, his best friend had been shot. If the police hadn't gone into the party to get information from witnesses, they never would have found Jeremy unconscious. The officers recognized the symptoms when they discovered him wearing the nasty bruise. The kids at the party never would have realized that his brain was bleeding inside his cracked skull and it wasn't the drugs causing his stupor. The doctors did express concern about the amount of drugs they found in his blood and special precautions — life-threatening precautions, they emphasized — had to be made in his treatment to allow time for them to dissipate from his system.

And there was no record of a Catrina Bergman or a Jamieson Otters anywhere in the hospital — not as a patient, nurse, doctor, employee or paramedic.

It was too much for Cassidy to deal with all at once. After a few days, though, when they were allowed to be together in Kyle's room, she let them have it. She started with Jeremy, blasting him for being such an idiot with drugs. She blasted Kyle for being too much of a daredevil on the motorcycle and Sukh for getting mixed up with people with guns.

She continued: "This was all your idea, you guys. You decided that we'd cheat fate, but all along, with your recklessness, we weren't cheating it at all. *We*, or should I say, *you guys* were tempting it. And because of your theories, you turned me into a basket-case. Worrying about you guys all the time. I hate this so much! I would like to beat some sense into the three of you, but by the looks of all the bandages you're wearing, your Gods got you all first!"

Each of the boys was humbled by Cassidy's words. She was right. They'd been reckless.

"I'm sorry, Cass," said Kyle. "I guess I was trying to prove I was invincible. I just kept pushing myself harder on the track thinking 'What could possibly happen to me?' I was winning. All the time. And I was actually getting a little famous." He smiled and raised his eyebrows at the boys. "It was so stupid, I know that now." He tried to hug her to him, but she pulled away from his arm.

Sukh stood, supported by crutches. It was easier for him to stand than to sit; the pressure of his leg on the stitches was too painful. "I've been pretty stupid, too," he said. "I knew my cousins were getting into all kinds of crap, guns and drugs . . . never mind what else. It seemed so cool. Once we all separated as friends, I just didn't care about school anymore. My life just became a 'what the hell?' kind of thing." He looked at the floor. He absent-mindedly twisted the Kara on his wrist. Looking back on his recent life frightened him. He did not want that life anymore.

They all looked at Jeremy. He'd probably changed the most, learned the most, hurt the most of all of them. He didn't know what to say. He lifted his head, smiled and asked, "Isn't she beautiful when she's angry?" Even Cassidy laughed as he pulled her to him and placed an exaggerated kiss on the side of her head before she could pull away.

Cassidy smiled reluctantly. "I hate this, guys. I miss you all so much and I've been so miserable. I've let myself turn into a paranoid worry-wart. I think about you guys all the time. I hate who I've become." She looked down to the bed where Kyle lay, not meeting anyone's eyes. She felt childish. Tears stung her eyes, but she wouldn't let them spill, not anymore. "I want you all back."

Sukh hobbled in closer to Cassidy. He wanted to touch her, to hold her, to show her he *was* back.

Jeremy squeezed her shoulder just as Kyle tried to sit up to touch her. "Awww, I feel a group hug coming on," Jeremy announced. He laughed as Sukh lost his balance, fell into both Cassidy and Jeremy and all three fell onto the bed, on Kyle's good leg.

Their giggles drowned out the sound of the opening door. Mr. Lockett walked in, carrying three small bouquets of flowers. He smiled when he saw them so happy for a change.

"Glad to see you all back to normal," he said.

When Cassidy saw him, she pulled out from the tangle of bodies on Kyle's bed and walked over to give him a hug. With her arms still wrapped around his waist, she said, "Guys, I have a confession to make. I told Opa."

Jeremy walked over to his Opa. He, too, gave him a hug as he asked, "Told him what?"

Cassidy looked at each of her best friends before she said, "Everything."

Silence. They'd made a pact not to tell anyone and she broke it. But she didn't care if that made them mad. She'd been left so alone by their foolishness. If it weren't for her confession to Bear and Opa and their consolation, she would have had a mental breakdown.

A huge sigh of relief escaped Jeremy. At first he hadn't wanted to tell anyone about their near death experiences. It was too weird. But after his visit to the church he wondered if the old woman's rosary was meant as a sign from God, permitting him to tell Opa so he could seek the peace he needed. He had been so alone.

Opa cleared his throat. "You guys have been through some pretty heavy stuff, lately. At first I couldn't believe what Cassidy told me, but I know you guys are the Miracle Teens. The strangest things seem to happen to you and I can only believe that something . . . supernatural is causing it. How you guys all ended up together in this hospital at the same time is unbelievable." He looked at each of the boys. They were all pale, but looked so much better than they had a few days ago. "And the press is curious about it, too."

Sukh didn't want to lose his friends again. He wanted to go back to the Cariboo. He knew Jeremy did, too. Hell, he even wanted to go back to school, so his family would be as proud of him as they were of Jaskirat and Gurinderpal. And Cassidy had just admitted that she wanted them all back. He was very hesitant to ask Opa's advice, in case he told them they should remain separated, but he took a deep breath and asked, "What do you think we should do?"

Opa smiled softly and shook his head. "I don't know, my friend. But I do believe in God, and I have always believed that if He has a plan for you, you should not fight the plan." He laughed and added, "Most people get small signs and callings from Him, but you guys . . . ! Well, you guys seem to need to be hit over the head."

He hugged Jeremy to him. "You especially, Jeremy." They all laughed.

"Being apart doesn't seem to work, though," Opa continued. "I think you need each other. Friends for life. And I don't know how I could ever give up friendships like that."

Kyle looked at Cassidy, Jeremy and Sukh. "Neither do I."

The room became silent as each of the teenagers considered where their lives together may some day end. At this point, they didn't care. It might be today, tomorrow, or in sixty years.

But they would keep their friendship unbroken.

43
Tempting Fate

"Hi, Kyle!"

Cassidy, Jeremy and Sukh turned toward the feminine voice behind them. Kyle rolled his wheelchair over to the excited, waving girl standing at the airport gate. He looked just as happy to see her there.

"Who's the hotty?" Sukh asked.

Cassidy turned to Sukh. "Her name's Ashley. You think she's hot?" She looked the girl up and down.

Sukh flashed a big smile. "No, she's a dog." He nudged Jeremy, who winked back at him.

Cassidy turned to Jeremy. "You think she's hot, too?"

Jeremy forced his face to lose the smile. He nudged Sukh with his elbow and said, "What he said. Bow wow!"

They watched Kyle talking and laughing with Ashley, who'd come to see him off at the terminal gates. Cassidy called her a "motocross groupie" and explained that Kyle had met her last summer. She didn't tell them about her suspicions about a relationship between the two, but she did say Ashley was at the track when Kyle got hurt. "She's probably just coming to see how he's feeling," she added.

Sukh sighed. "She could come over and see how I'm feeling anytime." When he turned to see Cassidy's stern face, he said, "I mean, *woof!*"

Jeremy chuckled. He put his arm around Cassidy and hugged her to him. "Come on Cassy. You're the most beautiful girl in all our eyes."

Sukh looked from Cassidy to Jeremy, recognizing the passion that passed between them lately, and added, "Yeah, but Cassidy, you're taken. If anyone's a dog here, it's Jeremy — a lucky dog."

Jeremy kissed the top of Cassidy's head. "And don't I know it."

Opa walked over to the kids, checking the five boarding passes. He'd volunteered to fly home with them. Between himself, Grampaji, Kyle's folks, Sukh's parents (who'd made an emergency trip back from India to be at their son's bedside), Bear, Jeremy's dad, Cassidy, Kyle and Jeremy and Sukh who were coming home to the Cariboo where they belonged, there wasn't enough room in their two vehicles. It took a while to figure out how everyone would get home, but the parents agreed to let the kids fly home to Williams Lake where Oma Lockett and Cassidy's parents would pick them up and keep them until the two cars made it back.

"They're going to start pre-boarding soon," said Opa. "Kyle, you'll need to pre-board because of your wheelchair. Sukh, will you be okay?"

"Leg's hurting a bit. I just hate sitting for too long." Sukh elevated his leg, resting it across the empty seat beside him.

Opa looked at Kyle talking with Ashley. He was popping a wheelie in the wheelchair and Ashley was cheering him on. Opa smiled, shaking his head, and turned back to Sukh. "That's why you get to fly. Less than two hours versus six in a car. Jeremy, how're you doing?"

Jeremy touched the bandage on his head. "Just a little headache, but nothing that some tender lovin' care won't cure." He gave Cassidy a squeeze.

She looked at his bandage. Every time she thought about his injury and how he got it, she got angry. He had almost been killed and it wasn't his fault. "I hope that idiot, Collin, is still in jail," she said. "They better charge him for what he did to you and to your poor mother."

Jeremy nodded. "My mom told my dad she kicked Collin out. My dad would have kicked him out literally, with his own foot, if she hadn't. He was so pissed at her for letting this happen." His dad had hit the roof at the hospital. He was angry enough that Collin had hit his ex-wife, but once he found out that Collin had laid a hand on Jeremy, his flesh and blood, he was fit to be tied. Thank God Bear was around and settled him down. If he hadn't, Jeremy was sure his dad would have gone to the apartment and earned his own assault charge.

Jeremy looked out the window. He didn't want to think about his mother, her parenting skills, her loyalties. She was a weak person. The only good thing about the time he had spent with her was that she was talking to his dad again. And his dad forgave her for leaving them. There was even something good about Collin hitting Jeremy. Two good things, actually. One was that he realized his dad really loved him when he saw how angry he became with Collin. The other thing was that his dad had seen through Bernadette. She had apparently whined so much about him coming down to the Coast to see his son in the hospital that his dad told her to take a hike. Yes! No more Bernadette.

They watched a flight attendant walk over to Kyle, speak to him and take the handles of the wheelchair. It was pre-boarding time. To their surprise, Ashley leaned her head close to Kyle's, whispered something in his ear and kissed him, right on the lips! Cassidy gasped, Jeremy chuckled and Sukh cheered loud enough to embarrass Kyle. By the time the flight attendant turned the wheelchair toward the plane, Kyle's face was flushed with embarrassment. He smiled, but wouldn't make eye contact with his best friends, even as he was wheeled right past them, and especially when they all made kissing sounds as he headed for the plane.

Cassidy raised her eyebrows as Kyle was wheeled to the front of the gate. When the flight attendant let go of the handles, Kyle pulled the chair into another wheelie, held the wheels just right to turn the chair in a spin. Anybody who saw him laughed, clapped or cheered. Except for Cassidy, who felt her heart in her throat. She had a mental picture of him flipping over on his back, rebreaking his leg and possibly getting a concussion.

She realized then that she could never be with Kyle. He would always be wild and she would always be terrified by his recklessness. She was fine with the fact that Kyle might have a new girlfriend, one who could relax around his antics. She'd felt terrible having to break up with him in the hospital, but she knew she couldn't keep the relationship going with Kyle when she felt so strongly about Jeremy. She'd been a little surprised at how easily Kyle had taken the news, but she wasn't surprised anymore. There *had* been something between him and Ashley. She turned to look at Jeremy's profile, snuggled closer to him, and let out a contented sigh. She hadn't been this happy since she'd been with him at the pond.

The flight attendant who had taken Kyle aboard came back and approached Sukh. "Hello, Sukhwinder? My name is Kitty and I'm here to help you board the plane."

Sukh smiled at the pretty woman, allowed her and Opa to help him stand up, and said, "Well, hello Kitty. Wow, that's an interesting name." He was flirting, but very badly. "You make me want to purr." He let out a low growling sound and looked down at Jeremy who rolled his eyes and moaned. Cassidy put her finger into her open mouth to indicate that she wanted to gag. Kitty laughed, which only encouraged Sukh, who smiled and growled again.

As Kitty and Opa assisted Sukh down the ramp to the plane, the general boarding call came over the public address system. Cassidy and Jeremy gathered their things and joined the other passengers in the queue to present their boarding passes and find their seats on the plane. In no time the plane was racing down the runway, angling upward and piercing the blanket of clouds that surrounded Vancouver.

They were going home. Jeremy looked through the small window at the last traces of the city disappearing far below as clouds thickened around the plane. He was relieved to leave the city behind. He was going home to the Cariboo, where he belonged. He now understood why his dad never wanted to come to the Coast. He doubted he would ever choose to come again. Leaning back in his seat, he squeezed Cassidy's hand and closed his eyes. He had everything he would ever want back in the Cariboo.

They sat in silence as the plane climbed higher, past the vapour of clouds to the sunshine that was always shining above. After the seatbelt light went off, Cassidy gently pulled her hand from Jeremy's, unbuckled her seatbelt and made her way toward the lavatory at the front of the plane. As she walked past Kyle she put a hand on his shoulder. He looked at her, smiled, touched her hand, but didn't stop his conversation with Opa. They were talking about airplanes. Cassidy looked across the aisle to where Sukh was sitting and she wanted to laugh. In the seat next to him sat a dark-haired, dark-eyed, olive-skinned beauty, and Sukh was making shooting sounds, his hands in the shape of a gun. The girl, who seemed about their age, was engrossed in his story of how he got his injuries. How could he get so lucky?

In front of them was the lavatory. It was occupied, so Cassidy leaned against the wall and waited. She looked into the galley, where she saw Kitty preparing coffee. Cassidy smiled.

Kitty smiled back at her and asked if she needed anything. Cassidy tipped her head toward the bathroom then said, "I've always wondered what it would be like to be a flight attendant. Is it as glamorous as it looks?"

Kitty laughed. "When I was your age I wondered the same thing. Do you think the waitress in the coffee shop at the airport has a glamorous job? Because, really, it's not much different."

Cassidy sighed. "But you get to travel, don't you?"

Kitty continued to gather items for the coffee cart. "From Williams Lake to Vancouver and back. Twice a day. If you think that's traveling."

"But don't you get to fly around the world?" Cassidy asked.

"Not with this airline. It's just a small commuter company. I live in Williams Lake and this is my run," answered Kitty.

The door from the cockpit opened and a man's voice called, "Cat?"

Kitty turned away from Cassidy, held the door and said, "Yes, Jim?" The door swung out, blocking Cassidy's view of the pilots and the airplane controls.

"Can we get two coffees here, please?"

"I'm getting right on it." She shut the door, turned to face Cassidy and froze. The young girl's face had turned white. The smile was gone and her eyes were wide open. She looked like she'd pass out. "Are you okay?" Kitty asked.

Cassidy's throat had gone dry. She tried to speak, but her voice came out in a whisper. "Cat?" She cleared her throat and tried again. "Cat? Is that your real name?"

Kitty looked at Cassidy, confusion in her eyes. She nodded hesitantly, then said, "Actually, it's short for Catrina. Why?"

Cassidy looked at the door to the cockpit. "And 'Jim'? Is the pilot's name . . . Jim?"

Kitty didn't like the way this conversation had turned. She didn't want to tell this girl anything, but answered, "The co-pilot. Why do you want to know?"

Cassidy looked from the door back to Kitty. She wanted to ask about Jim. Was his real name Jamieson? But she turned to look back at the passengers. She had to tell Sukh and Jeremy and Kyle that there was a Catrina on the plane before . . . before . . . before what? What would change if she told them? If they knew?

She looked at Sukh, writing down the email address of the girl beside him on his napkin. She watched Kyle and Opa talk about airplanes. She looked at Jeremy, his eyes still closed, unaware that she'd left her seat. She looked at the other passengers, the strangers who were on this flight, blissfully ignorant of their fate. She reached into her pocket and fingered something round and hard — her marble. She took another deep breath, one she no longer needed. The colour had come back to her face. She thought of how happy they all were again, together, and how much they'd suffered because they thought they knew their fates.

She didn't want to know.

She really did not want to know if Catrina's last name was Bergman or if Jamieson Frank Otters was the co-pilot of the plane. It was not her right to know. It was not Sukh's or Jeremy's or Kyle's right to know. It was God's right and only God's right. And He was the only one with the right to know! She cursed the day she ever found out who she would die with.

She turned back to face Kitty and said, "You know," she began with a contented smile and a shake of her head, "I *don't* want to know. I really do not want to know, not now or ever." She tried to smile to reassure Kitty that everything was fine. "I'm very sorry."

She walked back toward her seat, unaware that Kitty's gaze bore into her back as she went. As she walked past Sukh, she put her hand on his shoulder. He didn't stop talking to the girl beside him, but turned his head for a moment and put a little kiss on her hand. She turned to Kyle and Opa. This time Kyle kept talking and Opa looked up at her. She reached her hand into her pocket, pulled out the marble. He nodded, smiled.

Cassidy felt no fear. She had left all her fears in the hospital in Vancouver.

There were no tears. Those had all been shed in Opa's arms.

She sat calmly beside Jeremy. If Jamieson Frank Otters was on this plane, well . . . then he was on this plane. He might be the co-pilot. He might be one of the passengers. Or he might be in Tuktoyuktuk right now. It didn't matter.

She rolled the marble between her finger and thumb then held it up to get another good look at its blue centre. Again, she thought of the night in the gazebo. The night they had foolishly agreed to separate. She held the marble tight in her hand and thanked her God that they were together again.

She thought of her parents and her brothers. She gave them each a silent kiss as an "I love you," touching the marble to her lips as she thought of each one. She lifted Jeremy's hand and kissed it. He opened his eyes and smiled at her, putting his arm around her and pulling her closer into his embrace. Cassidy leaned her head against him, nestling in as close as she could to his heart, and closed her eyes.

AUDREY PFITZENMAIER has a Masters of Art in Children's Literature fom UBC, and has worked as a teacher/librarian and currently a Literacy Support Teacher. *Cheating Fate* is her first novel. Pfitzenmaier lives in Ladner, BC.